I0671501

Unforeseen

Viator Legacy Series: Book Two

Erin Lausten

Drago Fortuna Publishing

Copyright © 2014 Erin Lausten
All rights reserved. No part of this book may be
reproduced without expressed permission by the
copyright holder.

This book is a work of fiction. All persons, locations,
and events are created by the author or used fictitiously.

For information on permissions to reproduce selections
from this book contact - ElizaDFP@gmail.com
Drago Fortuna Publishing
Phoenix

To Mindy and Kelly

1

The door shut with a heavy thud. Lucius turned the dead bolt, sealing them into the most secure room within the *castellum*. Solid, steel walls stood between them and the bustling activity within the *viator's* center for operations. Derian pulled his Colt 1911 from the holster at his hip and checked the magazine. He looked to Lucius. "Good to go."

A stainless steel table lined the wall to the right. LED lights blinked from a silver box bolted permanently to the table. Lucius approached the box and pressed one of the buttons, then tapped in his security passcode. The room was the only location within the *castellum* where a *viator* could jump time. The rest of the facility maintained a buffer zone that prevented unauthorized jumps into and from the facility. With the highest levels of bureaucracy at work and hundreds of top scientists pursuing confidential projects, the security was abnormally high.

And the threat had never been more severe.

"Remember, you cannot return here. I have the timer set to close the window in five minutes. I will follow you once you have targeted Hailey," Lucius said.

"We have no idea what we'll be facing," Derian replied with reserve.

"Sounds just like old times."

Derian smiled and a hint of what made the man his best operative manifested in his movements. Derian lived for the hunt, adept at tracking men across time and continents. He was a deadly shot, strategically intelligent, and as loyal as any top soldier. Lucius wondered what it was about Hailey that made such an impression on his lead *venator*.

"I'm going to warn you. She might be cranky when we catch up to her," Derian said.

Lucius turned back to the table and entered the second series of access codes. "Just remember, we need information about the conspiracy. We have very little intel on the type of force we are facing with Nikanuur."

"Well then, what are you waiting for?"

With a snap, Lucius flipped a toggle switch and the system buzzed, initiating a field of energy that punched a hole through the buffer. The keen focus fell from Derian's eyes, and he faded from view, his body a bare impression of his solidified form. Then he was gone.

Lucius pulled his own weapon, a Walther PPK, from his hip holster. With no idea what the situation would be when he jumped, he preferred having the weapon ready. Several hours had passed since Hailey was been snatched from Derian's home deep in the mountains of Arizona. Now she could be anywhere.

They had no knowledge of how much manpower the conspiracy wielded. Several *venators* were reported dead from a devastating poison only a few weeks earlier. With Hailey's help they had the name of one of the men responsible. Nikanuur, her father, had a long history of dubious scientific experiments and questionable morals, but he'd lacked the support and funds necessary to be more than a minor threat. Now he appeared to have both. They needed to know who was backing the unstable scientist.

Lucius closed his eyes and sought the connection to Derian that circulated through his body. Nearly a thousand years ago, the two men connected through a blood exchange, a tradition within the *viator* that allowed a veteran to connect through time with someone new to the talent. Now he and Derian could find each other no matter the time or place.

Awareness of the blood pulsing through his veins aroused his senses. He grabbed onto the thread that flowed within, and prepared to follow Derian to Hailey. Opening his eyes, he watched as the room shimmered and began to fade from view.

The solid, steel door shook from a violent pounding on the outside. Closing the connection, Lucius rematerialized in the room and strode with irritation toward the door. Whoever interrupted his departure better have a good excuse. Now he'd have to begin the whole process over. The lights on the box flickered and returned to their original setting.

He flung the door open. "What?"

"Dude. Chill." Hailey stood before him, her eyes wide and Derian's gun gripped tight in her hands.

"What the hell are you doing here? Derian just left to find you."

"Right. I know. He found me. But then you disappeared and they didn't know why. So they sent me back here to find out, since they couldn't, you know..." She waved her hand in the air as though it answered everything.

"What are you talking about?"

"It doesn't matter. Look, something happens to you in like five minutes. You were supposed to follow Derian, but you never did. You disappeared and no one knows what happens to you."

He looked down at the young blonde woman, her hair pulled back in a messy ponytail and a new wariness in her manner. Her eyes darted behind him then looked up. Shifting from one foot to the other, she radiated agitation. Lucius returned his pistol to the holster and tried to stem the temptation to shake the woman. "Hailey, you stopped me from following him."

"I did? Wait, so if I hadn't stopped you, you would have gone after him?" Lucius crossed his arms and she scrunched her face, gesturing with the gun as she spoke, "Well that doesn't make sense. It's not like I am going to do anything that makes you disappear."

"Have you ever held a gun before?" He looked down at the weapon, now held loosely in her hand.

"Why does everyone keep asking me that?"

The door across the room opened and Millard from the data-tracking division entered. "Uh, sir, do you have a moment to look at something?"

Lucius raised his eyes to the ceiling and prayed for patience. He did not have time for any of this. "What is it?"

Millard coughed into his hand and darted his eyes into the hall. The weaselly man had nerves strung tighter than a suspension bridge and Lucius seriously considered transferring him to another division. Closing the door to the steel chamber, Lucius approached Millard. Hailey hung back, her stance ready.

When Lucius reached a few feet from the door, a shadow passed across the threshold and Millard scurried into the room. Behind him, a tall figure with sleek looks and familiar, malicious eyes stepped into the doorway. "Hello Lucius. It has been a while."

"What the hell are you doing here?" Lucius growled, his hands inching toward his pistol. Carlo Benanati had operated on the fringes of the *viator* community since the 18th century. After first jumping during the Italian Renaissance, he took to the life of a *viator* with natural ease. His talents and intelligence would have made him highly effective as a *venator*. Unfortunately, his moral compass had been established through the influence of the Medicis and Borgias. Since then, he'd served as a mercenary to anyone willing to pay the right price.

Carlo looked past Lucius to meet eyes with Hailey, raising a handgun to Lucius's chest, he answered, "It is never personal. You know that."

"Oh come on. I just ditched you!" Hailey said, holding her own pistol on Carlo, arms stiff and held at an awkward angle.

A smile slid across Carlo's lips. "Have you ever shot a gun before?"

"Oh my god. Yes! Yes I have shot a stupid gun before!" Hailey shouted as she pointed the barrel at the wall behind Carlo and pulled the trigger. The shot rang through the room, instigating a flurry of movement. Carlo dashed toward Hailey, his weapon still pointed at Lucius. Pulling his Walther smoothly into his hand, Lucius had it trained on Carlo in seconds.

Hailey shouted as Carlo slashed a hand out to knock the gun from her grip. It flew across the room as Lucius pulled the trigger. Unfortunately, he heard the ring of another shot first. Pain punched him in the chest and he lost focus. The familiar rush of a time jump started at the base of his neck

5

and the last thing he heard was his name falling from Hailey's lips.

2

A droplet of rain slid down the glass, leaving a trail of water for the early morning light to pierce and fracture into barely visible flashes of color. Grace traced a finger against the glass then wiped the built-up moisture on her slacks. The rain provided a mixed blessing. On one hand, her grandmother would stay away, unwilling to trudge through the wet leaves and pine needles to Grace's bungalow. That was a good thing. On the other hand, Grace wanted to visit her cousin on the edge of town and she wasn't looking forward to the walk.

She kicked the wall and slid to an unladylike slump on the floor. Her teeth ached and head felt like a beat-up treasure trunk. One look at her pained expression and her grandmother would know she'd had another vision. Grace cringed and pressed her palms into her eyes. The old lady would press her until she told the truth of it, then the council would be called, the town would get agitated and she'd be dodging dirty looks for the rest of the month.

What did it matter that she had visions of *viator*? She didn't ask for them. There was nothing she could do about it. And she certainly couldn't do anything about the warmth and excitement that pulsed through her every time she saw *him*. The looming, dark-haired *viator* with steel resolve in his eyes hadn't limited himself to her visions. No, he invaded her dreams as well. Watching her. Reaching out to her. It made for uncomfortable nights and frustrated mornings.

A soft patter of paws on the hardwood floor pulled her from her thoughts. Aristo slinked up to her, his tail curling as he rubbed his head against her hand. Grace pulled the tabby into her lap. A long scar ran from the top of his eye along his head in a long, white trail. She scratched beneath his ear and his purr vibrated against her belly. "You do not want to play in the rain either do you, friend?"

She pulled her hand away and his head followed, bucking against it with determination. A giggle rose and she sighed. He was nearly as insistent as her handsome *viator*. At least Aristo was tangible. A curt knock at the door startled her and the cat jumped from her arms to slide under the threadbare sofa.

A second insistent knock encouraged her to hurry. When she opened the door, a waterlogged Phillip grinned from the step. "Hello Gracey. I have something for you."

She beamed back at her cousin. She wouldn't have to make the soggy trek up to his place after all. "From the city? What is it?"

"Let me in and I'll show you." He pushed past her, stomping his feet on her rug and leaving a pile of pine needles and mud in a wet mound before striding into the kitchen. Cupboards banged open and shut as he scoured her stores. "You never have anything to eat."

"Yes I do. There is fruit on the counter."

His lip curled at the bananas blackening in a wooden bowl. "Good thing I brought you more. Do you even eat?"

Reaching into a drawer, she pulled out a packet of cheese crackers and threw them on the counter. "If you brought me food, why are you wreaking havoc in my kitchen?"

The wrapper tore and crumbs flew across the floor. Within seconds the crackers were gone. A tall, gangly man, Phillip constantly ate to keep up the flow of insuppressible energy. Mess and chaos were expected byproducts. And as long as he came to keep her company with endless tales of the world outside the community, she didn't care what kind of a mess he made. He dropped the wrapper in the wastebasket and turned to her with a grin. "I have the food in the truck. Thought I would bring it by instead of making you walk through the rain."

"That is very nice of you." She folded her hands in front of her and pushed up on her toes. "What surprise did you bring me?"

He reached behind his back, rifling with something tucked into his belt. With a flourish, he pulled out a plastic wrapped package, handed it to Grace, and sauntered into the living room where he plopped on the couch. With fingers threaded behind his head, he nodded at her to unwrap it.

Her hands trembled as she pulled apart the plastic wrap. It had been months since he'd been able to bring her something special from the outside. His monthly trips gave him ample opportunity but the necessity to hide it from the elders and other prying eyes made it a struggle not worth the repercussions. Not that the challenge didn't encourage him. Phillip loved pulling off a bit of subterfuge and Grace didn't mind being his excuse.

Beneath the plastic wrap, the glossy sheen of a book cover peeked out. Excitement thudded against her chest and she ripped the rest of the package apart. "Oh Phillip! The next Harry Potter book!" She wrapped her arms around the thick tome, swung around and beamed her appreciation. He grinned back at her as he pushed his hands against his knees to stand.

"I'll grab your groceries," he said as he sauntered out the door, the grin still shining across his face.

She slid her fingers along the glossy finish and traced the outlines of the young wizard and his friends. It was the perfect gift for a rainy day, and with Phillip delivering groceries to the community, no one would interrupt her. With the first page open, she shuffled to the couch and slumped against the pillows. Throwing her legs up, she settled in for hours of escape, barely registering the rustle of bags and hearty laughter as Phillip left to make his deliveries.

The hours passed and she'd hardly put a dent in the story. She laid the book on her lap and rubbed her eyes. The exhilaration from the engaging story was compounded by the excitement of pursuing the forbidden. Reading wasn't prohibited, but the only books allowed in the community were the ancient texts that had followed the *tiresians* as they moved from one hideaway to the next. Filled with thousands of scrolls from Greece, Mycenae, Minoa, Persia, Rome, the collection had once rivaled the library at Alexandria. Now it had no equal.

But Grace had grown tired of those texts over 100 years ago and had sought ways to expand her own collection. That collection now sat beneath the floorboards of her bungalow, hidden from suspicious eyes and protected from the authoritarian rule of her grandmother and the elders. A heavy sigh brought her shoulders off the pillows and she felt a sharp pain in her neck.

She swung her legs off the couch and stretched. The temptation to read for several more hours wrapped its fingers around her best intentions, but she pushed it away. She needed to savor the book, draw out the experience. Who knew when she would have another chance? A growl rumbled through her belly and she answered with a laugh. Perhaps Phillip was right, she hadn't been eating nearly enough.

A bright yellow apple sat on the counter where it had rolled from the hastily deposited grocery bags. She snatched it up and took a bite. The sweet tartness exploded in her mouth and she closed her eyes to the sensation. She was met with familiar dark eyes, brown as the richest soil and intense as a forest predator. Dropping the apple, she grabbed for the counter and missed. Her feet fell out from beneath her and she landed in a tangled mess on the floor.

By the time she got her bearings, the vision had receded. Relief and disappointment warred against each other. The clarity of her visions was sharpening, the details showing clear and crisp. This time she'd glimpsed concern behind the intensity of his eyes and it tugged at her heart. Why was this *viator* haunting her?

After pulling her legs into a manageable order, she ran to grab a jacket. Phillip might still be dropping off groceries and with luck she could get into his place and snoop around. There had to be answers somewhere.

****

Another box lay open at her feet, filled with nothing but moth-eaten clothes and random bits of trash. The *tiresian* community had settled in the south Oregon forest nearly 150 years ago and considering what she'd found in her cousin's stash, he hadn't thrown a thing away. Dragging the box to the side of the room, she hefted it on top of a pile of similarly trash-ridden boxes. She would haul them out to the small dump on the outskirts of the community as a thank you for the Harry Potter book. Of course, she'd need to borrow his truck and that would mean he'd have to teach her to drive. But if it were a benefit to them both, how could he argue?

Phillip's role as liaison between the *tiresians* and the world of humanity granted him an abundance of perks. Number one was the Victorian house tucked away on the outskirts of the community. In the wettest months they could be cut off completely from the outside and they needed a decent store of supplies to hold out until the rains ceased and the roads dried enough for travel. Phillip, as the man in charge of provisions, had the house all to himself. Before Grace had been granted her bungalow, she'd been terribly jealous of her cousin.

However, the grandest perk in her mind was the nearly unrestrained freedom Phillip enjoyed. Of course, he worked hard to maintain that freedom. If the elders had any idea of the constant flow of contraband he brought into the community, he'd be banished. And she'd no longer have a way to stem the constant threat of mind-numbing monotony.

In the corner, tucked beneath the eaves of the attic, she spied the tell-tale shape of a pinball machine. A smile spread across her lips as she stepped over several more boxes to get to the decades-old machine. The insanity required to bring the hunk of metal into the community had been memorable. While Phillip brought the machine in, she'd been tasked with creating a diversion. The night had been dark and wet. When she had let the horses out and coaxed them through the center of the communal buildings, the outcry had sent every able-bodied person into the fray. Slipping and sliding through the mud had created more chaos than it solved. The children woke and laughed at their parents who'd acted like confused rodents running through the streets. The only one that had maintained any sense of control had been Tymion, her fiancé.

She pulled at the dustcover. A piece of the worn fabric caught on the top corner and tore as the remainder fell at her feet. She frowned. Tymion was becoming increasingly insistent, demanding she commit to their betrothal.

He was a good man. A strong man. As the years passed he would move further up into the seats of leadership and she was meant to be at his side. As granddaughter to the oldest and most revered *tiresian* she would be expected to share the responsibilities and take her proper place. A marriage with Tymion was the first step along that road.

And she had absolutely no intention of ever making that a reality.

A slam from below the floor drew her attention. With haste, she threw the dustcover back over the pinball machine and hurried to meet her cousin. Her search unsuccessful, she'd have to ask him where he'd hidden the books. As her feet flew down the stairs her heels thudded against the hardwood, broadcasting her imminent arrival into the sparsely furnished foyer.

The house had been built for her grandparents in a happier time. But after her grandfather's death and her mother's betrayal the house had been abandoned until Phillip claimed it for 'the good of the community'. Her grandfather had been a quiet man, uninvolved in politics and happy to let her grandmother take the reins. It gave him time to spend with his granddaughter, something no one else had bothered to do. Pausing, she gripped the banister. She missed her grandfather terribly. His death had marked the beginning of a black time in Grace's life, one made more agonizing by the banishment of her mother. But, she kept fond memories of the house and refused to let the feud between her grandmother and mother mar how she felt about the old place.

She hit the carpeted first floor and padded toward the kitchen. Phillip rustled through several bags on the counter, his back to her, seemingly oblivious to her noisy descent down the stairs.

"Phillip."

He jumped and swung around. "Zeus in heaven Grace! What are you doing here?"

"Since when did you develop religion?" She perched on the nearest chair and folded her hands on the table.

He turned around and mumbled into the bags, his back stiff and shoulders tense. If she could snoop around the house so effectively he didn't stand a chance if the elders decided to inspect his operation. "Do not worry, everything was locked up tight. I simply used the spare key you lent me a couple years ago."

He faced her and leaned against the counter. Brushing a hand through his golden curls, he watched her with unusual intensity. "What are you doing here? I left you with a new book. That should have kept you busy for a week."

"More than likely a day." She ignored his snort of disbelief and consciously refrained from biting her lip. He wouldn't like what she wanted. She cursed his packrat tendencies. If she'd found the books before he'd returned she might have had a chance at him never knowing. "I need my mother's journals."

His hands fell down to his hips in limp shock. "Gods Grace, is that all? Althea would banish me if she knew I even had them. Think what she would do if she discovered I gave them to you."

"I need them." She tightened her fingers into white-knuckled balls. Something in her heart told her everything hinged on those books. None of it made any sense, but long ago she'd learned to have trust in her instincts. They were howling at her right now.

"No."

"Phillip–"

"No." He raised a finger, ready to argue further.

"I am having more visions of the *viators*."

His hand dropped and he looked out the small window above the sink. The day was still wet and grey and it cast a pall over the conversation. Rubbing his hand against the back of his neck, he looked up toward the ceiling. Grace rolled her eyes. Zeus wouldn't be writing the answers to their dilemma in the plaster of an old Victorian house. The ancient god hadn't responded to her prayers in the 300 years she'd been alive and he wasn't about to start now. "You know how they will react when they find out I am still having them. I have to figure out why I am having these visions and those journals are the only link we have to her. Maybe there will be answers for me."

He turned his back on her and rummaged through the bags. Grace sat quietly as he unpacked his supplies. Begging and pleading wouldn't help her convince him to help. Screaming and threatening wouldn't either. He had to come to a decision on his own. She just hoped he would do it sooner rather than later, she was growing tired of the onslaught of a steely-eyed *viator* that looked at her with hunger and possessiveness. Whoever the man was, she was determined to find an answer.

At first, she'd thought the visions had just been of a man. A simple fantasy, conjured by an overactive imagination bored with isolation. But one night she'd seen him jump time, shifting easily from a modern world to one filled with the trappings of ancient Rome. She'd run to her grandmother, at the time unaware of the gross animosity that existed between the *tiresian*s and *viator*s. She'd always known there had been bad-blood between the two peoples, but she never could have foreseen the level of vehement anger that would spill from her grandmother's lips.

Centuries ago, the *viator*s had enslaved the *tiresian*s. It hadn't been anything unusual for the time. The *viator*s had established a foothold within ancient Roman society and Rome had enslaved just about everyone. But the *viator*s knew the secrets the *tiresian*s held, and used that to their advantage. They exploited the *tiresian*s' talent for seeing the future, utilizing that knowledge for their gain.

But the *tiresian*s won their freedom and now kept to themselves, living outside humanity on what they considered their own terms. They hid in a desperate bid to avoid any contact with their ancient masters.

Grace hated it. She refused to believe that any people could hold malevolent intention and evil ambitions as a shared cultural characteristic. There had to be some redeeming quality to the *viator*s. There had to be some reason she felt an undeniable pull to know the man in her visions.

"Alright." Phillip sat beside her, his shoulders hunched while he softly drummed his fingers on the table. "But if anyone finds out you have them, you are on your own. I never

saw them before in my life and I would never think of helping you acquire such dangerous texts."

Grace placed her hands over his to quiet the drumming.
"Of course not. No one could ever imagine you doing such a
thing."

3

Thick rain threatened as Grace hustled toward her cottage. The two leather-bound books weighed heavily in her arms. Thin and brittle, they'd remained unopened for over a century. Phillip confessed he'd never looked at them and the thought boggled her mind. Had the journals been in her home, the mysteries within would have driven her to distraction.

Head down, she turned up the narrow trail that led between the trees and up the small hill to where her home sat nestled in a clearing. Privacy had been hard-won and if it had not been for the support and encouragement of Tymion, she would never have been allowed to break away from her grandmother's household.

That thought brought forth an image of Tymion's broad shoulders and bright, confident smile. Why couldn't she fall in love with him? He was good and kind. He supported her and was generous. Half the women in the community loved him, why couldn't she? As she approached the small porch and red door to her bungalow, she commanded away her questions. She'd tried for years to fall in love with Tymion with no success. There was little she could do about it now.

Aristo greeted her as she climbed the short steps to the door. "You silly cat, what are you doing out here? Did I leave your door locked?"

She turned the knob and stood aside to let the tabby in. He didn't move and stared up at her with unblinking eyes. "Don't you want to go in?"

He meowed then pivoted away. "Suit yourself." She turned to enter the dry promise of her living room and Aristo meowed again. When she swung back, he stood and walked down the steps, keeping his eyes turned toward her. "What do you want Aristo?"

The cat continued to walk, meowing every few feet. Intrigued, Grace dropped the journals on the antique side-table inside the door then followed him toward her garden. The cat's tail twitched as he walked and curled as he disappeared around the back corner of the house. Grace approached with caution. Whatever Aristo was about had her intuitive senses running hot.

Just as she reached the corner, she stopped and took a fortifying breath. It was probably just a mouse or injured bird–he was a cat after all. With her back straight she turned the corner and stopped in disbelief.

Aristo sat on the back of a prone man, one arm thrown above his head, the other tucked awkwardly beneath his body. Grace's heart stuttered and her voice caught in her throat. Aristo meowed and cocked his head in her direction. When she didn't move, he hunched over and kneaded his paws into the man's back.

"Aristo!" Her voice squeaked as she ran to shoo her cat off the man. Kneeling beside his shoulder, she reached a tentative finger toward his arm. "Pardon me," she whispered as she poked his side.

He didn't move.

She reached up and shook his shoulder. "Pardon me."

No reaction. Ivory-colored teeth pulled her bottom lip into her mouth. He didn't look like anyone she knew. He faced away from her, so she shifted to the other side and stifled a gasp. A crimson stain spread along his side, diluted by the rain that had soaked him through to the skin. Fear crept along her limbs, leaving goose bumps in its wake. Strangers rarely showed up in the community and they certainly never showed up face down in her garden with a bloody wound.

Mud covered the side of his face. Military cut, dark brown hair that approached black lay matted and muddy against his scalp. Leaves and detritus covered his body like sprinkles on a cupcake and his clothes were so permeated with the dirty dampness she doubted there'd be any saving them. Either he'd run through the forest in a mad dash or he'd been lying there an exorbitantly long time. Based on the amount of blood that mixed with the mud, she assumed the latter. He had to be moved out of the elements and his wound needed attending.

She stood to run for help when a glance at his face made her stop. Squatting, she reached toward his cheek and brushed at the mud. He looked so familiar, but she was positive he wasn't from the community. He groaned and shifted, lifting the rest of his face away from the obscuring mud.

She gasped. She knew him.

Hard lines and a strong jaw framed a rugged face. Lips that frequently thinned with resolve relaxed under the influence of unconsciousness. And should he wake and open his eyes, she knew they'd be hard as steel and brown as the richest mountain soil.

Rocking back on her heels, she considered her options. His appearance complicated things. When the elders found out a *viator* lay unconscious in their midst, they might just let him die in the mud. Her nostrils flared as she imagined the harsh words and uncompromising attitude her grandmother and others in the community had toward the *viators*. There was no possible way she would let them take centuries of bitterness out on this man. Not when he could have the answers to her visions.

Decision made, she shook his shoulder a second time to see if fortune would wake him and sighed when there was still no response. Dragging his long, massive, and unconscious body into her home would not be easy. She stood and wondered how her tiny frame could move a mountain.

Aristo returned and butted his head against her shin. "Well, do you have any ideas? He is your discovery." The cat meowed and sauntered away.

It took fifteen minutes to pull him from the middle of the small yard to the back porch. With a leg of his on each hip, she'd pulled and heaved. She'd seen a diagram of a travois in an old survival guide once, and thought how much easier such a device would have made her struggle. One look at the blood that clung to his clothing had her redoubling her efforts. She didn't have time for meddling with projects when she needed to get the man out of the rain.

Grace sat with a huff on the back porch stoop. With hair plastered against her neck and cheeks flushed from exertion, she wondered where she'd find the energy to pull him up the two stairs and into the bungalow. Aristo lay at her feet and sniffed at the *viator*'s feet propped on the first step. The cat turned an unblinking stare at her.

"What?"

He turned away and glared into the dense forest. Grace stuck a petulant tongue out at the cat. An uppity feline had no business making comments. She sighed and looked down at the unconscious *viator*. She had no idea how he'd ended up in her backyard. A barrier protected the community and had for over twenty years since they first discovered the technology. He couldn't have landed here. She looked into the trees. He must have hiked through miles of forest to find them, only to pass out from his wound. What were the chances that a lost *viator* would accidentally happen upon a *tiresian* community?

Next to none, which meant their existence was not as effectively hidden as the elders and her grandmother believed. Grace stood and stretched her back. There would be time enough to worry about all that later, now she needed to haul him to safety and ensure he didn't die.

She grabbed his feet and repositioned him so his head was facing the right direction. Then she squatted behind him and threaded her arms beneath his back and under his arms. As she pulled, her feet slipped, sending her tailbone into the hard ground.

This was not going as well as she anticipated. Aristo sidled up beside her and sat, cocking his head to look at her. Grace tucked a stray tendril of hair behind her ear. "Are you enjoying yourself?"

The orange and white tabby leaned down and began to lick his leg. "Lovely. You are a terrible assistant, I hope you know." Grace switched her legs and knelt on the ground. With the added leverage, she heaved and soon had his back leaning against her chest. Bloody mud soaked into her white cotton blouse. She pulled and they began the slow ascent up the stairs.

Twenty minutes later she had him lying on her living room floor, a dirty smear streaking all the way from the back door. She sighed and wiped her hands down her slacks. First things first, she needed to get him out of the wet clothes, warm and his wound taken care of. Then she could worry about the condition of her hardwood floors.

Heat rose up to her neck as she slipped the wet jeans from off his legs. She groaned when she touched the soaking wet boxers. Those would have to go too. Averting her eyes, she peeled them off, threw them across the room and hastily covered him with a blanket. His shirt clung like moss on a tree to a finely sculpted chest and abdomen. At his shoulder the grey t-shirt was stained crimson and the ragged fabric around the wound made it impossible for her to simply pull the shirt off. She went in search of scissors.

When she returned, her arms were stacked high with towels, rags, shears, and a bucket. She dumped it all on the floor beside him and grabbed the silver shears. One eye on the bloody hole in his chest and the other on her trembling hands, she began to cut through the fabric. She had no experience with doctoring. Beyond the occasional cut or bruise, she lived a relatively benign life. With luck, her inexperience wouldn't kill the poor man.

The angry skin oozed red as she removed the last of the fabric and dabbed at it with a wet rag. The minor blood flow worried her, but she continued to clean the area, watching his face for any sign of discomfort or pain. His lips tightened and eyebrows pulled together the closer she got to the wound. With her bottom lip between her teeth, she finished and covered it with a clean linen cloth. It was the best she could do.

She leaned against the nearest wall and watched her unexpected guest. His chest rose and fell steadily. The dirt gone, she saw a face that was achingly familiar and frightening. What was she going to do with him?

Exhaustion crept into her body and settled against her chest. Tipping her head back she let her eyes close. She should go to bed or at least lie down on the couch, but sleep claimed her before she had a chance to move.

****

A heavy fist banged against the front door, jerking her from a dreamless sleep. It took several blinks before Grace realized she needed to move. Stumbling to her feet, she stopped short when her toes hit the warm body on the floor. Pain-filled, brown eyes looked up at her and several beads of sweat trickled down his forehead toward the floor. She leaned down and placed a hand against his brow. Heat scorched her cool fingers and he flinched.

Another flurry of thuds hit the door. She grimaced and put a finger to her lips. Comprehension flickered in his eyes and she smiled in relief. Crossing softly to the door, she pulled back the deadlock and turned the knob. Tymion's square shoulders and worried eyes met hers when she opened the door a crack.

"Why do you have the door locked?" Tymion moved to brush past her.

Grace smiled, pushed him back, and hurried through the door, closing it behind her. "I came through the back this morning and completely forgot I had this one locked."

He narrowed his eyes at the door then glanced at her. "What happened to you?"

Grace looked down at the blood and mud soaked shirt then stifled a groan. How on earth could she explain this? He reached down and grabbed her arm above the elbow. "Are you hurt?" His second hand reached up toward her chest.

She blushed and pushed his hand away. "No, I am fine. I just–" Aristo sidled up beside her and sat at her feet meowing at Tymion. Finally the cat would be useful for something.

"Aristo brought me a present this morning. He became overly ambitious with a crow. Unfortunately, he forgot to kill it before bringing it into the house. It took me nearly an hour to get the poor thing out."

She glanced up at Tymion who glared down at the unimpressed cat. "It did not survive and the whole thing left a huge mess in the house," she said and motioned toward her shirt, "and on me. But we are unharmed. I just have not had the chance to tidy up yet."

He looked up at her and his eyes softened. "Would you like my assistance?"

Grace stifled a laugh. The thought of the overtly masculine Tymion with a bucket and mop painted a ridiculous picture. "No. I can take care of it. Believe me it looks quite a bit worse than it is."

He let out a relieved sigh and this time she couldn't restrain a giant grin. "Why are you here? Surely you did not think I was in need of rescue?"

His lips tipped up in the closest thing to a smile he ever gave and his eyes crinkled about the edges, twisting her stomach into a familiar knot. A number of the young women in the community would move mountains to have Tymion look at them the way he looked at her. "There is the festival tonight and you have not given me an answer yet."

Panic swelled and she pulled her lip between her teeth. She had completely forgotten about the festival. Tymion had asked her to accompany him nearly two weeks ago and she'd not found a single reason to refuse. It wasn't the thought of going with him that bothered her. He was always a gentleman, and she was sure to have a good time. But her grandmother and the rest of the elders would be there, watching and whispering. If she went with him, they'd almost certainly insist that the betrothal be acknowledged.

"Ty, I–"

His hands lifted and the feather touch of his fingers grazed her jaw. Her nerves sizzled, but not in anticipation. She wanted to cry. What was so wrong with her? "Ty, I just cannot."

He dropped his hands and stepped away. Silence built between them and she shifted from one foot to the other. His deep voice rumbled softly, "I wish I could convince you otherwise."

Grace dropped her head and whispered, "I wish you could too. Believe me with all my heart I wish you could."

When she looked up, his lips had thinned and his dark brows drew together then he pivoted around to leave. Grace felt the need to stop him, to explain, but she couldn't even explain it to herself. His back stood tall as he retreated and she knew he'd walk away from the situation strong and unmarked. Unfortunately, she was unlikely to survive this unscathed. Her grandmother would never let her live it down.

Grace turned the knob and entered the house. Her gaze met the empty floor. The *viator* was gone. Frantic, she stepped deeper into the room and swung her head in a desperate arc to find him. The door shut with solid finality and he leaned against it, his eyes dangerous behind their fevered depths.

Her heart thundered against her chest and she wiped her hands on her pants. "Hello. I am Grace, and you really should not be standing."

4

The woman had the largest, roundest eyes he'd ever seen on a human. They grew wider as she watched him and he wondered if it were possible to fall into their eddying depths. Like a siren song, she beckoned with each fluttering blink. She could make a killing as a mesmerist or fortune teller and that sent him a cannon shot of warning.

She took a step toward him, her hand outstretched to grab his arm. He straightened his back and glowered just as a piercing pain burned through his shoulder. She winced and dropped her arm. "I understand that you are wary, but you really need to lie down."

A fog filled behind his eyes and his knees buckled. Instantly her hands were at his side, easing him to the floor. She brushed a finger across his brow. "See, at least your body has some sense, even if you do not."

His head cleared but the weakness remained. Glancing down, he examined the bleached cloth that covered his chest, a spot of red spreading through the weave. "Now, you have gone and made yourself bleed," she huffed and pressed against the cloth.

"Christ," he growled at her and she flinched.

"I apologize. I know it hurts, but you have already lost so much blood. I am concerned if you lose more I will not be able to help you."

Lucius rested his head against the door. Her slender fingers continued to add pressure to the wound. A damp cloth slid across his forehead and he looked up to see her concerned expression focused intently on him. "Do you think you have the strength to stand and walk? I believe it would be better for you in my bed than here on the floor."

He nearly cracked a smile. That had to be the most innocent invitation to a woman's bed he had ever received. He couldn't help but look at the chest that heaved just inches from his face. Her breasts were full and quite possibly larger than a handful. But the sight lacked the usual draw when he realized the dark red stains that covered her previously white blouse were from his own blood. He looked into her eyes, now enhanced by a crimson blush crossing her cheeks. He felt a sudden need to apologize for gawking.

"I'm sorry. I did not mean to be rude."

Her hands fluttered in the air and waved away his apology. "Do not fret, you are injured, one cannot expect you to be courteous in your condition."

He frowned. One should expect courtesy despite any condition. He shifted and her fingers wrapped around his bicep. She smiled with encouragement and helped him to his feet. He kept one hand on the blanket he'd wrapped around his waist and scanned the room. When he'd been awakened by the knocking earlier that hour, he had found her asleep against the wall and himself significantly under-dressed. What had happened to his clothes? And how had he gotten into this woman's house in the first place?

Wrapping her arm around his waist, she led him through the small room, around an old couch frayed from years of use and through a narrow hall into another, even smaller room.

She stopped and left him to lean against the doorjamb as she shuffled away to turn down the covers. The bed was the only piece of furniture in the room, though it was less a sign of poverty than a necessity, as the King-sized bed covered all the available space. She returned and pulled him toward the bed.

"It's big," he said.

"I like them big."

His head came up fast but her bland expression betrayed no double entendre. "Who are you?"

"My name is Grace."

"Who are you, Grace?"

She settled on the foot of the bed and folded her hands in her lap. "You do not know where you are?"

"No."

"That is strange."

Biting back impatience, he kept his tone flat, "I appreciate your assistance, but it is imperative that I know where I am. There are things at risk here that I cannot explain."

"You are a *viator*," she said. The matter of fact proclamation took him aback and suspicion trickled uneasily along his spine.

"I ask again, who are you?"

She pursed her lips and did not answer. He pushed up on his elbows and swung his legs off the bed.

"What are you doing?" She jumped off the mattress and barred him from standing. "You cannot leave. You are injured. Someone quite obviously wants you dead and I went through a lot of effort hauling you into my home."

Lucius grabbed her arm and yanked her down to look him in the eye. "Then do not play games with me. Who are you? Where am I?"

"I-" she worried her lip between her teeth before continuing, "I am Grace and you are in Oregon."

He raised a brow and let her arm go. She hid her lies behind innocent eyes. He didn't have time to play guessing games with the girl. Hailey was in danger and he needed to get in contact with Derian. The pieces of the puzzle were starting to fall into some order. Closing his eyes, he focused on the connection he had to Derian, only to find it missing. He cursed. He would have to return to the *Domus* and find another way.

"You cannot jump here."

His eyes opened to glare at Grace. "What are you talking about?"

"We have a buffer. *Viators* are not able to land in the community."

"What community is that?"

Her mouth opened, then shut and she crossed her arms. Eyes narrowed, she considered him. "I do not know that I can trust you, *viator*."

"You seem quite familiar with what I am, but you have me at a disadvantage. It seems that I am the one in a treacherous situation, not you." He pointed at his chest. "And as I am wounded and incapable of walking without assistance, you hold the upper hand. What could I possible do to threaten you?"

She opened her mouth only to shut it again, then swung around to face the wall. The soft murmur of her voice spoken beneath her breath filled the air. While he waited patiently for her to finish arguing with herself, he attempted to jump time and met failure again. He was trapped. How could he have landed in a no jump zone? His last memory was the searing pain of the bullet ripping through his chest and the look of shock on Hailey's face as he faded through time. He must have landed somewhere and been brought in. But why and by whom?

None of it made sense.

"This may be the most foolish thing I have ever done. I have been taught from the day I was born to distrust you." She turned back, reaching out for him. Her voice softened when her fingers touched his skin, "And yet I feel that I can trust you. That I *have* to trust you."

She stepped back and folded her arms across her chest. "But if I find that the trust is misplaced, I will find you and I will make sure you pay for the betrayal."

Her fierceness prickled his skin and a glimpse of her vehement will peeked out from behind her naïve exterior. He said, "I give my word that I will bring no harm to you."

She rolled her eyes up to the ceiling. "If this were about me we would not be having this discussion." She sighed and sat at the foot of the bed. "I found you face down in the mud of my garden. Well, my cat did actually. But he could not do much to assist, so he brought me to you. Then I brought you into the house and cleaned your wound."

He raised a brow and shifted back against the headboard. This miniscule woman couldn't possibly have carried him into the house by herself.

"Do not look at me that way. I did pull you in here. It took a lot of work and a thank you would be appropriate."

"I thank you then," he said. She looked down, distracted and unsure. The way she bristled made her lips thin and little dimples appeared at her cheeks. He continued, "I apologize if I did not believe you were capable of doing as you say. It is quite a feat for anyone."

Her hand fluttered up and waved away his apology. "Yes well, someone else would have probably done it much faster." She looked down at her shirt. "And with less mess."

Again he had an excuse to look at her wonderfully full breasts, his breath caught in his throat and the room suddenly felt even smaller. "You still have not told me very much."

"Yes, I know. I just don't know how to say it." She brushed her hand along her pant leg. "I am a *tiresian*."

Lucius bit back a disbelieving snort. The *tiresian*s had died out nearly 800 years before and yet this young girl couldn't be older than her late twenties. He narrowed his eyes at her. *Tiresian*s aged much slower than most humans, making it likely she was nearly 300 years old. It couldn't be. "It's not possible."

"Any less possible than a bloody *viator* landing in my garden? No, it is possible and you are here. And unfortunately for both of us, if anyone finds out you are here I cannot begin to imagine what they would do. Although I can guarantee it would not be pleasant."

"Are you threatening me?"

"No. I am merely stating reality. The elders do not take kindly to outsiders in the community. They also have a hate for the *viator* that I cannot understand, but it is deep and irreversible. And so it seems you are stuck with trusting me to get you healed and on your way."

His stomach fell. If she were telling the truth, then he was essentially trapped in the most hostile environment he could imagine. The *tiresians*, if they were indeed alive, had good reason to distrust and hate the *viators*. All that stood between him and their version of retribution was this diminutive woman with haunting, brown eyes.

She smiled and said, "It is a good thing I like you. Otherwise you might not have a chance at all."

****

Lucius threw off the sheet and stood. The cool air reminded him he had no clothes to put on. His hands fisted as he drew the sheet toward his midsection and tied them around his waist. He wavered a bit as he let the tempest within his head settle. The bullet had traveled straight through his chest avoiding anything essential. It was fortunate for him that he would not need Grace to dig into his muscle to find the bullet. But it hurt like a bastard.

He flexed his neck and rolled his shoulders. Fresh pain lanced through his chest. It would heal and he'd have another scar to add to an impressive collection. The first, a long slice in his quad, had been put there by an enraged Visigoth nearly 2,000 years ago. This last was a gift from an enemy closer to home, one he should have seen coming. It was imperative that he return to the *Domus*. As *magister*, his responsibility lay in protecting the *viators* and ensuring that the threat Nikanuur and Carlo posed to the people under his care was handled. The five-mile buffer meant he needed to move quickly to find a location suitable to jumping time. He dreaded the walk if he could not find a vehicle.

Grace had left him to rest and he still hadn't processed the revelation of her people's existence. Unfortunately, there was little time to investigate the existence of a group thought to have disappeared into the ether of time. The current threat to the *Domus* was paramount and this would give the *tiresian* community plenty of time to disappear. A part of him figured it would be for the best. There was simply too painful a history between the two peoples.

He reached for the door knob, turning it slowly until he could crack the door and peek into the hall. Dense with silence, the cottage felt conveniently empty. He slid through the door and stole into the front room, the hardwood barely registering his step despite his enormous frame. Decades of experience as a warrior of Rome, as well as centuries tracking rogue *viator* taught his body how to move softly. He craned his neck to see over the tall back of the couch as he slid around the side.

Grace lay curled under a faded quilt, her arm hanging down the side and a book opened on the floor as though it had tumbled from her hand. Long black hair splayed out around her, curling over her arms and across the quilt toward her waist. Its rich sheen shimmered purple beneath the soft daylight pouring in from a side window. The sight intrigued him and he took an extra moment to sear the image in his mind, then turned away. Important matters required his attention and the distraction of an enticing *tiresian* with innocent eyes, and lips that taunted him could disrupt an already tenuous situation.

His pants lay over a kitchen chair along with the tattered remains of his shirt. Just as he slid a foot into one of the legs, a knock sounded heavily at the door. His head shot up and he cursed. The girl had more visitors than a Roman bathhouse.

A surprised head with a frizzy halo of black hair popped up from the couch. She blinked in his direction then swung back to the door as the knocking continued.

"Grace!" a shout pierced the air from behind the door. "Let me in this instant!"

Grace stood and the quilt slid into a heap at her feet. She looked toward him then down at the floor. Grabbing the book, she hurried to him and slammed it against his belly. "You have to hide. Take this."

"I am not–"

"If you want to get out of here before the next millennium, you had better hide. It is my grandmother. Believe me you do not want her to know you are here." She pushed him toward her bedroom.

"I am hiding from your grandmother?" The girl acted like an army of Gauls stood outside.

"Yes. Now go."

"Who exactly is your grandmother?"

She shoved him into the room and made to slam the door in his face. He stopped it with his knee. "Grace."

Her big eyes blinked up at him, wide with fear. "My grandmother is called Althea."

Lucius felt the blood drain from his head and he let her close the door. Somehow he'd managed to land in the lap of the granddaughter of the one of the most dangerous adversaries the *viators* had ever encountered. She was the woman that had led a bloody revolt against the *viators*, costing the lives of many of his compatriots. He sat heavily on the mattress and looked down at the young face of Harry Potter. How exactly would he get out of this alive? He doubted the young wizard with round glasses had the answer he was looking for.

5

Grace swung the door open wide. "Grandmother, I apologize, I was sleeping and did not hear you knocking."

The grey-haired woman looked up at her granddaughter, her cheeks red with irritation. "You sleep far too much. You should be down in the community doing your share."

As Althea pushed into the cottage, Grace raised her eyes to the heavens. "Please come in." She doubted the old witch would notice the subtle sarcasm in the statement. Why did everyone insist on invading her space? She'd never noticed until today how much it bothered her.

Althea swung around and propped her hands on her hips. The cut of her dress made her look more like a quilted pillow than a full-figured woman. Grace wondered if that was what she had to look forward to in her old age. It was not the most pleasant thought.

Her grandmother scanned the room. Disapproval heightened the tension as her gaze stopped at the clutter and well-worn trappings. Grace stopped herself from the temptation to defend her home. It was hard enough finding furnishings, let alone anything that looked this nice when they were cut off from society. But Althea wouldn't hear it.

"Would you like something to drink?" Grace asked.

"You should be down at the Hall helping to prepare for tonight. You have a position to maintain in the community. People expect you to lead by example." Althea threw her arm out to gesture at the room. "You are beyond 300 years old, Grace. When I was 300, I was leading our people to freedom! And still you lock yourself away in this hovel."

Grace bristled and moved away from the front door, not bothering to shut it. "This is no hovel. This is my home."

Althea may have been 300 when she led the rebellion against the *viators*, but she was well over 1,000 now. With luck she could push the old woman out the door.

Althea snorted and raised a fat finger to wave at her granddaughter. "Tymion deserves better from a wife." She looked Grace up and down and sneered. "And put on some decent clothes. A well-bred lady does not wear trousers."

Grace rolled her eyes. There were no well-bred ladies in the community, just well-bred cattle. "I am not going tonight."

"That is ridiculous."

"It may be, but I am not going." Grace's stomach spat fire into her chest. She put her hands behind her back and gripped them in a white-knuckled knot. What was she thinking? She couldn't stand her ground today. Such a refusal would not be tolerated and although her grandmother couldn't drag her down to the Hall herself, she'd find one of her minions to do that for her. But with her unexpected houseguest, Grace couldn't afford to have Althea's men snooping around the house.

She blurted out the only reasonable excuse that came to mind, "I have been feeling quite ill. I fear I will faint from the crush of so many in the Hall tonight. That would be a far worse situation than if I simply did not attend."

Althea squinted at her. "What is wrong with you?"

"I am simply getting over a cold, but it has made me dizzy and weak. I need a few more days to recover. I promise, after that time I will make an effort to prove myself worthy to you and to Tymion." Grace moved toward the couch, displacing several pillows as she made a dramatic effort to look ill. It helped that she felt sick to her stomach.

"I will send Endymion to attend you."

Grace did not want the ancient doctor showing up at her door for so many reasons. The *viator* in her bedroom was the least of them. "No, no, I assure you I am feeling much better. I just need to rest. The worst of it passed yesterday."

Althea frowned, distaste visible on her twisted lips. "I am not happy with you. But as you are ill, we will discuss this at a later time. There must be changes, Grace, or your life here will not be a happy one."

Grace looked at the floor. Tears threatened and she swiftly squashed them. Her grandmother already knew her weaknesses. She did not need to provide the woman with more to hold her hostage. The door shut with a thud.

She was trapped.

A rustle and a soft click preceded her guest entering the room. Grace scrambled to sit upright. Gods he was handsome. His hair was too short to look tussled, but she could tell by the slightly flattened side that he'd slept hard. The steel in his eyes hid all traces of exhaustion, but his skin had a grey tone that looked far from healthy. He should be in bed. "What are you doing up?"

His steady gait took him to the front door where he pulled back the thin, gingham curtains. Grace let a moment pass as he peered through the small window placed far too high for her use. He had to duck to look out the frosty glass.

How had she not noticed his tremendous height? Easily a foot taller than she, he made the room seem quaint and pathetically small. "You really should rest, you look like death."

His voice rumbled like the Snake River through a canyon, "I need answers." He swung around and pierced her with his gaze, initiating a tremor that started at the base of her spine. "How did I end up in your–" he paused and raised a mocking brow, "community?"

"I have no idea."

"I find that unlikely."

"Unlikely or not, I have no idea how you got to be here. I discovered you face down in the mud only hours ago. I had hoped that you could answer the same question." She grew tired of him staring down at her and stood. It didn't help. Moving around the couch, she crossed her arms. At least at this distance his head had to rise to see her.

His lips twitched. "You are aware of the history between the *viators* and *tiresians*?"

"I am. But I only know the version handed down by the elders. I imagine you have a vastly different interpretation."

"Perhaps, though they may be more similar than you imagine."

"Our version says your people enslaved ours. Because we had smaller numbers and an inability to jump time like you, we were susceptible and you took advantage. We had to disappear to save ourselves and we have been in hiding for centuries because of you." Grace watched him, his face a mask as cold and unapproachable as his cross-armed stance. A few flickers of response the only hint that anything she said impacted him. Were the stories true? Was he capable of the horrid acts and cruelty her grandmother preached? With his hard expression and lack of emotion, a touch of doubt crept into her skin. Had she let in a monster?

"It is true." His face didn't change a fraction and her heart thudded to a stop. In her visions, she'd read compassion and entreaty, not this cold detachment.

"Are you here to do that to us again?"

His head jerked up and his lips lowered in a mild frown. "No." Then as though a thought hit him, he dropped his arms from across his chest and gave the slightest smile. "No, however I can see why you would assume that. I honestly had no idea your people were still alive and I have even less idea how I landed here in the first place."

He turned back to the door and looked out the window. "I appreciate your hospitality." Looking over his shoulder, he sent a devilish grin, stopping her heart again–this time fear had nothing to do with it. His long fingers wrapped around the door knob. "Do you happen to have a vehicle?"

"No." Grace took a step toward him. "You are not leaving, are you?"

"Yes. There are things I have to do. Do not worry. You have nothing to fear from me. No one will know that you or the community is here."

That concern was the furthest from her mind. He couldn't possibly think about leaving in his condition. "You cannot go. You are hurt. I promise no one will know you are here while you recover."

He stopped before walking across the threshold. "Thank you for the offer but I must leave. Lives depend on it."

She closed the distance between them and grabbed his elbow, a jolt of hot awareness flaring as she made contact. His tension-filled eyes faded from view and were replaced by the image of his blood-covered body lying amid burning rubble. Heat burned her skin and the hairs on her arms stood on end. In the distance two figures huddled beneath swirling smoke. A young woman looked up with tear-streaked eyes then faded from view, her arms clutching the body in her arms. Grace looked down. Her *viator* stared up at her with vacant eyes, the vision of death ripping a scream from her lips.

Chills wracked her body and her knees gave out as darkness soaked her. Suddenly, she felt caught up in a current, floating in a whirlpool of warmth. Higher she swam until she felt the pull from the undertow take her back into the depths. "No," her voice croaked in a vain attempt to prevent the inevitable, "please."

"Grace." A sharp bark pierced through the muted effects of the depths, "Damn it woman. Wake up."

Her head jerked and she felt herself hurtle into a soft cushion. The bright light of the afternoon sun hit like cold water against hot skin as her eyes fluttered open. Her *viator* glared down at her, his arms pushing at her shoulders. Comfort and safety enveloped her. "I don't know your name," she whispered.

He rocked back on his heels. Somehow she'd been moved from the door back to the couch. She pushed up on the cushion, but he leaned forward and stopped her with a hand to her belly. "Don't move, you're still pale."

The steel and stone mask had lifted and the man from her earlier visions stared back at her. Sighing in relief that she hadn't been wrong about him, she placed her fingers on his wrist and squeezed. "I am well. It was simply a bad vision. It happens. Please, just let me up." Her throat ached and she wondered how long she had screamed. Had some-one heard her cries? "Was I very loud?"

"A bit."

"Oh gods." She brushed his hands aside and pushed against the cushions to sit. "They could have heard me. We must get you somewhere safe."

He chuckled and ran a hand down her arm. "You weren't as loud as that."

Grace peeked up at his amused lips then looked down, only to be faced with his remarkable chest. Despite being covered in the tattered remains of his shirt, the strength of muscle had her catching her breath. Memories of dreams and visions that had haunted her for nearly a year pressed at the back of her eyes. She squashed them. Some had featured his full lips and sculpted chest far too prominently.

His hand continued to brush up and down her arm, triggering goose bumps to rise up from her neck to her scalp. Each hair on her head felt as though it vibrated with anticipation. She stood and brushed past him. "I still need to know your name."

"Lucius Gratius Cossus."

"That is quite a name." She walked toward the kitchen and pulled out a rickety stool. It needed repair, but she found if she leaned to the left it served quite well as a seat. "Is it Roman?"

His expression inquisitive, he inclined his chin in response.

"Then you were around when the *tiresians* and *viators* clashed."

"Yes, but–"

Grace held up a finger. "I do not believe you were in-volved–at least not intimately. I am just curious. Perhaps you will tell me about what you remember sometime."

He kept an intense watch on her as he moved, each inch sucking a little more air from her lungs. By the time he reached the kitchen she'd be out of breath. "I would very much like to discuss this and many other things with you in the future." He stopped a foot from her and continued, "You are not quite like anyone I have met."

"What exactly do you mean by that?" she breathed.

This time he raised a finger. "Simply that one moment you faint and the next you are back to conversing as though nothing had happened."

Something certainly had happened, but Grace still needed time to process. Visions hit like lightning in a storm, a flash of image, a feeling, an impression. They hardly ever had substance or definition and this last had both. The meaning seemed pretty clear and she wasn't quite sure how to tell him. "It is complicated."

"I am certain it is." His eyes bore into hers as though he'd calculated her answers and waited for the solution. "And I would very much like to learn more, but I must go. Do you think you will be alright now?"

"You cannot go!"

He turned toward the door. "I *am* going."

"No! You do not understand." Grace hopped off the stool and chased him to the door again. When she reached out to grab him, she hesitated a half-second before wrapping her fingers around his arm. Nothing happened and she thanked the gods for their gift. "Wherever it is you are go-ing, you cannot."

His chest heaved with a frustrated breath. "I do not have time for this."

She pulled her lip with her teeth then let it go to say, "If you leave now you will die."

"That is ridiculous."

"It is the truth, I saw it."

He straightened and looked down his strong Roman nose at her. "You are certain?"

"Yes. I know it seems strange, but I know. I have never seen a vision so vivid. If you go, you will die and your friends will mourn you."

He ran a hand over his head and gripped the back of his neck. "This is not at all convenient."

6

Inconvenient did not begin to describe the issue. Lucius looked down at the delicate fingers wrapped around his arm. "Tell me about your vision."

She stepped back, dropping her fingers from his arm. "Would you close the door? If someone sees you, it would be quite unfortunate."

Lucius complied. He moved to the side of the room to stand beside a single-paned window and pulled back the curtains to keep an eye on the front walk. The last thing he wanted was to be caught off guard again by another visitor. The sound of Althea's voice had turned his skin to ice. It had been nearly a thousand years since he'd seen the woman, let alone heard the husky authority. There'd been evil intentions on both sides of that fight, but Lucius had witnessed firsthand the lengths this ancient *tiresian* would go to in order to protect what she believed was her right.

That this beautiful and kind woman with hair down to her waist came from the same family-line intrigued him. Beneath her cautious and naïve exterior lay a solid granite reserve, of that he was positive. How would Grace react when that reserve was needed? Lucius was the head of the *viator's Domus* for his ability to spot a person's strengths and talents as much as his leadership skills. Grace's measured comportment and intelligence was the kind that would have drawn his attention and allowed her to move up quickly in the ranks.

Except that she wasn't a *viator* and his inclination toward her was definitely not business related. He asked again, "What did you see in the vision?"

"You were in a burning building. In the distance were two people. A woman was crying." Grace pulled her lip between her teeth. "She was leaning over a man, I believe, and then she disappeared."

"A *viator* for certain. What did she look like?"

"Shoulder-length hair, I couldn't tell the color, but I am sure it was much lighter than mine. Other than that I could not tell much. She was fit, but that was all I could see."

"Probably Hailey. That was who I was going after when I walked out the door."

She looked down. "Oh." Then she raised her eyes, a small lopsided smile on her lips. "Are you close?"

"No." His stomach clenched and he realized he hadn't eaten in nearly two days. He glanced at her kitchen and laid eyes on a basket of fruit. "Hailey is a *novus*. A new *viator*. But she's caught up in a conspiracy and requires assistance." She'd come to his aid only to be captured and he'd been helpless to stop it. He had to get back to his people.

His stomach clenched again and he absently ran his hand over his belly. Grace narrowed her eyes then strode to the kitchen. "When was the last time you ate?"

"It has been a while."

She picked up a banana, walked over to the kitchen table and pulled out a chair. Two normal-sized people would barely sit comfortably at it. His giant stature would take up most of the space. Grace motioned to the chair. "Sit."

Lucius looked out the window again, reluctant to give up his vantage point. "Everyone is preparing for the festival tonight, so no one will be paying me any visits. At least not until tomorrow when, if I am lucky, the underworld will open up and suck me under before my grandmother finds me."

"You do not like her?"

Grace shook her head. "She is family and she thinks she does what is right by us."

"You disagree."

"It does not matter if I do." She returned to the kitchen and began opening the cupboards. "I hope you like pasta, it is about the only thing I have. My cousin is resourceful, but he lacks creativity when shopping."

"Grace. The visions–" She stopped pulling out supplies and looked directly at him. There was vulnerability in her expression, like she was frightened of his question. He continued, "You said you saw my death."

She turned away before answering, her reply barely a whisper, "Yes."

"Is it a certainty?"

She rested her palms on the counter. "I am not positive, but I do not believe so. If they follow the pattern of most visions, then no. What we see is a possible future that would happen should a particular action be carried out."

"So you see what could be. But there is no guarantee that I would be walking into the situation you described."

She picked up a knife and sliced into an onion, quick and efficient. "I know for a fact that should you leave and do what you intended, you would die." The blade flew through the onion, nearly sending him to his feet to prevent her from

48

slicing off a finger. No injury done, she slid the chopped pieces off the board and pulled out a green pepper.

"And so, you change your intention and you will not die." She paused halfway through the pepper and looked up at him. "At least, not in that way."

"It is an impressive talent."

"It has its value. In general, visions are vague impressions, much closer to what humans would call intuition, though far more powerful."

"You do not consider yourselves human?"

"Do you?"

Lucius didn't answer. The question of a *viator's* humanity had been debated for millennia. Neither the scientists nor the philosophers had come up with a suitable solution.

He glanced out the window again. Lush forest and a dreary sky were all that he could see. It made him uncomfortable. If someone were watching from the trees he would never know.

"Sit Lucius, you are making me nervous."

Her eyes sparkled and he was pretty sure nervousness was not her impetus for demanding he sit. But he complied nonetheless, turning toward the table.

Glass shattered behind his back.

"What was that?" Grace ran toward him from around the counter.

"Get back!" Lucius ducked beneath the window and slithered toward the kitchen. Grace froze, her eyes growing wide with confusion and fear. She shook her head and took a step toward him. He shouted, "I said stay back!"

The sniper would have his eyes on all the windows and exits waiting for his next opportunity. The kitchen, thankfully bereft of windows, provided Grace protected cover–for now. Listening for any sign that a force prepared to enter the house, he scanned the interior for the best place to resist attack. The kitchen, dining room and living room were combined as one open room. The short hall led to the bedroom, bath and rear door. They were entirely too vulnerable should anyone attempt to pin them inside.

And he had no weapons to use for defense. He cursed Carlo and Millard. Apparently they had not been satisfied that the first shot had done the job and now stalked him here to finish him off. He stood as he entered the kitchen. "Grace, do you have any weapons?"

"Weapons?"

"Yes, a handgun, rifle? Anything?"

"I have a shotgun for scaring away wild animals. But, I only have rock salt. I have never had a need for anything else." She glanced toward the hall. "It is in my bedroom."

Lucius headed toward the back of the bungalow, making certain to avoid exposing himself to the windows. A shot splintered the wall to his left and he swung around to see Grace fall flat on her rear, her mouth hanging open in surprise. "Get the hell back! Someone is trying to kill us."

"Kills us?" she squeaked.

"Just get back to the kitchen."

"But why are they trying to kill us?"

Lucius continued toward the rear of the house, keeping one eye pinned on Grace. He wouldn't put it past her to disregard his order again. Getting her safely away from the threat was his first order of business.

The windowless hall provided a safe haven as he approached the bedroom. The door creaked with a weathered groan as he opened it to peer in. Heavy, damask curtains covered the window above the bed.

With the bed taking up most of the floor space, he had to shuffle sideways to get to the small closet. The sliding door stuck from disrepair, required a solid shove to open it. A meager collection of plain dresses hung neatly beside an antique dresser. Two pairs of heavily worn shoes sat beside the long barrel of a shotgun.

Grabbing the stock, he pulled it out and scanned the closet for the rock salt. He found four shells shoved in the back corner of the high shelf. He loaded two into the shotgun and pocketed the spares. Grace, as short as she was, would never have been able to retrieve the shells in an emergency. He felt an unrelenting desire to scold her for being so unprepared.

A single woman living in the middle of the woods needed to be ready for anything. Not that rock salt was the most effective means for protection and certainly not against their current assailant, but it would do for the moment.

He returned to the front room and found Grace peeking over the kitchen counter. He smiled to reassure her. She grinned in response and rose. In each hand she held large kitchen knives. He frowned. "Those aren't going to be very effective."

She raised her brow. "It is better than having nothing. Now, are you going to tell me who is trying to kills us?"

"Me actually, they are trying to kill me. You just happen to be in the way."

"Is this a regular occurrence for you?"

"Not entirely, though I am not unused to the experience."

"Why?"

He slid along the wall toward the window and angled his head to get a glimpse of the forest. Nothing moved. From what he could tell, they were not dealing with a force that would take the bungalow. If they were, it would have happened already. More than likely they faced one, maybe two snipers hidden in the forest. He needed to draw them away from the building and from Grace.

"Lucius, are you going to tell me why they are trying to kill you?"

"We are having some power issues at the *Domus*."

"You're from the *Domus*?" Her voice squeaked and it drew his attention back to her.

"Yes."

"You are not just a minion are you?"

He laughed. She had made the comment with such hope. "No. I am the *magister*. I run the *Domus*."

"Oh dear, we really do need to get you out of here."

What exactly had the woman been taught about the *Domus*? Based on the history between the two peoples, it could hardly be good. But things had changed significantly, much of that as soon as he'd been appointed *magister*. He shouldn't have cared what she thought, but he did. She came around the counter, her eyes trained on the window but her lips set in determination.

"Stay in the kitchen," he barked and she stopped short then glared back in defiance.

"We have to get you out of here," she said.

"Yes, but you are staying in the kitchen while I draw them away from here."

"And what happens when you are gone and they come in here anyway?"

He doubted they had any intention of targeting Grace, but she brought up a critical point. How did he know she would not be threatened once he left? "Fine. We go now, out the back."

She bent forward and hurried toward him. He grabbed her hand to pull her toward the hall. When their hands met she gasped, stumbled and dropped his hand. "No. We need to go through the front."

"What?"

"Trust me." She tugged on his arm and pulled him toward the front door. She dropped his hand as she plastered herself against the wall beside the door. Her chest heaved with fright. Wrapping his fingers around the knob he turned it with measured patience, but before he could open the door she grabbed his wrist. "Wait." Her eyes fluttered shut then opened slowly. "It is alright. Go fast and to the right."

He didn't pause to question her, something told him to trust her intuition. His guess wouldn't be any more informed than hers at this point. The door banged against the wall when he pushed it open. Her hand in his, they ran for the trees. In his other hand he held the shotgun, ready should he find a target.

An explosion from behind sent them hurtling into the undergrowth. Grace rolled behind the thick branches of an evergreen then brought herself up to her knees to peer at the smoke and dust billowing from the back of her house. "Gods, that was close." She smiled up at him. "I am very glad I was not in there."

He frowned, a little uncomfortable with her unflappable response to the explosion. He'd never had the opportunity to work with a *tiresian*. The value and necessity of their skills had just become blatantly obvious. Unfortunately, the thud in his heart felt far more like terror than excitement at the possibilities. This beautiful woman may have died in a mangled mess of blood and muscle had she not seen what lay ahead. "Grace," he breathed and reached out to place a hand on her shoulder.

She swung toward him, grabbed his elbow and yanked him down in time to avoid a bullet before it buried itself in the tree. Wide-eyed, she said, "I think we need to get out of here."

"Stay close enough to touch."

Her lips trembled, but she smiled and let a sparkle tease at the side of her eyes. "I think that is a brilliant plan."

7

The shack hid beneath a multitude of branches, dry leaves, and creeping ferns. The last time Grace had visited the old building she'd been much younger–nearly 100 years younger. It had once served as a place for the solitude and privacy she couldn't find in her grandmother's household. Then she'd moved into her bungalow and the need for a place to escape had lessened. Sadness wrenched her heart as she witnessed the impact time and neglect could have on the things she loved. Then again, it had been her neglect that left it in such a state.

Lucius put out an arm to hold her back before she could enter the rundown building. "Let me check it out first."

Grace allowed him take the lead since she had little worry that trouble awaited them inside, at least for the moment. Her visions had led them along a zigzagging obstacle course through the Oregon forest. After an hour, she knew they'd lost the shooter but they continued to run until Lucius felt more comfortable. When she'd realized the direction they'd taken, she knew the frontier shack would serve them well until trouble died down.

Lucius popped his head out the door and motioned for Grace to follow him in. "It isn't exactly secure, but it will do for now."

She touched his arm as she passed. No visions flashed, giving her a sense of solace in their decision. Had there been danger there should have been something to tell her so. Her talent hadn't disappointed her yet.

The old wood creaked beneath her feet. The scent of rotted wood mixed with decomposing leaves flared her nostrils and the cool dampness of waterlogged walls permeated the air. She looked up at the ceiling to make sure it wouldn't crash in on them if she dared to breath heavy. "Secure is definitely not the word for it. But it is safe for the moment."

"You do not seem too upset by the situation," he said.

She shrugged. No one was more surprised than she by her reaction. "I will react later I expect. There is no point in worrying over past troubles now when so much remains to be seen."

"What exactly does that mean? What do you know about the future now?"

She shook her head and sighed. "Nothing. The future is as much a mystery to me now as it is to you."

"How is that possible? You knew down to the minute what would happen only a half an hour ago." His eyes narrowed but he relaxed enough to lean against the doorjamb.

"I do not know how it works. This is all quite new to me," she said. The elders told stories of similar experiences. That at times of extreme need, the visions could come clear and consistent. It had been just that talent which had drawn the interest of the *viators* during the age of Rome. It was also a talent that came with time and practice. How surprised her grandmother would be to discover it had found her so early.

The grasping fingers of branches had left their mark across his bare chest, his tattered shirt lost in their run for cover. She looked down to see snags and tears throughout her shirt. Once the heat of the moment passed, the cold would seep into their bodies. She glanced around the single room shack. The pieces of wood that lay scattered across the floor were far too wet to burn and she hadn't exactly planned for a night out in the elements. Shivers ran up her arms.

When she looked up, Lucius stalked toward her. She gasped when he pulled her close and rubbed his hands down her arms. Heat pooled in her belly as his action fanned tendrils of warmth through her limbs. She sighed and placed her head against his chest. A drop of water landed on her nose and made her blink. When her eyes reopened, his knuckle brushed the wetness away and he frowned at her as though the action confused him. She stared into his expression, lost in the moment. The pull she felt to go to him had her leaning toward him.

He lowered his hand and strode toward the door, keeping his back to her long enough for her to shake away the strange feelings. She could count the hours she'd known him on her fingers, she was a fool to blindly trust anyone in such a short time. But then her grandmother repeatedly named her a fool, so perhaps it was true.

She wandered to the far wall and slid down to sit, her back leaning against the moist wood. "I do not know how long you want to remain here, but I imagine long enough for your enemy to grow tired of waiting. That could be some time."

He glanced over his shoulder at her. "I shouldn't wait long. If it is who I think it is, he will find me soon enough."

Grace wrinkled her brow. He seemed so calm in the face of potential violence. "Who is he?"

"An old enemy that I thought had disappeared long ago."

"How inconvenient of him."

Lucius swung around. "What?"

"How inconvenient of him not to stay disappeared," she replied.

He crossed his arms over his chest. "You are a strange one, Grace."

She let the comment pass. Perhaps she was strange, she really didn't know. "Well, it was inconvenient for me at the very least. I was quite excited about preparing dinner and now we have nothing to eat and it is going to get cold."

Lucius strolled to her side and loomed. It was the only description to attribute to his stance. Tall, dark, intense, he seemed tailor made for a fantasy novel. Perhaps she'd discover that he was a dark warlock and he could magically create a warm cloak to throw around her shoulders.

He stooped down to sit beside her. His body blazed heat against her side where they touched. An arm snaked around her back and he pulled her toward him. She said, "Oh, wait, what–"

"Just deal with it. In the last five minutes all you have talked about is the cold."

"I am quite certain that is not true."

"Just deal with it."

She didn't argue. He was so warm and her insides tingled in a delicious way.

****

They snuggled close for nearly an hour when her arm alerted her to its dead state with a barrage of pins and needles. "Oh gods, that hurts."

"Shake it."

"That makes it hurt more."

Lucius grabbed her arm and started to rub. He was getting far too familiar with all the rubbing and snuggling, even if it did feel delicious. Grace moved her other arm to grab his wrist. Before she could extricate herself from his ministrations a flash of light and a picture of him covered the room. He was larger than real life, as though she watched him from mere centimeters away. His eyes stared with intensity and somehow she knew in this vision he was looking directly at her.

Her breath caught in her throat as she realized he was leaning toward her for a kiss. Her eyes fluttered closed as she waited for the taste of his lips on hers.

"Grace."

A rough shake of her shoulders greeted her instead. When she opened her eyes he loomed in her view just as he had in her vision. Only this time his eyes were shadowed with concern, not passionate intensity. A sigh escaped her lips.

"What happened? Was that another vision?"

It had most certainly been a vision, but it had been from her perspective. *Tiresians* never saw visions of their own future. It was thoroughly confusing. "Yes, but it was nothing really."

"Nothing does not cause disappointment."

"I beg your pardon?"

"You were disappointed when you opened your eyes."

"I most certainly was not." What rubbish. He fairly dripped with arrogance. The man certainly thought he knew her mind.

He leaned forward and she felt herself go cross-eyed. "Then tell me what you saw."

Grace pushed him away. "You seem to think you are entitled to all of my visions."

"Was I involved in this one?"

She bit her lip and worried it between her teeth. Her stomach began to ache, but from the strain or the hunger she wasn't quite sure.

"I will take that as a yes. In that case, I am entitled."

She didn't respond.

"Grace," he growled.

"You cannot intimidate me." She tucked a strand of hair behind her ear. The race through the trees had tangled it mercilessly. Now she yearned for a brush. Hungry, cold, an irritatingly demanding *viator*, and no brush–could things get worse?

"It is imperative that I am aware of anything that might impact our safety. Even something that to you seems petty or inconsequential could mean our life or death."

"Oh you do not need to get as dramatic as that. I can promise you this is no life or death matter."

"Grace!" His voice rocked against the damp wooden walls.

"Your bellowing is far more likely to threaten our safety." He opened his mouth and she knew without a doubt he'd match his last bellow. The man was a flash pan of heat and passion. "Fine. I will tell you."

He leaned back and looked at her through narrowed lids. She crossed her arms and frowned right back at him.

"What I saw was you and I think you meant to kiss me. That is all, nothing more. Very unexciting and not at all dangerous."

"Why were you disappointed?" His voice had lost the forest bear quality and coasted softly over her.

She turned her head and met his eyes, not quite sure what he hid behind his stoic expression. "I told you, I was not disappointed."

He quirked a brow but waited for her to continue.

"All right, I was disappointed." She turned away again. She would never survive this. She may not have died in the explosion, but he'd kill her right now with embarrassment. "I was disappointed that I woke before you could kiss me."

He didn't respond and she waited. The heavy thud of her heart throbbed up to her ears and if he said something, it was possible she would not have heard it. Was he trying to hide his mirth? He did not seem the type, but he was far too quiet.

She turned to peek at his expression only to be met with the same depth of intensity she'd seen in her vision. Her lips flapped open in surprise. "I do not want you to think I was asking you to–"

His lips slanted over hers and she lost her train of thought. He tasted of salt and timelessness–a wholly unusual experience. The nerves at the tip of her tongue tingled and her lips felt like they were filling with warmth and heady anticipation. His lips merged and mingled with hers, insisting she surrender to temptation.

The scent of him filled her senses, pine and loam mixed with salt and humanity. A rugged hand rose to cup the back of her neck and he deepened the kiss, pulling and teasing, his tongue darting into the tiny crevice at the corner of her mouth. Her heart thumped in a rapid staccato.

He pulled away and she thought the experience was far too short. Dark eyes, flecked with shimmering gold watched her. Convinced she'd forgotten how to breathe, she pushed the air from her lungs and stared back in wonder. "That was quite possibly better than ice cream."

His laugh punched the air and he quirked a brow at her, his lips now tipped in amusement. "I take that to mean you enjoyed it."

"Quite. Could we do it again?"

His head fell back and he laughed again, pulling her close to his chest, she could hear the rumble deep beneath his ribs. A happy spark spread from her toes to her head, dizzying and unexpected. Never had she felt the joy to be held by another like this. It was amazing, but also a bit frightening.

She pulled away. "I do not think the elders would approve of my behavior, though honestly I could not care less. You are quite the man Lucius Gratius Cossus. Do you think you could–"

He turned away from her, placing his finger against her lips. Grace stilled and listened. Low voices filtered in from outdoors, followed by the tell-tale crunch of boots snapping small branches. Lucius rose, pulling her with him and then blocked her view of the door. The shotgun leaned against the wall and she reached out to pull it into her arms. Lifting it to her shoulder, she pointed the barrel beside his arm and waited.

Familiar voices trickled in from behind the weathered door. "It is my cousin," she whispered into his back and lowered the gun. He didn't relax.

The door creaked open and Tymion's large frame loomed in the entrance. "Who in Hades are you?"

"You're still worshiping the old gods I see," Lucius growled.

Grace stepped around Lucius and put a hand on his arm. "All is well Tymion. He is a friend."

Phillip popped his head over Tymion's shoulder. "Grace? By gods you're safe!"

"Of course I am, why would you..." She remembered the explosion and frantic run through the forest. They must have investigated and found her home in wreckage. She cringed. While she and Lucius hid in the damp shack they must have been searching for her. Sending her cousin a smile that dripped with guilt, she stepped away from Lucius.

Tymion stayed her with his words. "Who is your friend, Grace?"

She blushed and glanced at Lucius. If they knew he was a *viator*, he would never get away. The anger against the time travelers ran too strong in the community. "He is just a man that got lost in the forest. Phillip, do you think you could give him a ride to town?"

Phillip started to nod, but Tymion shook his head. "Your house is missing two rooms, Grace. Try again."

She blanched. In her bucket of talents, subterfuge was dreadfully absent. "I–it was an accident. I don't know how it happened. I'm–"

Lucius grabbed her hand. "I am the reason for the explosion. If I leave, the trouble will follow me and leave you and Grace in safety."

Tymion's nose flared when his eyes caught sight of Lucius's hand covering hers. "I have the feeling that the story is significantly more complex than that." He put his hand out to Grace. Turning her head, she gave a weak smile to Lucius and strode toward Tymion.

She had to ensure that Lucius escaped, suspicion already shrouded everything they did. When she placed her hand in his, Tymion pulled her roughly from the shack. Three *tiresians* rushed past and grabbed Lucius, throwing him to the floor and binding his arms behind his back.

"Ty, No!" Grace tried to yank her hand from his grasp. "He's been injured, they will make it worse."

He continued to pull her away from the shack and Lucius. "There is nothing I can do. He is a stranger. The elders will want to see him. You are in enough trouble, you should not worry about a man you have only just met."

"Trouble? I am in trouble?"

He stopped, and swung her around so she faced him. His glare poured over her. "The books. They saw your books and the journals."

Her stomach flipped and fell until it settled into a heavy knot. Her life had just ended. They would never understand. They would never leave her alone now.

8

Grace shifted from one foot to the other. Nervousness rippled off her and he could feel it from across the room. Lucius had his gaze hooded, but watched all the figures as they waited. Althea kept her iron hand clamped down on her people as solidly as she ever had. She knew how to make a room sweat.

After trussing him up and pushing him through the forest, the *tiresians* had escorted them into a large hall, stark and lacking any of the comfortable amenities that usually marked a social space. The flat, windowless walls and polished wood floors were meant to intimidate. Seven tall backed chairs stood on a short dais against the far wall. The cavernous ceiling echoed each shuffle and carefully covered cough. It was a strange mix of ancient monarchy and puritan staunchness.

A man that hadn't lived through multiple reigns of caesars, kings, and dictators might have been intimidated. Lucius slumped against the wall, unimpressed.

A flurry of activity at the narrow, nondescript door beside the dais heralded the arrival of the elders. Five men and a single woman entered. Each wore the mantle of age, graying hair and stooped shoulders. Considering the long-lived nature of *tiresians*, it came as no surprise these people wielded such awe and reverence. Except age did not always indicate wisdom or strength, sometimes they were simply better at betting on the lucky throw of the dice.

The six took their seats, leaving the center empty. A few more moments passed before Althea made her entrance. Costumed in a long flowing robe made of the brightest red wool, she swooped across the floor, head held high and her gaze piercing the people that waited.

She sat with a flourish and the air whooshed from the room as the anticipation heightened. Lucius tried not to look bored.

"Grace, come forward." The ancient voice boomed, jolting Grace into motion. She stopped several feet from her grandmother, her hands clasped behind her back. Her spine straightened and her head tipped up. Althea's frown deepened. The woman had never been accustomed to people with a backbone. Warmth swelled deep inside Lucius's belly and a protective instinct ignited.

"I am not going to bother asking you what these," Althea motioned to a man that held a stack of charred papers and ruined books in his arms, "were doing in your cottage. You know that this is forbidden."

Grace stood unmoved and Lucius regretted not having a better view of the young *tiresian*'s face.

"Since you have repeatedly made it clear you do not respect the authority or values of our community, we will be taking steps to ensure you learn your rightful place."

A snort of derision escaped from Grace. Althea's head went back as though she'd been slapped and several gasps were stifled around the room. He wanted to applaud, but figured the gesture would be lost on the crowd.

Althea stood and stormed toward Grace. Grabbing the young woman's chin, she pinched it between her fingers. "You are far too much like your mother."

"Perhaps that is a good thing."

Althea struck Grace across the cheek, snapping her head to the side. Lucius lunged forward, only to be yanked back by the two men on either side of him. "You will learn how to behave here Grace or you will have a very long and unhappy life."

"It is already unhappy. I do not see that as much of a threat, *grandmother*."

Althea stepped back and squared her shoulders. She motioned toward Tymion who skulked at her side. "Take Grace to the community apartments. She can stay there until your wedding."

This announcement got a flicker of response from the hulking Tymion, but it was quickly hidden behind an uninterested exterior. Grace had not mentioned she was meant to be married. Lucius buried the news. It had not exactly been something he'd expect her to bring up, at least not until they'd shared the kiss. Yet she had not reacted as a woman eagerly awaiting marriage to another man.

Grace turned to the side and glanced in his direction. A blush crept across her cheeks. Was she also remembering the kiss?

Althea strode to the man holding the remains of Grace's books and pulled two thin leather volumes from his hands. She passed them to Tymion. "And once you have her settled I want these burned."

"No!" Grace swung toward Tymion and reached toward the books. "You cannot! Those are all I have left of her."

Althea turned her back on Grace and returned to her seat. "If you want to face her same fate, then please, continue your disobedience."

Grace stopped and pulled her bottom lip between her teeth. Then she opened her mouth to respond, but Tymion grabbed her roughly by the elbow and propelled her from the room. "Stop! This is not right! You cannot–" As she passed him, Grace met Lucius's gaze and dug in her heels. She swung around to the elders. "What are you going to do with him?"

"That is none of your concern."

"You are an evil, old woman! I hope everyone comes to realize it before it is too late."

"Tymion, remove her before she says something she regrets."

"I only regret I have not said this sooner!" Tymion had Grace out the door before she could continue.

Silence descended on the room like a heavy blanket of fog. Althea directed her attention to Lucius, but did nothing but stare for several moments. A number of the room's occupants shifted uncomfortably. Lucius kept his expression mild. Althea may play her people like keys on a piano, but the community would be served better by taking a lesson from Grace's strength.

"Bring him forward."

The two men grabbed at his elbows to lead him, but he was already walking toward the dais. Unsure of how to respond they hurried to sandwich him in, but a quick glare from him kept their hands from reaching out again. Althea's eyes narrowed at the exchange, her lips pursed.

"You remind me of a young man I once knew." It hadn't taken her long to recognize him. When she had last been at the *Domus* he served as a *venator*, an elite officer tasked with policing the *viator* and maintaining the authority of the *Domus*. Eight hundred years had passed and she no longer looked like the elegant and youthful woman she had been. Skin pulled tight at her cheekbones, but hung limply about her joints. Yet despite her body's frailty, Althea still held an aura of command and dominance.

"I am Lucius Gratius Cossus." A gasp escaped from several of the elders seated along the dais.

"The burden of leadership has left its mark on you, Lucius."

"Perhaps."

"Why are you here? What does the *Domus* wish with our community now? Have your kind not done enough?"

"I have no issue with the *tiresians*. You seem quite content in your kingdom, Althea. I bring no threat to you."

"That is difficult to believe. What I find strange is that the *magister* would come rather than send his army of *venator* to rouse us from our hiding."

That Althea kept tabs on the *Domus* and its leadership did not surprise him. It seemed quite in character. "It was a chance occurrence, I assure you."

"That, I am positive, is not the case. The only person that could have led you to us is my daughter. Had I known her expulsion would bring danger to our community I would have had her executed." Several eyes widened on the dais. There should not have been such surprise at the woman's Machiavellian nature. Perhaps they were too close to truly see the character of the woman who led them. The *viators* were all too aware of what she could do. Too many had died by her actions for them not to remember.

"I do not know your daughter."

"You lie!" Her voice careened across the room.

"You are quick to accuse her."

"Proof of her guilt stands before me."

Lucius declined to respond. Althea twisted truth like a cord of twine, knotting it so tight that reason could never break the bond. The interview would do nothing for him and he had to find a means to escape. Unfortunately, Althea would have to complete her performance before he could seek out his opportunity.

She stood to address her people. "My Family, before you stands the greatest threat to our kind that we have seen in 800 years. Once we were subjugated by the *viators*, abused, nothing more than slaves to their machinations. We risked everything to throw off the mantle of their dominance. We rose up and lost many of our brothers and sisters in our bid for freedom. I will not allow this to happen again. I will not allow a *viator* to destroy our hard-earned liberty."

She directed her gaze at him. "Lucius Gratius Cossus, *magister* of the *Domus*, your presence here is a threat to our livelihood. Your actions are an act of aggression against our people. You cannot be allowed to alert others to our presence and I cannot allow you to stay. Therefore I am forced to command your execution."

Several sharp exclamations echoed throughout the room, but when she raised her eyes to sort out the dissention, the room grew still. Lucius did not bother to react.

"He will be executed at dawn as outlined by our ancestors. Their wisdom and guidance will serve us well. May the Gods bless us and keep us from harm."

****

Grace wrenched her arm from Tymion's iron grip. She turned on him and shoved both hands against his solid chest. "This is wrong! You cannot do this, I will not allow it!"

"What exactly do you think you can do against her, Grace?"

"Her? The only power that old woman has is what has been granted by this community! Her strength lies in fear and her threat to us is not real. Not if we do not allow it! When does it stop? When do we stop being prisoners of a woman that seeks power over kindness? That cares nothing for the people she leads?"

Tymion stared down at her, his chiseled cheekbones prominent against a pensive face. He grabbed her elbow again and tugged her toward the multi-story apartment complex. Grace struggled against his momentum and he growled at her in a hushed voice, "We cannot have this discussion here. We will be overheard."

"Would you at least allow me to walk on my own?"

"No."

They remained silent the rest of the way. When they entered the apartments, they passed several wide-eyed young women confused by the stern determination of Tymion hauling a captive Grace. Her cheeks burned with embarrassment but she kept her head high. There was no shame in her situation, she was the injured party. She would not let the condemnation of her action dampen her resolve. For too long she'd hidden behind fear and secrecy.

They approached the stairs to the second floor domestic apartments and Grace yanked her arm free. "No one can see us now. I can walk on my own."

71

He frowned but allowed her independence, then hurried her toward one of the unoccupied rooms. When he shut the door, Grace swung on him. "You are a good and honorable man, Tymion. And in you I know beats the heart of a great leader. You must see what her autocratic rule has done. She speaks of the terrible times when we were nothing but slaves to the *viators*. But are we nothing but slaves to her and the elders? Are we not ruled by fear? A fear that they–"

Tymion raised a hand. "Please, Grace. You do not need to explain it to me. Do you truly believe I have not seen exactly what you have?"

"But you continue to do her bidding! You stand by her side as she subjugates us! How can you say you see what I do, yet you do not act?"

"You have spent far too much time in your cottage with your books."

"How dare you! It is the only freedom I have known. Would it be better that I follow the others like sheep? But even the sheep of Greece were allowed to roam the mountains!"

Tymion lifted his lips in a half-smile. "Grace, I have not acted because the time has not been ripe."

Grace opened her mouth to further berate him, but quickly shut it when she realized what he said. Had she truly been so blind that she did not know an undercurrent of rebellion lived in their community? "Why did you not tell me?"

He moved to the wall and leaned, crossing his arms against his chest. "Could you have kept your involvement a secret? How quickly she would have suspected you had she noticed you acting strangely. Instead she was content to know you hoarded books and outside goods. Spying on you and waiting for the time she could use it to her advantage."

Grace's stomach plummeted. "She knew?"

"Everyone knew. But it served us well. As her eyes were on you, we could work in secrecy."

"You used me."

"You served a purpose. Do you truly blame me? I do this for the good of our people. And in your way, you have allowed it to happen."

She couldn't blame him. But she did not like being played the fool. She turned her back on him and moved toward the twin-sized bed against the far wall. How quickly her life had changed. In the space of one day she had met the man from her visions and discovered a plot to unseat her grandmother. What more could happen? She settled on the mattress. "Althea must know something will happen. She has the long-sight. She can see things none of us can imagine."

"You know that visions never reveal the complete picture. She is aware of a potential rebellion, but she does not know from what quarter it will arrive. And now you and your guest have deflected the suspicion from anyone else in the community. She has her scapegoat."

A new side to Tymion revealed itself, one she had never expected. She hadn't exactly considered him stupid, but the keen intelligence and penchant for deception was startling. It made her uncomfortable to realize she'd been so naïve. "You knew. You knew this would happen!"

He laughed. "You are not the only one to have visions of this *viator*."

Understanding struck like a great god revealing himself in splendor. "You turned off the buffer. That was why he was able to land here."

Tymion did not respond, but the slight tic at his jaw told her all she needed. Grace felt a trickle of fear and began to wonder. Who was this man that she was meant to marry?

The door slammed open and a frantic Phillip burst into the room. "Tymion!"

"Great gods, Phillip. Close the door."

Phillip did as ordered then turned back to Tymion, his hands gripped tightly into fists. "Althea has ordered the *viator* executed. They prepare to do it at dawn!"

"No!" Grace jumped from the bed, ready to run from the room.

"That is not unexpected."

"Ty, you cannot let her do this."

Tymion frowned at her, his eyes cold and calculating. "No, if he dies there will be nothing to keep her from turning her suspicion toward us."

She let her chin drop toward the floor. If that wasn't a possibility would he let Lucius die? She shivered at the thought that Tymion could be just as ruthless as her grandmother. He may be a better leader for their people, but her instincts were strong. She could never love this man.

9

The room they locked him in had no windows, dirty walls, and a damp, earthen floor. Lucius prowled, checking for chinks in the hand-hewn logs, but it wouldn't matter. The only way out lay beyond an oak door fixed solidly on well-oiled hinges. Leave it to Althea to maintain an impenetrable prison to hold her captives and terrify her people. He clenched his fists. Something had to break. There had to be a way out.

Three hours later, he leaned against the wall as the cool air of night seeped in through the imperceptible holes in the wall. The ceiling had sprung a leak in several places, allowing steady streams of droplets to fall to the ground. She may maintain the locks, but she neglected the room enough to ensure the inhabitants stayed miserable.

For two thousand years he'd had more time than he knew what to do with, now he found himself running short. Funny that his instinctual jump into the *tiresian* community would kill him when a shot to the chest had not. He touched the puffy skin around the injury and allowed a faint smile to touch his face. Grace had the fight of twenty good Roman soldiers. He prayed to whatever god would listen that the beautiful and kind *tiresian* would find a way to escape her grandmother's clutches. He rested his head against the wall and looked to the ceiling. Now to determine a way to solve his own dilemma.

A thud against the door startled him and in seconds he stood to the side of the entrance, just out of sight of the person who opened the door with hesitant precision. He flexed his arms. This might be his only chance.

"Lucius?"

Grace's tussled, black hair hung over her face as she stuck her head in the room. She squeaked when she saw him against the wall. "Gods, you frightened me."

Turning her head to motion to someone behind her, she shuffled into the room. One of the men that escorted him to his prison followed, a frown marring his features and hard eyes keeping a wary watch on Lucius.

Grace gave a tentative smile. "We have to hurry and keep quiet. Anyone could happen by." She reached out to grab his arm, but stopped when she looked back at the guard. "Aaron, we have to find a way to make this look as though I overpowered you."

The guard scoffed and rolled his eyes. She put her hands on her hips and glared back at him. "Well, it could happen." She bristled when the guard laughed. Lucius had to restrain himself from a vocal agreement. She said, "I could get branch from outside and hit you over the head. They would believe that."

This sent Aaron into a bent-over peal of laughter that even irritated Lucius. The man clearly lacked the proper respect. "You need to apologize to the lady."

"Excuse me?"

"Apologize."

Aaron straightened his back and puffed out his chest. Lucius took a step forward. "I may not be certain of the circumstances or why it seems you have been chosen to aid us. But I know this, in ten seconds I could have you on the floor with five broken bones and no way to scream for help."

In a flash, Aaron went for the small pistol at his hip. Lucius had the man's arm pinned behind his back and several fingers pressing into his larynx before the weapon could be drawn. "Are we clear now who has the advantage?"

The man gurgled and Lucius accepted that as an acknowledgment. He let him free but pulled the pistol from the holster and tucked it into his own waistband. "Now, apologize to the lady and let us move on."

The apology lacked genuine feeling, but Lucius let it pass. Grace blushed under the attention. "All right, we still need to make it look like I was able to overcome you. I suggest we have it look like I hit you with a branch. Then we can leave."

"Come on, Grace. Every action movie has a scene like that in it. No one will believe it."

"When have you seen action movies, Aaron? You know those are forbidden."

He rolled his eyes and turned to Lucius for help. There would be none found in that quarter. Lucius peered out the door. The night enveloped the landscape in darkness and it gave a false sense of timelessness. They had to move fast.

"They will believe it," Lucius said. When Aaron opened his lips to argue Lucius interrupted, "Althea has made it clear she feels her granddaughter is capable of deceit and trickery. And if she does not believe her able to disable you, she will assume someone from the outside assisted. If it would make you feel more masculine, I could shoot you in the leg."

Aaron blanched. "No, the branch will be fine."

"Good, now let us finish this."

Aaron took the hit with relative honor, though the man flinched several times before the deed was done. Lucius would have preferred shooting him. Grace turned her head at the violence, but kept her thoughts quiet.

She led them through the night, her soft voice warning of barriers and hazards as they went. It hadn't been necessary, as his eyes grew accustomed to the low-light of the moon, but he didn't bother to alert her to the change. Focusing on a task could keep fear at bay and the cool tenor of her voice sang sweetly in his ears.

It had been a long time since he'd found pleasure in the company of a woman. Many of those that he'd had contact with over the past several hundred years were under his command and off-limits. Strange, that he enjoyed the time with her even in the heat of suspense. Grace grabbed his wrist and stilled suddenly.

"What do you see?"

She let out a relieved laugh. "Nothing that I did not expect, thank the gods. Come this way. They are waiting for us over the ridge."

Grace threaded herself between several branches, holding her hand out to him as she went. The scent of pine and decomposing vegetation assailed his nose as her feet stirred up the forest floor. They hiked up to a ridge, ducked under more branches, and stepped onto an unpaved road. Two men stood beside a beat-up pickup truck, their heads together in quiet conversation.

"Ty," Grace said.

Ty and Phillip looked up at the sound of her voice. "What took so long? Were you seen?" Ty said.

"No, Aaron was just being difficult. Can we leave?" she said.

The lanky Phillip hustled to the driver side and slid into the front seat. "Grace you get in the cab with me. They will ride in the back."

Grace looked up at Lucius. "Is that all right?" She reached toward his injury. "Will it make it worse do you think?"

Lucius wrapped his hand around her fingers and rubbed his thumb along her knuckles. "It will be fine."

Tymion cleared his throat and pushed Grace toward the truck. When she'd turned her back to them, he glared at Lucius. "She's not for you, *viator*."

Lucius didn't bother to respond. The man had staked a claim but it seemed Grace had a different opinion of the relationship. It didn't matter. He had to leave Grace in the hands of her people. Hopefully they could provide the protection she needed from her grandmother. That Tymion felt proprietary meant she would at least be kept safe. Perhaps when the crisis at the *Domus* had been settled, he would seek out the enchanting Grace. But until then, he could make no claim himself.

They climbed into the bed of the truck and took off down the rocky, rutted road. The gun he'd confiscated from Aaron sat cold against his back and he shifted to ensure he'd have access should it be needed. The hard eyes of his companion seated across the short, metal bed hadn't softened. There was nothing altruistic about the motives for his release, of that Lucius was certain.

He scanned the surrounding landscape. The sniper that had attacked earlier that day could very well be hidden in the foliage, waiting for another opportunity. Somehow Carlo

learned the first bullet had not done the job and sent someone to finish what they'd started. Either that or Lucius had
more enemies than he anticipated. The forest remained silent
and the ride uneventful.

After an hour on the road they pulled to the shoulder.
Tymion motioned that they should get out. Grace appeared
at his side when he swung off the tailgate. "We just passed
beyond the buffer. So you should be able to jump now."

Her smile trembled as she reached out to grab his arm.
Her eyes lost focus in the glow of the brake lights. It seemed
the woman couldn't touch him without having visions.
Dropping her hands, she blinked. "You need to be cautious.
There are several threats that you will face."

"I imagine there will." He grabbed her chin between his
fingers and tipped her head up. "Take care of yourself,
Grace. I will be just fine."

"You need me. I can go with you."

"Where I am going, you cannot follow." He glanced at
the men standing to the side, both with crossed arms and
scowls as they watched the exchange. "Let them help you. It
would upset me if you came to a bad end on account of me."

She rolled her eyes and stepped away. "Fine, go be he-
roic. I will stay here and hide from my grandmother until
the men decide it is time to do something effective."

"Grace."

"Just go." She sighed and cocked her head to the side.
"There are people counting on you. Do not worry. As you
said, I have my family to take care of me."

Lucius couldn't help but doubt her sincerity. However,
as he had said, she could not follow him through time. He
looked to the two men, then stepped several feet away. He
kept his eye on Grace as he focused on the place at the back

of the neck where fear and anticipation sent his nerves into a frenzy. Long ago he'd conquered the fear, learning to trigger the jump consciously and with little effort. A tingle started from the neck and ran its fingers through his limbs until he could see the world around him dissolve. Grace's hand, held up in farewell, burned itself into his memory.

His vision restored and the sleek, modern lines of his living room came into view. Pulling the gun from his waistband, he scouted his home, cautious of the fact that his enemies could have anticipated his return. A thorough investigation of all the rooms eased his mind and proved the house was empty.

But someone had been there.

Doors that should have been closed stood open, papers had moved, objects were slightly off from their original position, and a definite sense of trespass clung to the atmosphere. He expected Carlo had come to visit. But the man would have found nothing. As *magister* of the *Domus*, he knew better than to leave sensitive information in plain sight.

He ducked down the long, dimly lit hall. Passing the master bedroom, he turned into a guest room. Unless the intruder had an above average understanding of architecture, they would miss that the room was far too small to account for the size of the house. The wainscoting that lined the walls provided a deceptive sense of continuity. At the corner, he flipped a piece of the ivory-colored wood and it swung up on hidden hinges. Beneath the wood, a small button had been installed. When he depressed it, a locked panel disengaged and he pressed against it to open a narrow cubbyhole.

Along the wall hung several weapons, including an ancient gladius, shield, and spear. He trailed a finger along the well-polished bronze. Prior to his first time jump as a *viator*, he'd served in the Roman army, working his way through the ranks until he'd earned the right to lead a hundred men. They had been a dominant force, unrivaled, until the day they faced the Visigoths. One Roman walked away from that fight.

He shut his mind to the memories. Retrieving his shoulder holster, he strapped it on, tucking his Walther away. He was fortunate to have another, since the first had been lost during his run-in with Carlo. The gun felt comfortable in his hand, and he preferred its compactness to some of the others in his collection. He pocketed the extra ammunition and reached into a cupboard to extract a spare hard drive. The metal box contained copies of the most sensitive documents from the *Domus*. It was only a matter of time before Carlo found his way back to the house, intent on discovering the secrets that had eluded him.

Time began to strike warning into his intuition. After two thousand years passing through time, he'd begun to feel the ebb and flow of disturbance and threat. An unexpected addition to his talents, he didn't question that which had been proven but not explained. Danger approached. How unfortunate that he could not determine the quarter from which it would come. Perhaps then he would have been prepared for the conspiracy which now plagued the *Domus*.

He locked the cubby and readied for his jump. The next stop would have to be the *Domus*, but the danger there would require far more alertness than he felt. He needed to rest, an hour, perhaps two, before he investigated the extent of the damage done in his absence. Focusing on the base of his spine, he let his mind settle on a distant time in a place that none knew and where, for a few moments, he could rest without threat of discovery.

10

Grace stared at the little pickup and pulled at her bottom lip. She could hardly touch the pedals, how did they expect her to drive it all the way to Portland?

"Stop biting your lip. You're going to pull it clean off one of these days."

She glared at her cousin. If he'd bothered to teach her to drive years ago when she'd begged him to, she wouldn't be in this predicament. Grabbing the keys from his outstretched hand, she flounced to the front. Excitement fluttered in her stomach. Or perhaps it was dread. Either way she was finally getting out of the community and away from her grandmother's influence.

Phillip jumped into the passenger seat as Tymion stood outside, his arms crossed and his glare illuminated by the bright headlights. She peered nervously over the dashboard. "He is going to get out of the way, right?"

"He's twenty feet away Grace, he'll move long before you reach him."

She snorted under her breath. They had far more faith in her abilities than she did. Following her cousin's instructions, she adjusted the seat and steering wheel until her feet could touch the pedals. She felt like a child on a giant throne. Her fingers shook as she turned the key in the ignition.

Three hundred years on this earth and she was finally in control of a growling machine. Fantasies neglected to produce the requisite fear. Could she ever have been prepared for this moment?

"Just ease your right foot on the gas."

Grace placed one foot on each pedal and pressed down. The truck lurched forward then stopped.

"Gods Grace, one at a time." He slapped her thigh. "And just use your right foot. You switch between the two. Never press both at the same time."

"You neglected to mention that."

Phillip's heavy sigh seeped into the darkness. "I should go with you. You are going to get yourself killed."

"And then they would know you were a part of this conspiracy against them."

"It would be better than the alternative."

Grace eyed Tymion as he shifted impatiently on the rutted road. "No. You have work to do here. I can do this." She moved her left foot away from the brake and pressed on the gas slightly. The engine purred but didn't move. She added more pressure and it inched forward. The crunch of wheels on gravel brought visions of bones cracking under the massive machinery. Years of boredom had given her far too much practice with fantasizing. The truck kept going and her calves shook from the tension in her muscles.

"Breathe."

She let her foot off the gas and it rolled to a stop. Phillip laughed. "Gracey, if you don't breathe you will pass out before you reach the bottom of the ridge. You are doing fine. Add a little more pressure to the gas and just keep your eyes on the road."

"By Hades, we don't have time for this," Tymion said.

Grace squeaked. Tymion had come up to the side of the truck and stood at her open window. She said, "I am doing the best I can."

"Do it faster," Tymion said.

She turned her head to him and snapped, "If you had bothered to include me in your rebellion I might be more prepared for this. But as you chose to use me as a tool instead, you will have to be patient."

He leaned into the window and growled, "Althea planned to execute your *viator*. With him gone, do you think she would have any difficulty substituting you or Phillip for the honor?"

It was the truth, but it didn't change the fact that Tymion was a bastard. She pressed heavily on the gas and the truck spat gravel and dirt at him as they barreled down the road. Phillip slammed his hands on the dashboard and let loose a string of expletives.

"I have had quite enough of your cursing, Phillip. Now tell me how to drive then show me how to get out of here."

She gripped the wheel with granite determination. The desire to leave the town behind banished the fear that held her captive. No one would tell her how to live anymore. The sooner she got away, the sooner she could learn to live.

An hour later, Grace turned onto a deserted, paved road. The yellow lines stretched into the black distance. Once, when she'd been a teenager and fed up with the restrictions, she'd hiked all the way to this road. The terror of the unknown had been debilitating and she'd huddled beneath a stand of trees until her cousin found her. He never told the elders how far she'd gotten, but the punishment was severe nonetheless. Five days locked in the same prison where they'd found Lucius stopped her from attempting the same again. That and the fear.

She tightened her fingers on the wheel. No one could rule her anymore. Not her grandmother, not Tymion and not her fear. Beside her sat a giant duffel bag filled with clothes and necessities. Those necessities being a dozen of her favorite books she'd kept hidden in Phillip's house. In them she'd found a font of knowledge. The real world may have been missing in her life, but at least she'd read about it. Now she could finally see it.

Tucked beneath the books were her mother's journals. Tymion had returned them when he'd explained the plan. As soon as she found a place to settle, she would scour the books for answers to her past and perhaps find solutions for her future. Her mother left nearly 150 years ago, exiled by her grandmother. Grace could still see her stricken expression as they hauled her away, anguish in her eyes as she bid a distant farewell to her only daughter, too young to understand what was really going on. Grace was an adolescent and, at the time, she blamed her mother for leaving her. Now she knew better.

Whatever her mother did had been kept secret. Secrets were the mark of the *tiresians* and she was tired of them.

The massive machine gliding down the road required all her focus and she let the night take away the worry. The sense of freedom slowly began to ease into her soul.

She approached the entrance to a vast highway. A huge truck, larger than her bungalow, barreled past and she pulled to the side. It was early morning and there were few vehicles on the road, but those that were flew by at such speeds she wondered how she could possibly share the road with them. The flutter of fear enveloped her again, then anger surged. There were things more important than fear.

She pressed the light on the truck ceiling and pulled out the map her cousin had provided. He'd taken a pen to her route, illustrating the way to a small apartment waiting for her in Portland. There she would find enough provisions for a month and the money to get more. He promised to visit her as soon as it was safe to do so and then they could plan her next step.

Except she wouldn't be there.

When she'd touched Lucius's arm before he'd left, she had indeed foreseen tremendous danger. Again, she had seen far more than the usual brief flash of image. The action played out in vivid detail. Lucius and another man faced two adversaries, the confrontation violent and terrifying. Then she'd seen the woman Lucius called Hailey, her powers unique and unlike anything she'd ever read about.

But stranger still, she had seen a vision of herself, from Lucius's perspective. He had been looking right at her as she stood in front of a bright purple couch covered in blood. Then the vision flashed to a piece of mail on the small table beside the couch.

The address on the envelope was burned in her memory and with it the certainty that Lucius needed her to be with him.

She scoured the map until she found the name of the city in southern California. Riverside seemed so far away, the distance between where she was and where she needed to be stretching out along the expansive state. A sense of impending threat encouraged her to toss the map aside and press her foot to the pedal. She had no idea how long the drive would take, but she knew she had to get there as soon as possible.

****

The ground crunched under his boots as he approached Louisa's Boarding House. It had been several years since he'd sought refuge in this sparsely populated New Mexico mining town. The challenge was remembering the date of his last visit. A *viator* could not jump to a place and time where he'd been previously. Beyond this, there were few limitations to where and when he could go. But it wouldn't do to land in a time when Louisa didn't already know him. They had a good thing going, so he aimed for landing at a time only a few months since his last visit.

As he lifted his hand to knock on the whitewashed screen door, it swung open. A wide-eyed urchin threaded past him and down the pinewood porch steps.

"Arthur don't you dare go down by the creek!"

Lucius grinned as he pulled off his broad-brimmed felt hat. Louisa halted when she caught sight of him standing at her door. "Mr. Luke! You look like you've been drug by a horse and spit up by vultures."

"Things have been complicated."

Tipping back her head to look at him, she grinned. "Well they always are with you. Stop hovering at the door and come to the kitchen. I just put on a pot of coffee."

Louisa's feet echoed across the room as she led him through a small foyer over well-worn hardwood floors into the small but tidy kitchen. Seated at a table pushed against the far wall sat a rugged man hunched over a cracked mug.

"Sheriff."

89

At Lucius's greeting he turned, a frown marring his sun-baked skin. "Mr. Luke."

"Don't pay any mind to his grumpy disposition. He's just unhappy with my opinion." Louisa picked up a wooden spoon from the counter and pointed it at the sheriff. "And don't you think I will be changing it neither. What you're planning is nonsense."

Lucius considered walking right back out the door. Louisa and Sheriff Clyde Randolph had an off and on relationship that seemed more off than on lately. He wanted nothing to do with their squabbling. The morose sheriff just grunted and Louisa turned her attention to Lucius.

"Well, now that you are here you can help me talk some sense into this addle-brained man."

Lucius put up his hands. "I don't think that–"

"Don't you dare wipe your hands of this!" She slammed down a mug of coffee at the only open chair at the table. "He's going to go get himself killed."

With a barely restrained sigh, he sat and settled the coffee between his hands. Those couple hours of peaceful sleep were looking farther away. "What's going on, Randolph?"

"He's decided he's going to run off and–"

Lucius cast a stony glare at Louisa and she clamped her mouth shut. When he turned back to Randolph, the man had a smirk teasing his lips. "There's been some trouble out in Lincoln County. I've been asked to come out and give a hand."

Lincoln County was the site of a brutal range war between competing factions. Both sides suffered casualties and it would launch the infamous Billy the Kid's nefarious career. Lucius saw the resolve in the man's eyes to do the honorable thing. Randolph was a good man and a damn good sheriff. The town would be far worse off if he were lost in a political battle with little redeeming purpose.

But the *viators* walked that fine line between living with mankind and watching from the distance. Millennia passed and they still had no idea just how much influence they had on the world of humans. It was a tough choice. One Lucius preferred to avoid when at all possible.

Louisa stood at the counter, gripping the handle to the cast-iron coffee pot with white knuckles. He cursed under his breath. The decision had more or less been made for him. "There's nothing good that will come out of that war for you, Randolph."

The sheriff straightened his back and pierced Lucius with a glare. "Now Mr. Luke you are a fine, upstanding man, but I don't see how your opinion on the situation much matters here."

"You listen to me, Clyde! When Mr. Luke has something to say you best pay close attention."

"Louisa, please." Lucius stood and looked down at the sheriff. "I understand your reservations, but if you go to Lincoln County there's a good chance you won't come back."

"I ain't a coward, Mr. Luke."

"I never said you were. But you got priorities and those are to this town, not to another man's war." When Randolph opened his mouth to argue, Lucius braced his arms on the table and leaned in to within a half-a-foot of the stubborn man's face and growled, "It ain't your fight."

With that he spun away and stalked to the door. He'd wasted enough time. He needed rest before he could leave to fight his own battles. Louisa's hushed voice followed him from the room. "Don't you argue with me, Clyde. That man

knows things. I ain't never been steered wrong by him before."

He made his way to the small bedroom that Louisa kept
open for him at all times. Long ago he'd discovered a need
to establish a safe place to rest when things got hot. When
he'd been a *venator*, he'd frequented more isolated locations,
with few people and less hospitable environments. As the
magister, his responsibilities kept him stationary, but the
need to get away never lessened. The small house in New
Mexico provided a more comfortable place to get away. One
where the people were friendly, but generally left him alone.
Perfect for a man that seemed to always be wandering.

The door to the bedroom stood closed and he pulled a
key from his pocket to insert into the lock. When the door
swung in, he was greeted by a clean and simple room, left
just as he'd last seen it. A rush of air escaped his lips. The
familiar room allowed a sense of peace to seep into him and
the rising anxiety faded. Now he could rest and prepare for
the inevitable confrontation that approached.

11

The halls echoed with the sound of his footsteps. Not even the customary administrative assistant scurrying from his scowl could be found. Lucius kept a hand on his Walther as he canvassed the property. A sick feeling of dread welled from inside and he realized so much had already been missed during his absence.

He'd considered traveling back to a time just after his jump to see if he could stem the tide of disaster infecting the *Domus*, but experience and good sense kept him focused on Original Time. When a *viator* went back with the intention of changing the course of time, it inevitably created a domino effect that never went the way intended. It was better to stick to the present, the furthest time had gotten, a time when things were much less complicated.

The door to his office stood open, its gaping entrance an indication that it had already been emptied of anything of value. Not that he hadn't expected it. Lucius ducked into the room. The simple furniture and clean tile floors were undamaged. However, the simple couch his assistant installed in an attempt to make the head of the agency appear more approachable, was pushed out of alignment. Its cushions were hastily thrown back in place. Piles of paperwork littered his dark-wood desk. He restrained himself from stacking them neatly as he checked to see if his computer tower had been removed.

The hard drive was ripped from the tall box and when he pulled open the drawer he discovered all the jump drives were gone as well. They'd done a thorough job in cleaning him out. He stalked out of the room. Fortunately, he rarely left sensitive material on his computer. Any thief with half a brain would know that, which is why they'd scoured his home as well. But Lucius hadn't been appointed *magister* because he thought like everyone else. He had to think ten steps ahead.

Those ten steps weren't enough to prevent him from being caught off guard by Carlo, but hopefully it was enough to limit the damage. Lucius kept his gait unhurried, despite the sense that his time in the *Domus* was limited.

Roderic, his chief researcher and data manager would have seen the tide turn and made adjustments. Lucius was counting on that. He only needed one more thing before he could meet back up with Derian.

The lab had been sealed with tape along the door cracks. Lucius frowned. Had an accident occurred which necessitated the quarantine of the *Domus*? It would explain why no one haunted the halls. His finger slipped beneath the tape and sticky residue clung to the paint as he ripped it from the door. It may look like a biological accident, but his intuition suggested a cover-up. More than likely the accident had been used as a convenient excuse to send the hundreds of employees away. Whoever orchestrated the current crisis must have ties high in the *Domus* to affect such complete chaos.

The knob turned easily and he slid into the lab. His hand found the light switch and he illuminated the room in a wash of harsh, artificial light. Equipment shelves hung open and the contents were completely removed. Not even a test tube remained. Lucius folded his arms across his chest and contemplated his adversary. Had there been a run on Bunsen burners at the local lab supplier? Why would they take all the equipment from the lab?

He crossed the room, his footsteps barely registering a sound on the cool, ceramic tile. At the corner, he pushed his foot into the floor. The tile clicked and he bent to remove the makeshift lid to reveal a box in the floor. Inside hid three vials and a slim hard drive just like the one he'd retrieved from his home. A scrap of paper was tucked under the drive and Lucius unfolded it. Roderic's flowery script flowed across the page in unusual brevity.

Council compromised. Destroyed rest of samples.

-R

Lucius stood and pocketed the vials. The *Domus* had been conducting numerous research projects on the nature and physiology of the *viator*. In recent years Roderic had broken through several barriers that plagued them for centuries and finally made significant discoveries. Most of those discoveries were innocuous and positive, but a few had the potential for severe repercussions should the knowledge fall into the wrong hands.

With the data retrieved, he prepared for another jump. Only one more place to stop before he reconnected with Derian.

The wind sliced into his bare arms as his body solidified. Snow-capped mountains ringed the Ochiara Dara, creating a rocky bowl for the solitary visitor. A weather-worn shack tilted slightly to the right, its wood walls holding out against 500 years of abuse. He and Derian would need to make repairs to the decrepit building if they intended to utilize it in a time after 1400.

He turned from the building and trotted across the plain. The valley and shack was a place of refuge since Derian had first jumped. In 1066 Lucius found the man here, young and frightened huddled against a boulder. Unlike Lucius, who'd known about his *viator* legacy from a young age, Derian had no idea about the power he wielded.

At the far end of the valley he reached a rocky outcrop. Between two boulders he reached down and swept away the dirt until the cool metal of an ammo box touched his fingers. He pulled it up and retrieved his pocket knife. Years buried in the unforgiving environment in the Ochiara Dara had created a crust of rust around the warped box.

The thin metal of the blade sank into the crease and he pried the lid open. The glint of gold drew his attention to the few pieces of Derian's past he'd kept safe within the box. A brooch cast in intricate Anglo-Saxon design, a wood spindle whorl, and a small braid of hair were all the man had left of his family and existence prior to life as a *viator*. The objects reminded Lucius he needed to move quickly to reconnect with his old friend.

He placed the hard drives and vials in the box then resealed it. The electronics would not last in this environment, but he had no intention of letting them sit there for long. With the *Domus* unsecured, he would have to establish a new headquarters, but first he had to circle the wagons and determine the extent of the threat.

He replaced the box and stood. Harsh clouds covered the sun and the wind flung its cold fingers against his cheeks. It was time to leave.

Focusing inward, he sought the thread that connected him to Derian. It had been known for years that when blood was shared between *viator* a connection was established which allowed them to find each other in time. This ability allowed family members to stay close to their offspring. It became common practice for mentors to exchange blood with new *viator* to aid in guiding them through their new capabilities.

He and Derian had exchanged blood nearly a century ago, long before Roderic had developed a synthetic method that strengthened the ties. Even so, the thread still ran strong through his veins. The back of his neck tingled and he let his body fade from the Ochaira Dara.

An outrageous purple couch burned his eyes when he landed. Who in their right mind would have a couch that color? He scanned the rest of the room and found that the rich purple ran as a theme throughout, as if a Roman wine shop had exploded beneath the decorator's over-eager hand.

"What the hell are you doing here? Don't you know how to knock?"

Lucius swung around. A short woman with thick black hair, a cropped t-shirt, and men's jeans hanging far too low on the hips stood at the door to the room. Her hands were propped on her hips. "You gave me a hell of a scare. I could have shot you."

"Reena."

"It's Poppi now."

Lucius raised a brow. He vaguely remembered Derian mentioning it. Reena–Poppi had been a thorn in the side of *viators* for as long as he remembered. Luckily, she had never grown attached to him. The same could not be said for Derian.

"What are you doing here?" he asked.

"What am I doing here? Sugar, I just asked you the same question. I get my answer first."

"Don't play games with me. I'm here to see Derian. Where is he?"

She flapped her hand in the air and turned away. "He's busy."

Lucius restrained a growl then strode to the hall across the room. Three closed doors lined the wall. He approached the first, turning the knob in his hand to find a miniscule and immaculate bathroom with even more purple than the awful living room. Moving to the next room, he reached for the knob when a thin-fingered hand clamped on his wrist.

"Don't," Poppi hissed into his ear. "They haven't had much time together. Please just wait."

An unusual hint of sincerity shined from her eyes, encouraging him to drop his hand from the knob. He frowned, but let her lead him back to the front rooms. Patience was hard won, but he'd give Poppi her few moments.

She placed a glass of water in front of an empty seat on the kitchen table then went back to the sink for a second glass. "Sit down, *magister*. We have some time to wait. You look like you could use a break."

He sank into the cheap, Windsor-style chair, certain if he put too much weight on it he'd turn it into matchsticks. Poppi turned around and he finally got a good look at her. Bruises covered her cheekbones and several cuts had only recently scabbed over. "What happened to you?"

She joined him at the table. "I won't lie to you, sugar, things have been crazy. Had a couple near misses. Could have used you around." She looked at him expectantly. He didn't reply. Poppi may have the outward impression of working in the best interest of the *Domus*, but he knew well enough not to count on it. There were few whose loyalty he did count on. Derian was one. Roderic the other.

"Hailey's with him, I gather," Lucius said.

"That's right. He got shot and she's taking good care of him."

Lucius was out of his chair and striding to the door before she'd finished her sentence. The sound of the chair crashing to the ground distracted him and he turned back toward her. Poppi stood inches from him, her eyes dark with purpose. "I told you to leave them alone. He's fine. He doesn't look any worse than you do. So sit down and give them another twenty minutes."

"What's your game?"

"I'm not playing games right now, damn it. For once would you believe I want something for my great-granddaughter? She's been beat up, torn apart and abused. Derian hasn't had it any easier." She reached up and grabbed his upper arm. "Please."

"Fine." But he still didn't like it. There were things that needed to be done.

Twenty minutes dragged like nails across sensitive skin. Poppi spent the time fidgeting in her seat, her glare pinned to him as if waiting for him to make a move. He put his hands on the table and shut his eyes. Patience had its place.

Finally, she stood and walked out of the room. He heard her knock and yell for the others to join them in the kitchen. Lucius remained seated. In the few minutes he'd been forced to wait, his long limbs stiffened and the strain from the last few days settled into his joints and muscles.

Hailey entered the room, her shoulder-length, sandy blonde hair hastily brushed and her clothes rumpled. Bruises on her face were a sickly yellow. Had anyone gone through the last few days unscathed?

"Dude!" she squealed.

Derian followed her into the room at a quick pace, his stance ready and wary. When he caught sight of who sat at the table he stopped short, a flicker of surprise quickly replaced by the usual, unworried expression. Lucius nodded at his friend. "Derian."

"Lucius." He nodded in return.

"How did you? But I saw you..." Hailey stuttered and her brows creased.

Lucius cracked his neck to ease the pressure. "It's a long story. We don't have time for it right now."

"He's been a little impatient. But I told him he had to give you two a little more time. Nearly had to tie him down," Poppi chimed in. Hailey blushed and glanced away and Derian looked up to the ceiling. Diplomacy was not one of Poppi's strengths.

"Does she really have to be here?" Lucius asked.

Hailey jumped to her great-grandmother's defense. "Yes she does. She's been a bigger help than you have."

Lucius refrained from responding. The ancient *viator* may have proved useful, but it was unlikely to come without a cost. Having traveled time far longer than even Lucius, she'd developed survival skills few would find redeemable. Poppi always had ulterior motives and they only served one person–Poppi.

Derian pulled out a seat and joined Lucius at the table. "Tell me. What's going on, Lucius?"

"The *Domus* is shut down."

"Yes, I know. A good portion of Roderic's staff were relocated to Carpathia."

That was not good news. Lucius stiffened his shoulders. Carpathia was a *viator* stronghold established to house the greatest secrets, as well as the greatest threats to the *viators*. It was a prison, one no *viator* ever hoped to see the inside of. The management of Carpathia fell to an extension of the *Domus* that Lucius supervised along with all the other departments. There was no doubt that the conspiracy had its hands at the highest levels of the *Domus*. Lucius was pushed from power with as much effectiveness as a hangman's noose.

"How much do you know about what happened after you were shot?" Derian asked.

"Not much. I was only able to jump again a few hours ago. I went to the *Domus* and it was completely locked down. No one was in the building. All the records were either missing or destroyed. I couldn't find a single thing that could tell me where everyone went or exactly what happened."

Poppi listened to the exchange with far too much interest. Not all the records had been missing, but he intended to keep his cards close to his chest. Lucius pressed his palms into his eyes. He needed to determine a plan of action.

12

Derian filled Lucius in on the rest of what happened during his absence. The conspirators had established a laboratory in Babylon where they experimented on *viators* to develop methods to amplify abilities. Hailey's expression grew strained as they described the actions of the head scientist, Nikanuur, her father.

"He's a bastard. They've been using pregnant woman and children. And you should have seen what it did to the older *viators*. They've gone completely nuts. I don't know if they will ever be able to recover."

She took a deep breath and Lucius jumped in. "Were there others in charge at Babylon? People other than your father?"

"Yes. Carlo was there. He's a real piece of work. I think he enjoys being a sick and twisted monster."

Lucius agreed. Carlo Benanati had taken his training under the Medicis in Renaissance Florence and made it a personal art.

"And there was this woman and two other men. They didn't tell me who they were, but they tried to recruit me to their cause." She spat out the last word.

"Their cause?" Derian asked.

"From what I gathered, they want to have a more management-style role in human affairs. I think they plan to enhance their abilities to grow an army that can handle taking over the world."

He could have been surprised, but Lucius expected such would be the case. If a force could be developed with enhanced *viator* abilities, then no human or *viator* could stand in the way of world domination. But they still didn't know exactly who they were fighting against. "We need to get a hold of Roderic. He will have insight on how far they could have gotten in their research. And possibly who the players are in this."

Derian shook his head. "Roderic was arrested and taken to Carpathia. They claimed it was treason. Rusa has been removed from the Council as well."

Lucius sat back in his chair. That was inconvenient. He needed Roderic. As one of *viator's* most gifted scientists and strategists, Roderic was essential to the defense of the *Domus*.

"Do you think it's true? The treason?" Hailey asked with wide eyes.

"No. Whoever is manipulating the situation needed him gone. It gave them the excuse to get rid of Rusa as well," Lucius said.

"Rusa can't be the only one on the Council that isn't corrupt," Hailey answered.

"There are several good *viators* on the Council. But we don't know what has become of them. They may have been removed like Rusa, or worse. We can't know," Derian said.

The Council of Seven was established over two thousand years ago, around the time when Lucius first jumped. Before that time, *viators* existed ungoverned. They were nei-

ther policed for their actions nor protected from the repercussions of a life with few boundaries. The Council oversaw
the development of the *Domus* during the Roman era when
it became essential that some kind of organized oversight
exist. The catalyst was a war that many *viators* had not survived. Lucius feared they may be headed toward another.

He stood and stretched his limbs. The chair had been far
too uncomfortable. "With the lab destroyed and the *Domus*
empty we are low on avenues to pursue. We need to get Roderic out of Carpathia."

Lucius looked to Hailey. Her father used her as his most
daring experiment. From birth she'd been changed, given
enhanced capabilities. So far it meant she was developing
her skills as a *viator* faster than any had ever done. She also
had the unexplainable ability to land in no jump zones. It
was something that gave them a significant advantage over
the enemy. Out of the corner of his eye he saw both Poppi
and Derian tense.

"Is this place protected by a no jump zone?" Hailey
asked.

"Hailey. It's too dangerous," Derian said. Lucius kept
his eyes on Hailey. Something was going on in her mind.

"Oh I know it is, but not for the reasons you think." She
turned her attention to Derian. "There are some unexpected
side effects from what my father did to me. Next time I
jump, I could turn into a raving lunatic."

"What kinds of side effects?" Lucius asked.

Hailey shrugged. "There seems to be some degeneration
in the brain. Different people react differently. They did tests
on several of the *viators* I saw in Babylon. One became violent. Like an animal." She blanched and looked away. "An-

other just sat on the ground and rocked. It was a little freaky."

The comment was no doubt an understatement. Derian looked sick to his stomach. Poppi threw up her hands and started an angry tirade in an ancient language that even Lucius did not recognize. He rolled his eyes to the ceiling and stopped his prowl beside Hailey. "This is inconvenient."

"Dude, you have no idea."

He laughed and squeezed her shoulder. "You have the most interesting way of describing how you feel."

"You knew about this and you still tried to jump with him?" Poppi stopped her rant long enough to turn it on Hailey.

"Yes."

"You're an idiot," Poppi replied. At that, Lucius was lost. Something happened at Nikanuur's lab and it was clear that the three had yet to come to grips with the situation. At this point he was having a hard enough time tracking the pertinent details. Add the fact all three were emitting high emotional signals and he felt things were getting out of hand.

Hailey was the first to realize he hadn't followed the conversation. "Derian was unconscious in a burning building. They're mad at me for saving his life."

"How exactly did you save his life?"

She tipped her lips in a half-grin. "I jumped him."

"Not possible." It wasn't just impossible. It was ridiculous. The shear mechanics of bringing physical matter with a *viator* was complex and the skill was limited to the most experienced. Even then the amount that could be transported was minimal–clothes, a gun, perhaps a small box were about what could be handled. But not even small animals were successfully transported, their bodies far too complex. It just couldn't happen.

"You know, when it comes to me let's just throw all those assumptions out. Ok? I did it. Period." She stood and moved toward the door. "It doesn't matter. So let's drop it. I have some stuff for you guys to look at."

For a moment all three *viators* just stared at the empty space she'd left. Lucius frowned. If Hailey could do such a thing, Nikanuur might have been able to replicate it in others. In many ways such a skill could be indispensably valuable, in others it could threaten everything they had accomplished for millennia.

Derian stood abruptly and followed Hailey from the room. Worry tugged at Lucius. Derian was obviously attached to the woman. In general it would not matter, but he wondered how his top *venator* would function when his thoughts and emotion were so focused on another. With the crisis at hand, they couldn't afford to have divided attentions.

Poppi started to yell again. Lucius prayed for patience. He almost believed the woman had feelings for her great-granddaughter. He crossed his arms, propped a hip against the table and watched the ancient woman throw a tantrum. After the other two had been gone several minutes his patience faded. "Sit down. You are doing nothing to help the situation."

"You're a bastard, Lucius."

He stood and grabbed her arm. "I may be, but I know that Hailey doesn't need you acting like a child. You are one of the oldest *viator*. When will you start acting the part?"

"You have no idea what you are dealing with, *magister*." She bared her teeth and spat out his title like it had gone sour.

"Why don't you explain it to me then?"

She ripped her arm from his grip and flounced to the other side of the table. There she made a long and pronounced show of sitting. Lucius flexed his fingers and sat in his own seat.

Hailey returned and settled in the chair beside her great-grandmother. She placed six vials onto the center of the table.

Lucius took one, lifting it into the light. "From the lab?"

Hailey hummed an affirmative. A small rubber stopper sealed the vial. When he removed it and sniffed the inside, the harsh scent of acid burned his nose. He closed it and traded it for another. This one had a much less intense aroma. Not quite void of scent, it had a more subtle set of ingredients with a slight metallic undertone. He did the same for the other four vials. Only one was different from the others, with an organic scent, almost sickeningly sweet. When he finished, he returned them all to the center of the table and folded his hands.

Poppi looked like she would jump down his throat if he didn't fill them in on his observations. "Well?"

"I'm not certain," Lucius said.

"Did they all smell the same?" Hailey asked. She'd begun to tap her finger against the table.

"No. There were three distinct scents."

Poppi grabbed one and started to sniff at it. "What are they?"

107

"One took away Derian's connection to me. Another is supposed to help prevent the brain degeneration," Hailey said.

Lucius and Derian looked up in surprise. The enemy had discovered how to cut the ties between a *viator* and *praeceptor*. Blood was also used by the system to track *viators* through time. Once the data was entered into the system the *viator* was essentially tethered to the *Domus*. Was it possible that the same thing that removed the thread that connected Derian and Hailey could also mask a *viator* in time?

Poppi was significantly more upbeat about the news. "That's great. We can figure out what is in it and make more! But there are three. What is the third?"

"Poison," Lucius said. They knew a fast-acting poison was being used to assassinate *venators*. If his hunch was correct, they now had a sample and could possibly discover an antidote.

Hailey let out a long exasperated sigh. "It seems there is now even more reason to free Roderic from his prison."

Lucius agreed. He stood and looked to Derian. "We will have to take the traditional route."

"I'm going too," Hailey said as she stood.

"No," both Lucius and Derian replied.

Poppi laughed. "Do you think you can stop her? She'll just jump and beat you there."

Derian opened his mouth to argue, but the doorbell rang before he could begin. Hailey took it as an excuse to leave the room. Derian looked to Lucius, a frown marring his face. Where they were going was dangerous enough for an experienced operative. Hailey would have no idea what to expect nor what to do when things got dangerous. And they would most certainly get dangerous.

A pair of feminine voices came from the front room. Lucius recognized the second but hoped, for her sake, it wasn't who he thought it was. He strode from the kitchen and stopped just inside the living room. A perplexed Hailey stood with her hand on the door. Standing beside the atrocious purple suede couch was Grace, her arms hugging a giant duffel bag easily two-thirds her size. His jaw tensed.

"Grace."

When she saw him her smile widened in relief. Dumping her bag on the couch she vaulted toward him, throwing her arms around his neck. Her enthusiasm encouraged a quick smile to cross his lips. But he clamped down on the urge to return her embrace and set her away from him. "What are you doing here?"

"I told you something terrible was going to happen."

"And I told you to stay home."

She leaned back to look him directly in the eye. Her's glinted with determination and he imagined this would get ugly before he could get her out. "Hailey would you mind giving me a moment?"

The feisty blonde snorted, but granted him his privacy by returning to the kitchen. He turned his attention back to Grace. "You can't be here. It isn't safe."

She took a step forward and poked him in the chest. "You need me here. I know that for certain. I appreciate your desire to protect me from whatever is threatening you, but you can't. I have seen it."

"What do you mean, 'you have seen it'?"

"When I touched you that last time and told you there would be danger I also saw myself. This never happens. We never see ourselves in our visions. So I know it is important that I be here." She took a small step back and crossed her arms.

"That is ridiculous. You said yourself that the vision is what would happen should you continue your current intention. Perhaps if you had not come the danger would not have occurred."

"In my vision you survive. What if my presence is the factor that ensures that?"

"There is no way to know that," he growled. The temperature at the base of his neck rose and it had nothing to do with jumping time.

"Of course there is not. But what if it does? I could not risk that." She smiled up at him. Clearly thinking she'd won.

The problem was he could not come up with a logical reason to send her away. Except that he did not need the distraction. "Damn it woman."

Her smile widened even farther. "Come on then, introduce me to your friends. I did not mean to interrupt you from your discussion."

She stepped around him and entered the kitchen. He lifted his eyes to the ceiling in a quiet plea and followed. Grace already had her hand extended to Hailey. "I am sorry. I did not properly introduce myself. I am called Grace."

Hailey looked a bit dumbstruck as she shook the outstretched hand. "Do you mind me asking when you first jumped?"

Grace looked to Lucius before answering. "Oh I am not a *viator*."

Poppi lurched toward Grace and all attention shifted to her. She clenched her fists and snarled, "You aren't a normal human either, are you?"

Lucius took a step toward Grace as she stumbled back a foot. Her hand fluttered to her chest as she adjusted to the assertive question. He put his arm around her shoulders and glared at Poppi. There was no call for her to be accusatory. An involuntary growl erupted from his chest when Poppi poked a finger at Grace.

"What are you?"

"Poppi, don't be rude." Hailey stood and put a hand on her great-grandmother's arm.

Grace relaxed. "No. That is quite alright. She is correct." She stepped out of his arms and sat in the seat he previously occupied. "I am *tiresian*."

"I knew it! You people always look like possessed dolls."

Lucius took a step toward Poppi, but the quizzical look on Derian's face made him pause.

"Poppi!" Hailey smacked her great-grandmother's shoulder. "Seriously, chill."

Derian looked to Lucius. "How exactly did you find yourself a *tiresian*?"

Lucius grabbed the chair beside Grace, keeping a wary eye on Poppi. "I fell into the situation. It isn't pertinent."

Grace stifled a giggle beside him and her eyes sparkled when they met his. She was taking the situation far too lightly. She had no idea what she'd walked into and the danger she was in. She raised a brow at his stern look.

"How exactly did you find him? You put a spell on him didn't you? You have him mystified as your love slave right?"

Grace clutched her fingers and he could feel her body shake with restrained laughter, but she only let Poppi see

111

her roll her eyes. "That is all silly superstition. Lucius simply looked at some of Hailey's mail. That is all."

Poppi swung her accusatory glare on him. His expression challenged her to continue with her argumentative questions, but for once, she kept quiet.

Hailey looked toward Derian, then to Grace and Lucius. "Ok, seriously people. What is a *tiresian?*"

"Oh dear. She is a new *viator* then? I thought with what she did that she was much older." Grace looked down and threaded her fingers together.

"With what I did? What?" Hailey's voice rose in a pitch which nearly reached the same annoying quality of her great-grandmother. Lucius was in no mood to deal with both of them. Derian, always aware, reached up and took Hailey by the hand. She immediately quieted.

Grace recovered from her confusion and smiled. "No matter. I can read the future. All my kind can. Your friends are shocked to meet me because it is rumored that we are all dead."

"Dead?" Hailey asked.

"It is a long story."

"I'm sure. So, you're here why?"

"Perhaps she saw something quite alarming."

Everyone swung around at the unexpected voice. Carlo and Nikanuur stood in the living room, each wielding their weapon of choice. Carlo held a Berretta 9mm pointed at the group in the kitchen looking less than his usual well-kept self. Nikanuur stood beside him, shifting nervously with his hands clenched around a nasty-looking pole weapon.

Hailey was the first to respond. "Are you frickin' serious?"

13

Lucius and Derian sprang to their feet and blocked the women from the dangerous men. Grace stepped to the side, behind a wall that hid her from the living room. She glanced at Hailey who stepped between the two men and eyed the threat with relative calm.

"Quite chivalrous gentlemen. I still want those vials," the swarthy-looking man said. He had a gun pointed at the Lucius while Nikanuur held his pole nervously at Derian. Grace pulled her bottom lip with her teeth. So this was the moment her vision had shown. Unfortunately, she had only seen the aftermath. Was she supposed to do something? Or was she to just stand there stupidly, waiting for the events to unfold?

"No," Derian said.

The gun shifted to point directly at Derian's chest. "Do I really need to shoot you a second time?"

Hailey jumped in, "No. I'll get them for you."

"Please do and don't keep us waiting."

Hailey turned and went to retrieve the vials from the table. She looked up in surprise when they weren't there. Grace frowned. They had been there just a moment ago; she didn't remember anyone moving them. Then she saw Hailey clench her fist and shake with anger. Grace was uncomfortably confused until she realized Poppi had disappeared as well.

Their eyes met as Hailey turned back toward the men. A strange mix of uncertainty and resolve reflected back from the *viator*. Grace felt out of her element.

"What is the problem, Hailey?" the man with the gun barked at her. Grace flinched. What would happen to them now? Her vision promised they survived this. At least that's what she thought she saw. What if she were wrong?

"Um," Hailey stalled. A loud buzz sounded from the room and Grace peeked around the corner to see the nasty pole weapon ignite. Its bulbous head glowed red and hummed with heat. She had never seen anything like it, though considering her sheltered existence it wasn't a shock. But everyone else seemed just as wary of its power.

Hailey stepped between Lucius and Derian and approached the evil-looking pair. Grace decided Hailey had to have more courage in her pinky than she ever would. "So, listen, we have a bit of an issue. Poppi, sort of ran off with the vials and…"

"I suggest you find them."

"Seriously? I doubt she's hiding in a closet. She's long gone and you know it."

At that point Grace stopped hearing what was going on. Her neck started to tingle and a loud rush stormed through her ear canals. She placed her hands over her ears and cringed beneath the weight of the sound. The hairs at the back of her neck felt like they were being pulled out one-by-one and her eyes burned. What was happening to her?

A shout and a shot punctured through the cottony fog that enveloped her mind, but she paid little attention to it. The world could end outside and she wouldn't notice. Her vision turned white and she fell to her knees as everything went black.

She woke with her head cradled in Lucius's lap, concern etched into the creases beside his eyes. Had she fainted? She'd never fainted before. Embarrassment colored her cheeks. "What happened?"

He tucked a stray strand of hair behind her ear. "You fell. Are you feeling alright?"

Grace sighed in relief. He was nice enough not to state the obvious. She'd fainted like a southern belle at a summer afternoon party. "I feel much better, thank you. I am not certain why–" She scrunched her face, something big must have happened while she was out. "What happened to the men with the weapons? Is everyone all right? Hailey!" She tried to sit up, but he held her down by the shoulders.

"Hailey is fine. Physically at least. She had to shoot her father. But we are safe–for now."

Her father? Which one of those awful men was Hailey's father? She turned to her side and pushed up. He shifted and his arms came around her waist. "You don't have to get up. You may still experience dizziness."

She flapped her hand at him. "I am fine, really. I am no shrinking violet, I assure you."

"Grace, I don't think…"

The pause told her far more than the words. So he did think she'd fainted in fright. Her heart clenched and she scooted away. Why did it matter what he thought? Maybe it had been the fright that made her head feel like it would explode and carry her away on a painful wave. She pushed her thumbs into her temple and kneaded quick circles into the pressure point. He stood and held out a hand to help her stand.

She mumbled a thank you then stumbled toward a chair. Resting her elbow against the table, she braced her head in her palm. Through the door she saw the blood-soaked purple couch exactly as she'd seen it in her vision.

She sighed. At least she knew she'd been right on that count. Lucius leaned toward her and asked if he could get her anything. She waved him away. A few minutes later a cup of tea slid in front of her and he walked into the living room to assist Derian with removing the couch. The gesture made her smile. Tea would be just the thing. It almost made up for the fact that he thought she'd faint when things got dangerous.

Wrapping her hands around the mug, she let the steam rise toward her face and soothe her. She watched as the two men shoved and pulled the couch toward the door. Eventually, they had it wedged halfway through and took a quick break, their bodies heaving with the strain. Lucius was still recovering from his wound and she wanted to scold him for pushing himself, but she doubted he'd appreciate the gesture.

A sound to her right drew her attention away from the men. Hailey came up beside her, the strain of the day showing clearly in every part of her body. Grace said, "I'm sorry you had to shoot your father."

"He was an asshole."

Grace started with surprise. The vehement response spoke of a painful history. It wasn't so much the comment as the ease at which it was stated. Straight talk had never been one of her strengths. Grace looked to Hailey and wondered if she hid her fear and pain behind a mask of bluntness as much as Grace hid it behind polite, circular conversations.

Hailey knuckled her eyes and looked as though the world had settled squarely on her shoulder. Grace reached out. "Is there anything I can do?"

Shaking her head, Hailey pressed her fingers into her temple. Grace knew the signs of a raging headache. "Do you want to go to a doctor?"

Hailey glanced toward the two men as they finally moved the couch out of the living room. Grace wondered if she even heard the question. "Hailey?"

Finally, Hailey looked down as if she'd only realized there was someone beside her. Then her eyes cleared and she responded, "No, I should be better after some rest."

Grace held out a hand and Hailey threaded her fingers through hers. She hadn't had many friends in her life, but something about this blunt-speaking woman made her want to make a connection. Grace looked at their joined fingers and wondered what it would be like to finally have a friend she could count on.

Once the men returned, Hailey shooed Grace and Lucius toward the master bedroom, then pushed Derian toward the guest room. When Grace opened the door she smiled at the purple curtains and the purple and gold paisley bedspread. She turned to Lucius who failed to hide his grimace of distaste. "Purple is not one of your favorite colors?"

"Not in this quantity–no."

The room was quite a bit larger than hers. She winced as she remembered her room was now nothing more than a pile of rubble. The ever flourishing vegetation of the Oregon forest had probably begun to reclaim the land. Hopefully, Aristo had found a sympathetic friend in the community. Guilt ran a hand across her heart, but she pushed it away.

Phillip promised to look after her cat. She had to trust in that.

Lucius pushed past her toward a connecting hall leading to a tiny bath. The soft rush of running water from the sink had her craving a shower. She wondered if Hailey's friend would mind if she took a quick one.

When Lucius returned, he threw a towel at her. She asked, "How did you know?"

He stopped and raised a brow. Grace stomped past him. So he wanted to pretend he could read minds, fine. She could see the future and it included a hot shower with the refreshing scent of soap.

When she emerged from the shower, he'd propped his back against the head of the bed and his eyes were closed. She finished toweling off her hair and dug through the chest of drawers for a shirt long enough to cover her in modesty. Hailey had told her to help herself to whatever she needed, but she'd learned they were staying in a stranger's house. One Hailey knew, but a stranger nonetheless. So, Grace kept a tally in her head. Somehow she'd find a way to pay back the unintentional Good Samaritan.

She tugged a t-shirt over her head and it fell to midway down her thigh. It seemed there were advantages to being a small woman. The feel of the soft fabric and the fresh scent of dryer sheets had her smiling in bliss. Dryer sheets were a novelty in the community. When Phillip would deliver a box, the sheets went fast, as everyone eagerly vied for the opportunity to feel snuggly fresh.

Grace glanced at Lucius. He would probably rip the shirt she wore in two if he tried it on. His square chest rose gently and his large hands lay in his lap. Gods he was magnificent. How terrible would it be if she walked over and ran a hand over his broad shoulders?

A single, brown eye opened, catching her open stare. Heat surged into her cheeks and she turned away. "It is your turn. I am certain I did not use all of the hot water. It was still quite steamy when I got out."

"I'm sure it was." He pushed himself from where he lay and swung his feet to the floor.

She stepped to the side as he passed her to take his turn with the water. He glanced down and the corner of his mouth tipped up in a slight smile. Smiles seem to be rare for him, although this wasn't the first time she caught him tempted by the expression in her presence. It had to be a positive sign, didn't it?

The thin door shut and the water turned on. A bit of relief settled as solitude enveloped her. She hadn't had this much interaction with others in a long time. With the exhausting drive, harrowing traffic and unexpected violent crisis, her body had yet to come to grips with the last 24 hours. Hundreds of years of mind numbing boredom had suddenly been supplanted by terrifying action and excitement. A giggle erupted and she clamped her hands over her mouth. Gods, she must be having a bit of a breakdown. She had the ridiculous desire to laugh hysterically.

The water ceased its rush against the glass walls and she tried desperately to tamp down the rising tide of hysteria building up from her diaphragm. The whoosh of a towel let her know she was running out of time. Three large breaths. The air went in as a gulp and left in a rush. The door opened and he walked back into the room, the towel tucked snuggly about his waist. His chest a reddish-brown from sunlight and a little too much heat from the water.

He stopped and stared back at her. And she completely lost it. The tide of laughter broke free like a maelstrom, reaching a pitch that could have cut glass if she hadn't slapped her hand across her lips. Her sides clenched and her eyes filled with hot tears. Her other arm went across her belly as she tried desperately to control the tempest.

Lucius just leaned against the wall and watched. Mortification mixed with the inexplicable laughter until Grace was positive she'd bust in two. "Why are you-" she hiccupped, "why are you just," she hiccupped again then drew in a huge breath. "Why are you just standing there?"

He straightened and approached her. The bed dipped as he sat, sending her rolling toward him. His arm wrapped around her shoulder and he tucked her head against his chest. "I am not good at dealing with hysterical women."

She pushed away from him and glared. "I am not hysterical." Then another barrage of laughter erupted and she fell back onto the soft, billowy comforter. So she was a little hysterical. Giving in, she let the laughter escape unfettered and ignored him as he stared dumbfounded at the wall. If the roles were reversed she'd have no idea what to do as well.

Finally the laughter waned and the convulsions quieted. Her sides ached and throat felt scratched but her body finally relaxed. And she was tired. Gods she was tired. Lucius stretched out beside her on the bed and looked into her face as if he could determine her mental state just by staring into her eyes.

"I feel better, thank you. I do not believe you need to worry that you share a room with a madwoman any longer."

"I never thought that."

"Oh? I certainly did for a few moments. Tell me Lucius, how do you handle the excitement?" She turned onto her side and closed the distance between them. He traced a finger across her jaw-line.

"Time and experience. I have had a lot of both."

Her finger itched to trace the line that defined the muscle of his bicep. What did it matter, he had already touched her. Tentatively, she reached out and stroked him with a single finger. Warmth seeped from his skin, seeming to surround him like a blanket.

"How old are you?" she asked.

"Nearly two thousand."

Grace blinked. *Tiresians* lived long lives as well, but her grandmother, at 1200, was close to reaching the limits. Two thousand years and he didn't look a day over 40. "That is astonishing. You must have seen amazing things in a life so long."

"Quite amazing." The way he stared at her, she thought for just a moment that his response wasn't about memories. Grace stifled a yawn and he pulled away. Suddenly, the warmth that had settled around her left as though sucked through a vacuum.

"We need rest. There is still much excitement ahead and we will need all the energy we can find." He pulled a pillow out from under the comforter and threw it on the ground.

Grace sat up and peered over the side of the bed as he settled on the carpet. Her feet could attest to the scratchy nature of that carpet. "We can share the bed. It cannot be comfortable down there and you are still injured."

He turned onto his side and faced away from her. "While I would like nothing more than to share the bed with you, I would find the temptation too great and I would not get the rest I need."

"Temptation? What kind of temptation?"

"Go to sleep, Grace."

"But I really do want to know. What kind of tempta-tion?"

He didn't answer and she tried not to pout. She was nearly positive she was the cause of the temptation and it made her feel fluttery all over. But it would have been nice if he told her exactly how he was tempted so she wouldn't spend hours staring at the ceiling wondering what it could be. She'd given up hope when he finally answered.

"I would find it impossible not to spend the entire time touching you."

Her stomach surged like hummingbirds at a sugar store. The confession hadn't helped. She still stared at the ceiling, imagining just what it would be like with his hands all over her body.

14

Someone was watching him. His eyes flew open to find wide, brown eyes staring down at him. His heart stopped thudding and he let his lids close. The woman had an uncanny way of making him feel uneasy and exposed. His body tightened in response to her gaze and he took a few moments to pull together his control. The rebellious nature of his desire made the struggle significantly more difficult than he appreciated.

The bed creaked as she moved on the mattress. When he felt confident that he had himself back in order, he opened his eyes again. Her tiny feet dangled off the side and she leaned forward, a silly smile shining in the daylight. "Did you rest well?"

"Well enough."

"I think you would have been quite a bit more comfortable up here."

He pushed himself up on his elbow and kept his expression bland. "What are you about, Grace?"

Confusion had her sitting up straight. "I am not sure." She pulled her legs up and crossed them Indian-style. "What are we going to do now?"

He pushed his body up and shifted until he leaned against the wall, his arms resting against his bent knees. "We are going to take you and Hailey somewhere safe."

"Safe? But I thought with Nikanuur dead."

"There are far bigger threats than Nikanuur facing us."

"Oh. But what are you going to do?"

"Derian and I will be going to Carpathia."

Her expression darkened at the name. It was no surprise she recognized the place. Originally built during the Roman Empire, although significantly expanded in the Middle Ages, many *tiresians* had been imprisoned there. Many were left to die. Lucius did his best to limit its function to holding only the most dangerous quarry, but that was long after the *tiresians* disappeared. He'd never been given the chance to help right the wrongs done to her people.

"But why?" she asked.

"A friend is imprisoned there. It is essential that we free him. The knowledge he has may be the key to understanding the threat to the *Domus*."

"I have to go with you."

"No."

She crossed her arms and tipped up her chin. "You need me. You need my vision. I can get you in and out. It is what your people used us for in the past, is it not?"

"No." There was no way he would let her go to such risk. She'd already done it far too many times.

"Be reasonable. I am the only way you can guarantee it would be a success."

"Damn it woman!"

She grinned. "You know that when you get upset I know that I have won?"

The desire to truss her up and throw her in a closet seemed reasonable at the moment. She hopped off the bed and headed to the bathroom. He took the respite from her presence to pull on his shirt and check on the others. The door to the spare bedroom remained closed but he could hear rustling through the wall. He thought better of knocking and went to the kitchen.

Grace may have thought she'd won, but he had no intention of letting her join them on the mission. They had no idea what to expect at the fortress. With the conspiracy procuring it for their purposes, it could be easily assumed the place would be well guarded. Since Derian and Hailey assisted in destroying the Babylon laboratory the conspiracy would be extra wary of intruders. Carlo would have also noticed Nikanuur had not completed their murderous assignment by now.

The first priority would be getting the four of them out of the area. Then he would find a suitable place to hide Hailey and Grace while he and Derian extracted Roderic. With Carpathia protected by a jump buffer, it limited the options to normal human travel. He may have to call on some old acquaintances.

Grace sauntered in and hefted her duffel bag onto the kitchen table. "Do you think Hailey's friend would mind if we borrowed breakfast?"

Lucius leaned a hip against the kitchen counter and shrugged. She was not going to be happy with his plans. "Grace, about Carpathia–"

"Good, you're up. We wanted to talk about the same thing" Hailey walked through the door and Derian followed close behind. "So, what's the plan?" She pulled out a chair and sat, waving Grace over to join her. A bright smile splashed across Grace's face.

Lucius slanted a look at Derian, who'd taken a relaxed stance at the door of the kitchen. He eyed both women with undisguised wariness.

"I will be calling someone I know in the area. You and Grace will be safe there until we return," Lucius said.

Grace's eyes widened with hurt, but Hailey beat her to the vehement verbal response. "Save it Lucius, we're going with you."

"No. I appreciate your desire to help. But it isn't safe. We cannot be concerned about the two of you while we are also trying to retrieve Roderic. You just do not have the training."

"I think the last two weeks of hell have been plenty of training."

"Hailey." He put a strong warning in the depth of his voice. She crossed her arms and looked to Grace for support. The two women were clearly on the same side. Lucius looked to Derian for assistance, but the man just shrugged.

"She will just jump them and with her track record they will end up in the middle of the American Civil War or something just as dangerous," Derian said. Lucius frowned at him. He'd expected more support. Derian continued, "It may also be advantageous to have a *tiresian* as a guide. It was how they helped us in the past."

Lucius gave a curt shake of his head. "She has no experience."

Grace piped up, "I got you away from the gunman."

Hailey's head snapped up. "What gunman? You forgot to tell us about a gunman."

Lucius looked to the ceiling. Could things get more complicated? "There was a sniper at Grace's house. I believe it was Carlo, or someone he sent to finish what they had started at the *Domus*."

Grace turned to Hailey. "I was able to foresee the threats and get us to safety. It was quite invigorating."

Lucius looked down at her incredulously. Invigorating was not exactly how he would have described the experience.

"Well great. Then we both have experience," Hailey said then looked to Lucius. "So how do we get to Carpathia?"

Derian's face mirrored his own pained expression. The whole situation was a train wreck. Hailey stood with a huff and started to pace. "You two are being no help here. We will all be better off doing this together. Last time I got *left* somewhere I ended up in the middle of a firefight. You have no way of knowing that where you leave us will be safe. So get over it and let's figure out options."

He let it go. Apparently it would be a battle easier won on a different field. "We'll need to take a plane to Kiev."

"Kiev, as in Ukraine?" Hailey frowned.

"Yes," Lucius replied then turned to Derian. "I need you to contact Andrij. We will need supplies for the hike in and any intel he has on what has been going on in the area. Have him put together gear for inside as well."

Derian's sternness matched his own. They would need weapons and supplies if they were to be successful in what would, more or less, be a very real version of 'storm the castle'. At this point he intended to leave the women outside the fortress, out of the action. But they would need protection as well. The whole idea rubbed him the wrong way, but

Derian was right. Having Grace along to that point could be useful.

"Do you have your passport?" he asked his top *venator* and the man shook his head. It didn't matter. Lucius lacked his as well and Grace was unlikely to have one. "I will need to procure documents so we can travel. Hailey, do you have one?"

"Dude, I hardly ever left Los Angeles County."

Lucius asked for paper and a camera, spurring Hailey to rustle up supplies from another room. Luck was with them and she found an inkpad as well. Within twenty minutes he had what he needed and walked to the living room. He hated jumping when people stared. "Get packed. We leave in half-an-hour."

"Half-an-hour? How are you going to get us passports in half-an-hour?" Hailey asked from the kitchen. He would let Derian answer that question for him. The room faded from view and he focused on a rundown warehouse in the depths of Los Angeles.

"Shit, Lucius! You should know better than to do that to a man with chronic paranoia!"

A dark-haired man with a receding hairline, made more prominent by the tightly pulled back ponytail, stood across the cluttered room, a bag of Doritos in one hand and a gun held in the other. Lucius stepped forward from between two file cabinets. "Marvin. You look stressed."

Marvin put down the gun and brushed his cheese-covered fingers down his right hip. "Of course I'm stressed. You're supposed to be dead."

"Who told you that?"

"Just your entire staff. The interoffice instant messaging went nuts after you disappeared. You know most people don't use that for business? Do you know how much productivity gets sucked away with instant messenger and email?"

"What are you doing monitoring my people?"

"Oh come on man. How else am I going to keep up on what's going on? You aren't exactly the most open employer I have."

Lucius let it go. Consultants were always a challenge. The kind that specialized in what Marvin did were even worse. However, in this case the man's idiosyncrasies may solve a quick puzzle for him. "Do you monitor the email as well?"

"Look man, I understand privacy and all, but I can't help it, you know. I have this condition." Marvin brushed his hand over his head, leaving a bright orange line of dust in the slick black hair.

"Just the answer, Marvin."

"Yeh man, I do."

"I want to know why everyone left the *Domus*."

"Well shit, you should have just asked. The Council sent them home. The email came from your assistant."

Lucius just stared at Marvin.

"Right. Let me pull that up for you." Marvin sat in his swivel chair and swung it around to face what he often referred to as his 'command center'. Three giant monitors hung on the wall. Several hard drives were scattered across the desk and a pair of gloves sat to the side with wires extending from the fingers. When Marvin caught him looking at the gloves he went on excitedly, "What do you think? They're a prototype, but I think I am really onto something good. Keyboardless typing, man. You can type on any flat area. It's a little cumbersome right now, but eventually I want it so you can even type in the air. How cool would that be?"

Lucius shot him an annoyed look and Marvin swung his head back to the monitor. "Right. Ok, so here it is. Sent out about three hours ago."

Lucius leaned over the man's shoulder. The email had indeed come from his assistant. Essentially, it stated that due to security concerns the *Domus* would be closed indefinitely. The staff was to leave immediately and only return when contacted. He stood and took several steps from the desk. His assistant was constantly trying to soften him up, make him more approachable. She would never have sent such a curt and cold message.

"She did not send that email."

"You mean they hacked her account?" Marvin pivoted the chair around and leaned back, the loud groan of the exhausted springs echoing against the metal walls.

"Yes. Can you find out who did?"

"I don't know man." Marvin shook his head but stopped when Lucius sent him another deadpan glare. "I can try. I can't promise you anything."

"You say you are the best."

Marvin leaned forward and the chair popped back to vertical. "Sure, but I can't perform miracles."

Lucius raised a brow.

"All right, some miracles. But don't expect it this time."

Lucius held up his hands in defeat. Then he plopped the packet he'd brought with him on the desk and slid the digital camera out of his pocket. "I have another project for you as well."

"What? That first one wasn't enough?" Marvin picked up the packet and began pulling out the sheets of information. Lucius handed him the camera.

"I need four passports, ID cards, everything. I have it listed on the sheet. There are fingerprints, identifying information, photographs, everything you should need."

"She's cute," Marvin said when came to the picture of Grace on the tiny digital screen. Lucius restrained a growl. When the man reached the picture of Hailey, he whistled. "Now this girl is more my type."

"That's Derian's girl."

Marvin groaned and threw down the packet. "You *viators* get all the hot chicks."

"Two days. Bring it to the address I listed in the notes."

"Ah come on man. You know I have other clients."

"None that pay as well as I do."

Marvin narrowed his eyes. "Some might."

Lucius ignored him and prepared to jump. He landed back in the apartment where Derian, Hailey and Grace waited with their bags packed. A knock sounded at the door and he turned to answer it. Marvin's timing was unbelievably convenient. The man stood on the small platform to the apartment, a bundle of papers under his arm. Lucius held out his hand for it. "What did you find out about the email account?"

"I don't know man. It's weird," Marvin said. Lucius waited for him to continue. The man always seemed to want conversation when all Lucius needed were answers. "Right, well, the email came from Rusa's computer. Don't know what you can do with that."

Lucius thanked him and sent him on his way. Rusa had been the head of the Council for over 500 years and one of

Lucius's staunchest supporters. He was also Roderic's grandfather. It just did not add up.

15

Grace stared through giant panes of glass at the beast of a machine they were about to enter. People bustled around her and if Lucius hadn't stood sentry at her side she knew she'd have been caught up in the river of passengers moving from one side of the airport to the other. But she was determined not to let her nerves show. He'd already made it quite clear he did not want her on the trip.

She hugged her mother's journals to her chest as a nasally voice made announcements from speakers in the wall. Lucius grabbed her hand to lead her to the door and her heart skipped for a moment at the contact. They stood in line while a man in uniform spoke to each person that entered the plane. Shifting from one foot to the other she glanced behind and Hailey smiled from where she waited with Derian. Never having been on a plane either, Hailey seemed to understand Grace's anxiety, but she handled her nervousness significantly better. Grace wished she could discover the young woman's secret. She was 300 years old and feeling like a timid teenager all over again. It was quite embarrassing.

They made it through the line and found their seats. Hailey slumped into the chair beside hers and the two men settled in the row behind. Grace looked out the oval window at the people hustling about, preparing the massive machine for takeoff. In the distance, she could see another plane as it backed away from the terminal. She buckled her seatbelt.

It seemed to take forever before the plane finally began to move. Her knuckles turned white as she dug her fingers into the hand rest. When it picked up speed, she felt like her stomach was left behind. Hailey grabbed her hand and the two of them stopped breathing until the cabin settled back to normal.

After a while, Grace's nerves stopped buzzing and she dared to look out the window. Thin clouds obscured pockets of land and the whole experience of being high above the earth took on a surreal normalcy. Hailey grinned when the stewardess stopped at her side. "Two Bud Lights."

Two cool cans were placed on the tray Hailey had pulled down and the stewardess moved on. "All right Grace, you said you wanted to try beer. This isn't great beer. But it will give you a general idea."

She popped the top of one and handed it to Grace. Lucius leaned over the seat. "Grace, have you had one of those before?"

"No. But I have always wanted to try."

"Maybe now is not the time," he said.

"Now is the perfect time. We have hours of nothing in front of us. We're good," Hailey said. Then popped open her own can of beer.

Grace grinned. Lucius could be a bit of a curmudgeon. The cool can tasted metallic against her tongue and she took a tentative sip. She grimaced.

"Yeh. It's an acquired taste." Hailey tipped her head back and swallowed a much larger sip.

It took a while, but eventually she got most of the beverage down. It wasn't so bad after her taste buds grew used to the flavor and she found the notion of being thousands of miles above land worried her less. Hailey finished another beer and started chatting. Most of the conversation was directed toward Grace's existence as a *tiresian* and she answered the questions with an eye to the people around them. What would the humans really think of their conversation?

Despite the odd topic, no one showed any interest or concern over the two women spinning fantastic tales in the cabin. Did no one pay attention to the people around them? There was such disinterest in the humans that shared the space, strangers in close proximity doing everything they could to maintain a buffer of indifferent privacy. She felt overwhelmed and out of place.

Hailey's chatter served to distract Grace from the foreignness that surrounded her, providing a pillow of calm between her nerves and the knowledge she had no experience to help her deal with reality outside the community.

In addition, she discovered that in the three centuries of her life, she really hadn't done much. Not if Hailey's life was the norm. Grace resolved herself to change that now that she could.

Hailey leaned in with a conspiratorial nudge. "So, what's going on between you and Lucius?"

"I don't understand."

Hailey leaned in a little closer. "You know."

Grace stared back. Was she talking about the visions? Grace hadn't revealed much about those. She supposed someone would be curious about how it worked, but Hailey was unusually indirect about it. "What do you want to know about it? It can be hard to explain."

"Boy, do I know that."

Grace giggled. She could imagine how difficult it would be to describe time travel to someone. Even she, raised with a basic knowledge of the *viators*, had no idea how the process worked. The first time she'd seen Lucius fade away had her all the more curious. "Most of the time I only see flickers. But when it comes to Lucius I see so much more."

"Flickers?" Hailey leaned back, confusion on her brow.

"Yes. They are like impressions, feelings–occasionally a flash of an image. But with Lucius I see events unfold. Sometimes they last as long as a minute." She blushed at the thought of the last. The longest vision she'd had of Lucius was much more like a dream and hadn't happened yet. At least not to her knowledge. The person he'd been in bed with during that particular vision was hidden from her.

"Your visions?"

Grace cocked her head in response and Hailey laughed. Then she leaned in again. "I meant, are you and Lucius an item? Are you two, you know…"

"You mean romantic?" Grace whispered. Hailey grinned and slowly nodded. "Oh, no. Not really."

"Really? You seem close though."

Grace looked down at her lap. She didn't think so. A single kiss didn't mean they were romantically involved. Did it? And he made it clear any attraction he felt was unwelcome. "He does not want me around, actually."

"Dude." Hailey turned her head to peek between the seats at the two men sitting behind them. "I don't believe that for a minute."

"You say that a lot. I am not certain what you mean."

"I say what?"

"Dude."

At that Hailey burst into a loud laugh. Several passengers across the aisle looked over. "Dude is by far the best word in the English language."

"I know that it has had numerous permutations through history. But you use it in ways I have never read."

"Well. It used to mean a city slicker. It was a derogatory term for men from back east that didn't fit into the west. But it was picked up by the California surfers and then teenagers. When I grew up, dude was required to be said in every sentence. That and certain swear words that I have tried to use a little less. I just can't seem to get rid of dude."

Fascinated, Grace gave a tentative smile. "But what does it mean?"

"Well. It can mean just about anything. Mostly a feeling. For instance, let's say you said something I wasn't expecting. I would say 'Dude'," the word came out short and changed in pitch toward the end. "But if you said something I didn't agree with I would say 'Dude'." This time the word was said low and long.

Grace giggled. Then tried it herself, "Duuude."

Hailey threw back her head and let loose another of her hearty laughs. Lucius peeked over her head. "Tell me you are not teaching her to speak your language."

Both girls fell into a fit of giggles. Grace hadn't had this much fun in...well, ever.

An hour later, the conversation waned and Hailey fell into a fitful sleep. So vibrant and positive when awake, the impact of the situation showed as bluish shadows beneath her closed lashes. Grace didn't know everything that happened before they'd met, but she could tell now it taxed the new *viator* far more than she allowed it to show. The minuscule blanket slid to hang from one knee and Grace adjusted it back over Hailey's scrunched body.

Leaning down, Grace pulled her mother's journals from beneath the seat. The scent of old paper wafted up as she opened the first book. She ran her fingers over the carefully scribed Ancient Greek words. It had been a long time since she'd seen the language of the ancients. No one really knew when the first *tiresian* saw visions. But their mythos attributed Tiresias, the blind prophet of Thebes, as their Father. It had been a time when people with their abilities were held in high regard and could openly practice.

She sighed. But these words didn't connect her to that past. Instead, they were the closest she'd been to touching her mother in over 150 years. She started to read.

Three hours later, she looked up to find Hailey gone and the lights turned low. She closed the first book, put it aside and rubbed her fist into her eye. So much had been covered in the thin volume. Sporadically updated, her mother had filled the pages with bits and pieces of her life before Grace's birth.

It began just after the revolt against the Roman *viators* when her mother entered adolescence. She described the exodus from Constantinople amid the confusion of the Crusades. While it continued with their trials in discovering a new land to settle, far away from their old enemies, Grace began to pick up hints of discontent and frustration her mother felt under Althea's leadership. It struck a chord of familiarity in her heart.

An announcement came over the intercom and everyone hustled back to their seats to prepare for landing. Hailey popped back into her seat and buckled herself in. As the plane descended toward the earth, she reached over and grasped Grace's hand. "No problem, right? They land planes all the time with no problem."

Grace returned her weak smile and closed her eyes.

They made it to New York. Grace held close to Hailey as they maneuvered through JFK International Airport. As they wound through the crowds, Lucius and Derian made a small buffer of space for the women by staying on either side of them. A constant aura of awareness seemed to emanate from the *viators*, strength and a predisposition toward protection a common characteristic between the three. Grace let them encourage her along, happy to allow them to be her guide in the unfamiliar waters.

Hailey kept up a constant chatter, explaining the nature of Los Angeles traffic patterns and how the current conditions in the New York Airport couldn't compare to the terror induced by a million people in two-ton death machines going eighty-miles an hour a foot from your own vehicle. Grace experienced a touch of that on her harrowing journey to meet up with them in California but the disinterested and nervous crowds about them seemed, to her, to be just as treacherous.

They made it onto the next plane and Grace immediately pulled out her mother's second journal. Eagerness to start again was only half the excuse. In truth she needed to distance herself from the overwhelming pocket of humanity. The noise, proximity of strangers, and overwhelming new sights she'd witnessed in the airport had her nerves rattled. Hailey promptly fell back to sleep. Grace envied her, but knew she would have no rest for quite some time.

She was exhausted when they finally arrived in Kiev. Several tense moments followed as they made it through customs, but the documents Lucius acquired held up against the focused inquiry. They hurried to retrieve their bags and the men gave a reluctant warning of caution before leaving to secure transportation.

After a short while, Hailey waved Derian over as he pulled up to the sidewalk in a silver sedan. Lucius untucked himself from the passenger seat and retrieved Grace's bag from the sidewalk. She hardly noticed as they threw the luggage in the trunk. She started in surprise when he touched her elbow.

"What? Oh, I am sorry. Thank you for getting my bag." Grace's voice was barely a whisper. The trip had been draining. But that wasn't the problem. No, the problem lay in her finishing the second journal. She had no idea what to do with the new knowledge. Lucius guided her toward the car, a quizzical look on his face. She blinked up at him, then looked away.

The others piled into the car and Derian eased them into traffic. He seemed significantly more confident at the wheel than she had, but then, he apparently had much more practice. Much more practice at a lot of things. Like time travel. She opened her lips to speak then thought better of it. After all, she didn't yet know the implications of her discovery.

She thought back to her mother's journals. The second one started just before Grace's birth, a little after her mother returned from a self-imposed exile, heartbroken and pregnant. For the first time in her life she understood the sadness she remembered in her mother's eyes. For the first time in her life she understood the animosity her grandmother had towards her and why she never felt like she fit in.

She knew her father. And he was a *viator*.

16

Andrij ushered the four travelers into his pocket-sized apartment, slapping his hand on Lucius's shoulder as they walked down a narrow hall into a sparsely furnished living room. In the corner, a tiny kitchenette with just enough counter space to hold the stack of dishes waiting to be washed and a mini-microwave.

"I am glad to see you alive, my friend." Andrij's Ukrainian accent slipped like thick syrup over his words. He motioned toward a thread-bare couch, where Hailey and Grace took tentative seats on the very edge, their nerves finally fraying under the tension. Lucius hoped they could stop long enough for decent rest before they began their trek into the Carpathian Mountains, otherwise, the women would be unlikely to make it out of the foothills.

"No one is happier than I to be alive."

Andrij laughed with a deep rumble. Then he asked for assistance with moving the supplies from his hidey-hole in the closet-like bedroom.

"I have procured what you requested," Andrij said as he slung several hiking bags over his shoulder. "Do you truly intend to take the women with you?"

When Lucius grunted his reply Andrij shook his head in commiseration. "I do not envy you this trip. I would go with you but..."

Derian scoffed, "Andy, you never get involved."

Andrij shrugged, but his temperament remained solemn. "This trouble with the *Domus*, it is not good. I fear it is bigger than any of us can handle."

They returned to the living room and laid out the supplies across a circular table. Derian unzipped the bags, to inventory the supplies to accompany them on the trip.

Lucius turned to Andrij and crossed his arms against his chest. "What have you discovered?"

"It is not good. Activity has tripled in the area since you were reported dead. When you called, I sent a man up to see the fortress. My cousin, he is a good man. Very strong constitution. He came back worried. Too many men walk the walls there."

"Armed?" Derian asked.

"Very. Even two men with your experience will find it difficult. Very dangerous. With them–" Andrij cast a sidelong glance at the women. "I am concerned. Leave them here. I will make sure they are safe."

"Not going to happen," Hailey called from the couch. "This argument is getting really old. When are you guys going to remember I fought with Nazis?"

"Hailey, you didn't fight Nazis. You were captured by Nazis," Derian replied as a slight smile pulled up at the corners of his lips.

Hailey sputtered, "Yeh, well I did fight pirates."

He looked up and raised a brow. Hailey narrowed her eyes in response and said, "Don't even start with me."

Lucius felt relieved that at least Grace looked suitably worried. With the situation as daunting as Andrij described, her value as a *tiresian* just multiplied. Overconfidence would be detrimental. Unfortunately, so would a lack of confidence. "The women will do well. I have complete faith in their abilities."

Grace turned her big, brown eyes to his, slightly questioning. Uncomfortable, he turned back to an unconvinced Andrij. "We need a place to rest before we make the trip."

"My Aunt has a nice place. It is halfway between here and the mountains. Plenty of room for you to rest. Her husband worked in oil. Made lots of money then died and left it to her." He shook his head. "She is crazy, but we are in luck. She is on vacation in America."

It would do. Then they could get underway. The outlook at the fortress concerned him. The conspiracy had gone to a lot of trouble to capture Roderic and there was no way to know what condition they would find the surly scientist. Lucius held a hand out for Grace. Her eyes unfocused as their skin touched. When the light again lit in their depths, she gave a tremulous smile. "Nothing surprising in that one. I think I need to sleep."

He pulled her into the crook of his arm and led her to the door. They all needed sleep.

The next day they drove for hours to the Carpathian Mountains. When they reached the furthest point for vehicle travel they left the rented sedan under a mask of darkness. An hour-long exhaustive trek over one of the low hills at the base of the mountains brought them to an old hunting shack. Lucius had used the shack several times in the past when traveling to Carpathia for business. Luck held that the conspiracy had not discovered it. They settled down for a few hours of sleep.

Early the next morning, as sunlight bathed the landscape in a warm, yellow hue, they set out onto the mountain trail. The women held out better than expected. After twelve hours he stopped them at an outcrop which provided suitable protection from the elements. Grace let her bags fall, slumped against a boulder and pulled out her water, closing her eyes to the waning sun.

"This is the boundary of the jump buffer. From this point you have to memorize the way in. If anything happens, return here and get to safety." Lucius addressed the whole group, but looked worriedly to Grace. There was a risk for Hailey if she jumped, but should it be an emergency, she could leave. Grace provided a complication.

Hailey dropped her bag beside him. "Don't worry. If things get crazy I will get her out."

"That could be very dangerous for you," Derian said.

She waved him off and looked pointedly at Lucius. "Don't worry. She's worth the risk. Don't you think?"

Grace opened her lips to respond then closed them as if thinking better of expressing her words. She turned her head away from them and gazed into the distance.

They set up camp and prepared for another rustic night. He spent an hour instructing them on what he expected while in the fortress, but intentionally neglected to mention that Hailey and Grace would wait outside for them. When they woke the next morning, an excited tension filled them all as they cast off the supplies they wouldn't need that day.

The hike toward the fortress passed quickly and quietly. Grace let out a long held breath when they caught sight of the fortress. "That is imposing. The stories do not give it justice."

"There have been many changes made since any of your people were housed here." It was a mild way to state the fact that *tiresians* had once been imprisoned behind its walls. But it was a history he could not change and unfortunately words couldn't soften the black reality of that part of *viator* and *tiresian* relations.

"It looks like something out of a medieval fantasy," Hailey said, her voice breathy from the steep ascent into the thin, mountain air.

"Most of the fortifications were made during the thirteenth century. After the fall of the Eastern Roman Empire our people moved our central operations here," Lucius said.

Derian's eyes shimmered with memory. It was where Lucius trained him as a *venator*. The two men had worked together for centuries before Lucius was appointed *magister* and the *Domus* was brought kicking and screaming into the modern era. That process necessitated a move of operations away from the fortress into a more hospitable location in the American southwest.

"So what's the plan?" Hailey asked.

"We wait until dusk." Then Lucius would tell the women they would wait for the men outside the fortress walls.

That conversation did not go well. As the sun dipped below the silver fir and spruce trees, Hailey confronted him, her hands on her hips. She hissed between her teeth, "Like hell, Lucius! We did not hike all this way, to wait out here for you. We can help you in there."

"Hailey–" Derian warned.

145

"No. Look, I know I might be worthless in there, but you need Grace. And if things get bad I can get her out. So you need us."

"Damn it, Hailey. This is not negotiable," Lucius growled.

Grace put her hand out and touched his arm. Wrapping her fingers around his wrist, she pulled him behind a small stand of trees. He waited as she gathered her thoughts. When she spoke, her voice could barely be heard, "You are correct that I should not go in there with you."

He let out a relieved breath. Finally, someone was thinking sensibly.

"But I have to go with you."

He threw up his arms and turned away.

"Please listen to me." She walked around him to force his attention. "I can do what I did at my house here. And you know that will help more than anything."

"Do it from here."

"Once will not be enough. You know that. I can only give you a few moments like this. You need me inside with you."

"I do not like it."

"You have made that clear. I do not like it either."

He clenched his fists and tightened his jaw. What she said made sense. He'd known it all along, but he and Derian could do this without her aid. The risk was too great.

"I think you might like me just a little."

He swung his head down and a tiny sparkle reflected back from her darkening eyes. She put her hand to his arm and lost focus. When she returned her attention to him, her face grew marred with a frown. "We need to go."

"What did you see?"

A grin split her face. "You were helping Hailey up crumbling stone stairs. I believe we find an old entrance to sneak in."

Lucius ran a hand through his short cut hair. He knew just the place. Damn it but the women would be with them. He looked suspiciously at Grace. She wouldn't lie about what she saw. Would she?

He watched as her tiny figure sauntered toward Hailey and Derian. When she told them she won the argument, Hailey let out a sharp hoot of victory and picked up her bags. He felt a tic in his jaw. Somehow he'd lost complete command. This could be a serious problem.

Derian took Hailey aside and went over the use of the weapons he had strapped to his utility belt. She took a handgun and slid it into the holster Andrij had provided. Grace stood awkwardly to the side and Lucius approached her, then dug his hand into the little bag she'd carried up the mountain. His fingers curled around a small semi-automatic pistol and he pulled it out. "Have you ever used one of these?"

Grace shook her head. Lucius pointed out the safety and how to use the sight. He handed it to her and she tucked it into the holster on her hip and gave him a reassured smile.

When ready, Lucius led them along a narrow, over-grown trail which encircled the fortress. As they drew closer, they could make out the shadowy guards patrolling the ramparts. Bright orange torches lit the night sky every hundred feet, enhancing the medieval ambiance and bringing ancient memories to the surface. He held out a hand and halted them when they reached the farthest corner.

The stone foundations were cut straight from the mountain, giving it granite strength and a permanence which seemed inherent in medieval castles. Trees and brush had been cleared forty-feet around the perimeter with a thirty-foot wide trench to discourage unexpected guests.

"How are we supposed to get over that?" Hailey asked, her voice breathless.

"We don't," Lucius said, leading them away from the gaping chasm between them and their target. A quarter-mile along the mountain slope, the brush became nearly impenetrable. Lucius ducked to his knees, peering beneath leaves and branches. Satisfied, he stood and motioned to Derian.

With a machete in hand, Derian chopped the branches and cleared a path wide enough for them to pass through. Several feet in, a small hole just big enough for a man to crawl through opened into the mountain side.

"A secret entrance. Of course there's a secret entrance," Hailey grumbled when they ducked through the crumbling rock into a small cavern. "You know, Lucius you are about as bad at providing information as Derian. Would it kill you to give us a little more detail?"

He pulled out a palm-sized Mag-light from his bag and lit the way. Each slip and misstep through the natural cave tunnel echoed, but Lucius remained unconcerned. The side entrance was one of the few secrets in Carpathia he'd held. The tunnels meandered through the mountain in a spider web that could easily disorient the inexperienced visitor. He and Derian discovered the tunnel entrance eroding out of the wall of a small storage room 700 years ago. They spent years exploring the depths until they found the exit the four just used to gain access.

At the time, neither man had known the upheaval in the status quo they would face, but for some reason they kept their discovery secret. It was perhaps one of his more fortuitous decisions. Two hours later, he pulled the group to the side. The entrance to the storage room lay only a few hundred feet ahead. "Hailey, if anything happens that we cannot escape you must take Grace back to Andrij. He will help you to a safe house where we will meet up."

In the yellow light, the short movement of her acquiescent nod showed against the stone wall. He gave silent thanks that she finally decided to listen to his direction. Hopefully it would continue for the rest of the night.

When they reached the entrance, Derian pulled aside the wood and rubble they used to seal the door hundreds of years ago when they'd closed Carpathia down as the central operations for the *Domus*. Beyond the rubble was a wall of bricks. Concerned they may have a need to access the caverns again, Lucius installed the wall without mortar. He pulled out a compact entrenching tool and prepared to knock out the bricks to clear the way.

Grace grabbed his arm. "Wait."

He stilled. She kept an iron grip on his wrist for several moments then suddenly released the pressure. "It is all right now. But we must move fast. There are three guards in the hall beyond the first room. They will be facing the opposite direction when you open the door. Be prepared."

Lucius let out an unconsciously held breath and lifted the tool to strike. Derian and he made quick work of the wall and all four of them scrambled over the rubble into the room. Grace and Hailey brushed dirt from their clothes as Lucius listened at the door. The muted sound of footsteps passed and he waited another thirty seconds before opening the door.

With weapons drawn, he and Derian entered the hall, ready to incapacitate whoever stood on the other side. Just as Grace foretold, three guards stood ten-feet to the left, all three facing away from the two approaching men. Dressed in black t-shirts and cargo pants, the guards blended into the darkness, but so did their opponents.

Derian snuck up on one, wrapping his arm around the man's neck and swiping his legs out from beneath him. The man hit the ground with a thud and Derian had a Glock to his head before he could move. Lucius had his pistol pointed at the other two before they could reach for their own weapons. Derian grabbed his man by the scruff of the neck and hauled him up, motioning for all three to move back to the storage room.

Hailey and Grace joined them in the hall as the three guards were shoved into the room and locked in.

"You had the keys?" Hailey asked, her face incredulous.

"Of course I have the keys, I am the boss."

"Right, of course you had the keys. So *boss*, when we are done with all this, remind me to talk to you about a missing manual."

17

Derian and Lucius flanked the women as they snuck down the dark stone hall. A rumble of voices floated down from a narrow set of stairs. Lucius hurried them past, toward the deeper sections where the prisoner cells were installed. A wrought iron gate sealed the stairway leading to the lower levels. He reached into his pocket to pull out his keys.

Grace grabbed his arm. He waited for her vision to clear before continuing to dig in his pocket, but she tugged on his elbow. "He isn't down there. We find nothing if we go that way."

Lucius pulled his hand free of the pocket. The sound of the voices grew louder, so he hustled them through the hall and down another set of stairs leading to what had once been barracks. He put his hand on a heavy wood door. Grace touched him then nodded once. Her visions came reliably, making the process easier than he wanted to admit. They shuffled into the dark room and waited.

The voices echoed as they passed the stairwell then faded into the distance. "What now? Should we split?" Derian asked.

Splitting the group would allow them to cover more of the facility, but he was reluctant to have Hailey separated from Grace. He contemplated leaving the two with Derian and striking out on his own to find the elusive Roderic. Grace grabbed his arm again.

"That is a bad idea. You end up captured." She reached for Derian. "Yes. I am certain of it. We need to stay together."

Derian stared down at the little woman. "This is taking some getting used to."

Hailey sniggered. "Now you know how I feel. So what's the alternative?"

"We move fast." Lucius cracked open the door. The hall clear, he waved the three out and back up the stairs.

For an hour they ducked from oblivious guards and checked every room they came across. "They do not seem as diligent as they should," Derian remarked.

Lucius agreed. The facility seemed on low alert, suggesting overconfidence in their security. They continued their reconnaissance until the only locations left lay in the very center of the fortress. Hidden behind a giant, stone pillar, Derian and Lucius consulted. "It's dangerous. Even if they aren't expecting it, they are sure to notice us."

Lucius frowned. Was it possible they had removed Roderic from Carpathia? They'd gone on the intelligence given publicly at the *Domus*. Had they made a terrible mistake? Grace reached over as she had continued to do periodically through the night. She sucked in a breath this time and when she returned to the present her face was ashen. "They have him here."

"You know that for sure?"

"They are holding a man in the central courtyard. He is light-haired, broad shoulders." A smile touched her face. "And he stands just as arrogantly as both of you."

"That's Roderic. Alright, we will go up to the ramparts to see if we can get a good vantage point," Lucius said.

When they reached their destination, Lucius looked over the edge of the ramparts and down into a wide, open courtyard. Hundreds of men milled about, their hands on various weapons, both modern and experimental. He spied a number with the same pole weapons Nikanuur wielded at the apartment. Lucius regretted leaving behind the one they procured after that confrontation.

Roderic stood in the center, his arms restrained behind his back and several men standing guard on all sides. The irritable Scot scanned the area, worry creasing his forehead. Grace sat beside Lucius, her back leaning against the stone blocks. She let out a deep breath then turned to him. "You have to trust me."

"What?"

"Just trust me."

A commotion erupted on either side of the ramparts. Derian and Lucius whirled around as two sets of guards advanced on the four of them. "Damn it."

Grace gripped his arm and looked up pleading. "Don't fight."

"What?" he growled. What was the woman up to? The guards reached them and Derian grabbed Hailey to shove her between him and the men threatening with weapons ready. Grace moved to place herself between Lucius and the enemy, preventing any clear shot he may have had. Lucius turned back to see Roderic struggling against his captors.

They were out of options. Lucius removed his hands from his pistol and held them out for the guards to see. A path cleared and Carlo sauntered up to confront them. "I

153

had wondered if you had gotten lost." His nasty grin slithered across a triumphant expression.

"Don't you have small animals to torture?" Hailey said from behind Derian.

"A pleasure to see you again, *cara mia.*"

"Seriously? A pleasure? You are such a slime ball."

Derian put his hand behind him to stay Hailey's rant. Carlo sneered then turned his attention to the small woman standing before him. "And you must be Grace. Such an interesting creature you are." He held out a hand and one of the guards handed him a thin, leather-bound book.

"That is mine! I left it with–" she turned her head to look back at Lucius. "I left it with Andrij."

That explained why Carlo had been ready for them. How deeply had Carlo sunk his claws into the *Domus*? Was there anyone left to trust?

Carlo motioned for three men to take Grace and she took a quick step back until she stood between Lucius and Derian. "Remember I told you to trust me?"

Lucius looked down at her. Grace kept her eyes on Carlo and the advancing men. "Grace?"

"Duck," she whispered.

"What?" Derian asked.

"Get down!" Grace shouted, then grabbed both men by the arm and fell to the ground. Lucius and Derian both followed her to the hard granite and Hailey quickly joined them. A shot pierced the air and took out the man standing directly in front of Carlo. Chaos erupted as another shot connected with a second guard.

Shouts and gunshots filled the air as the guards searched for the shooter. Several ran toward the small group huddled on the rampart floor. Grace placed her hands on each side of Lucius's face. "Now you can fight."

Lucius sprang into a crouch and pulled the gun from his holster, firing off several rounds at the men headed their way.

"Don't shoot the girl! I want her alive!" Carlo shouted over the cacophony of sound.

"Hailey! Get her out of here!" Lucius ordered.

Hailey wrapped her arms around Grace then shouted to Derian, "Remember where I went after Tom Roy's? We'll meet you there!"

It took a few extra moments, but then the women faded from view. Lucius and Derian were pinned down. The guards retreated to the two ends of the rampart and used the tower doors as cover. Lucius looked over the side to see that the entire courtyard was a milling mass of running guards. Across the yard Roderic head-butted one of his captors and another went down under a well-placed bullet.

Lucius scanned the yard for where their miracle assistant set up their ambush point. Across the courtyard, on the opposite rampart a flash of movement preceded a falling object. When it hit the ground, an explosion ripped apart the men attempting to scale the wall. A second object careened from the heights, only this one had arms that flailed as it fell. The figure took the landing hard but rolled and jumped to their feet in an instant run. Long blonde hair flapped behind her in a tightly weaved braid.

"Is that Lidiya?" Derian asked as he reloaded his weapon.

"It seems to be." The woman ran at a breakneck speed toward Roderic, two guns out as she cleared a way for herself. "I say we join her."

"Brilliant plan, *boss*."

Lucius glared at his friend. "That woman is a bad influence on you."

Derian laughed as he reached into his bag and retrieved two grenades. He pulled the pins and threw one in each direction down the rampart. Just before he swung his body over the edge to make the forty-foot plunge, he replied, "She is incredible, isn't she?"

Two explosions impacted the stone walls, sending debris rocketing through the air. Lucius catapulted over the side and followed Derian in the near suicidal jump. Pain lanced through his body when he hit, but the momentum took him through a roll and lifted his body up before it brought him to a complete halt. Derian was already up, punching a surprised guard in the nose and pulling his gun to shoot at an advancing group with the menacing pole weapons. "Now be honest, Lucius. You missed this when you worked that cushy desk job."

"There was nothing cushy about that job," Lucius replied as he shot several bullets to discourage others from coming closer. "And your job was never this exciting."

"Maybe it was and I just left out the details."

"You're getting delusional in your old age," Lucius said.

Derian took off in a trot toward a fumbling Roderic. "Come on now, grandpa. You have a thousand years on me. Get those old legs pumping. We have a lab rat in need of assistance."

For the first time in years, a giant grin spread across Lucius's face. He indeed missed the excitement of working in the field. They reached Roderic and turned their back to him to provide a cover of fire. Lidiya had already begun removing his bonds.

"Ye haven't brain between the lot of ye. Ye bloody stupid *venator*. What part of this dinna look like a trap?" The more worked up Roderic got, the stronger his accent fell to its origins.

"Shut up you stupid neandertal and stop moving. I cannot get my knife through rope with you squirming like fish." Lidiya answered, her Ukrainian accent oozing just as thick.

"Damn ye lass. What were ye thinking coming after me?"

"You were afterthought. I came to kill a man."

Lucius and Derian kept the attackers at bay as the four of them moved toward the front entrance of the fortress. A giant wood and iron gate barred them from escape. Around it stood twenty armed men. "I dinna think that is the way to go."

Derian pulled out two more grenades. "Lidiya, do you have any more in that stash of yours?"

She'd already pulled three from her own bag.

"Jesu lass, ye are a computer geek, not a commando."

Raising a sardonic brow to Roderic, she pulled the pins and heaved them in the direction of the gate. Derian added his to the bunch and the four of them ducked behind several large supply boxes. Screams and splintered wood followed the explosion and the four of them ran back into the fray. With bullets and explosions in their wake, they high-tailed it out of the fortress and into the mountain wilderness.

They didn't stop their sprint until they reached the boundaries of the jump zone. Lucius brought them to a halt and addressed Derian, "Where did Hailey take Grace?"

"To the beach."

"We're in a war-zone and the lassies get to go on vacation?" Roderic rubbed his jaw where a nasty bruise began to flower.

Lucius ignored the ornery man. "We need a place to set up operations. The usual are all unsecure. And we have to be careful who we trust."

Derian looked behind them, his stance wary. "Do you think Andrij sold us out?"

"I don't know. He could have just as easily been coerced. But we cannot know for certain. We need a place no one knows or would suspect."

"Pick a time period. We'll find something that works," Roderic said.

"We need a lab. Someplace secure. We have work for you to do." Lucius wracked his brain for a suitable solution. Roderic grumbled about wanting to join the ladies on vacation while Derian kept a watch on their perimeter.

"My mother's lab."

All three men turned their attention to Lidiya. She'd bent over and was tightening the laces on her combat boots. Roderic scoffed, "It would have what I need, but every *viator* knows about your mother's lab."

Lidiya stood and stretched her back, then speared Roderic with a glare. "Not that lab. That was destroyed days ago by the same bastard I was trying to kill in there. We can go to my mother's secret lab."

"Why does Irene have a secret lab?" Derian asked.

"She lived over 3,000 years. You learn not to trust people when you live that long." She pulled a folded piece of laminated paper from her supply bag.

"What do you mean by lived?" Roderic asked.

Lidiya unfolded the paper and handed it to Lucius then looked to Roderic. "She died in her lab."

Roderic sucked in a breath and Lidiya turned to stare into the darkness. Lucius took out his flashlight and shined it on the paper. It was a map of San Jose, California. A large, red circle ran around a residential neighborhood tucked behind a university. "Is this it?"

"Yes," she whispered. He barely heard her over the anguish in her voice.

"We leave now. Meet there in original time." He handed the map off to Derian and prepared to jump. The only thing that would assist Lidiya with the pain was time and time was running low.

****

Water filled her nose and she broke through the surface with a sputter. Hailey floundered beside her, filling the air with a multitude of choice curse words. Her foot touched sand and Grace was able to find purchase in the shallow water only to be knocked down by a wave barreling toward the beach. Hailey grabbed her arm and hauled her back to her feet. The two women waded to shore then fell with exhausted grunts onto the hot, dry sand.

"Sorry about that. Last time I jumped here I landed on the beach. I'm still trying to figure out this time travel stuff."

Grace didn't respond. Her stomach gurgled from swallowing too much warm saltwater and her head spun from the disorientating jump through time. The sun beat on their skin and they were enveloped in a muggy cocoon from the water evaporating off their waterlogged bodies.

"Come on. Let's get in the shade. I don't know how long it will take for Derian to catch up with us." She stood and held out her hand. Grace wrapped her sand-covered fingers around Hailey's and stilled as a vision swamped her senses. Fear and anxiety clutched at her heart as a murky image of the dark-haired adversary from Carpathia filled her mind.

Just as suddenly, the vision cleared and a concerned Hailey stood a nose-length away. "Are you alright?"

"Yes, thank you," Grace said as she pushed herself up. Sand flew as she brushed the dry particulates from her jeans. They trudged across the sand. When Grace stumbled, Hailey reached out to help, but stopped just before she touched her. Grace appreciated the forbearance. The visions had been coming on stronger and with more frequency. She'd never had much physical contact with others in the community. Due to the nature of their talents, the *tiresians* limited the touching of others.

Frustrated, she focused on getting to the rocky shade beyond the beach. Tall palms rose above the lower lying trees. A gentle breeze cast sand against her skin and sent a chill across her arms. They fell to their knees under the shade of a leafy tree and sat quietly for a few moments, gathering their strength.

"You saw something didn't you? When you touched me, you saw my future."

"I did. Nothing solid, just a flash of an image. It was the dark-haired man from Carpathia."

Hailey groaned, "Carlo. Figures."

"He frightens you."

"Oh yeh he does. I was hoping he'd forget about me. But he's like a roach, every time you lift a rock he scurries out." Hailey picked up a pebble and threw it across the sand. "I'm pretty sure he saw me jump with you. It's not exactly a common skill for the *viators*, so he's going to be back on my ass again."

Grace looked down at the ground and twirled a tiny stick in her fingers. Carlo might have an alternate view of their jump. If he had her mother's journals then he knew she was half-*viator*. Would he assume she could jump time as well? Could she?

"You know three weeks ago I was bored out of my mind working in a cubicle. The highlight of my day was wondering what I would have for lunch. Now I can't even remember when we ate last." Hailey threw another pebble and let out an aggrieved sigh. She rubbed her stomach and looked up at into the branches. "I hope Derian shows up soon. I'm starving."

"He knows where we are?"

"Yep. We met up here once, about a week ago. He'll remember it."

Grace picked up her own pebble and rolled it in her fingers then squinted toward the horizon. Three dark dots appeared just over a low lying cloud. "Does he know *when* we are here?"

Hailey stopped, her arm mid-throw and swung her head to Grace. "Ah hell. I didn't think about that."

18

Lidiya opened the door to the craftsman-style bungalow and let the three waiting *viator*s into the entry hall. Hardwood floors registered their heavy booted steps and the scent of time settling into unused space flowed around them. Roderic slumped onto a flower print couch. "Where's this lab?"

Derian took the bag from Lucius's arm and laid it on a coffee table then asked Lidiya for the restroom. She pointed down the hall then turned back to Roderic. "Lab is in cellar. The neighborhood generally keeps to themselves, but mother wanted to keep eyes away from her work."

She left the room for a moment and returned with a pad of paper and a pen. "I have access codes here. You will find what you need downstairs. Here is list of local suppliers for additional materials."

She shoved the papers toward Lucius, but he grabbed her wrist instead. "Where are you going?"

Granite eyes stared back at him. "I have a man to kill."

"Don't be foolish. You will do better with us. There is nothing to gain from rushing into trouble," Lucius said.

She wrenched her wrist from his grasp and slapped the papers against his chest. "There is everything to gain from doing just what I intend to do. You have job to do, *magister*. But I no longer work for you."

Lucius took the papers and she swung around to pick up her bag. When she stood, she'd already begun to fade from view. Roderic shook his head. "That lass is as hotheaded as my father."

"Your whole family is hotheaded," Derian replied as he returned to the room. Roderic grunted in response.

There really was no argument there. Lucius had worked with Roderic's family long before the man jumped his first time in eighteenth century Scotland. Twins born in Minoan Crete, Rusa and Irene were instrumental in the new direction the *Domus* took after the fall of the Eastern Roman Empire. Rusa focused on the administration and development of a viable bureaucracy. Irene, on the other hand, had a passion for serving their people through research and knowledge. Interestingly, Roderic had followed in his aunt's footsteps as had his cousin Lidiya. Unfortunately, they'd both inherited Rusa's legendary fury.

Roderic pushed himself to his feet. "I might as well check out this lab."

"I must leave to retrieve the hard drives," Lucius said.

"You found my note then," Roderic said.

"I did. You saw this coming."

"Not soon enough. They were still able to get a hold of the majority of the database. Just not the most sensitive research."

Lucius expected as much. The information in the database would give the enemy a significant advantage. Every *viator* registered with the *Domus* would be traceable through the system. If the conspiracy set up a system that could pinpoint locations in time, they would all be vulnerable. Lucius said, "It is imperative that we find a way to mask our signals."

"Aye, if we're lucky, Irene will have set up a no jump buffer. If I can reactivate it, we should be relatively safe."

Derian pulled his bag onto his shoulders. "I need to find the girls."

"Find them? Don't you know where they are?" Roderic asked.

"I know where. Just not when. Hailey forgot to mention that part."

Roderic raised his eyes to the ceiling. "That girl has been trouble from the start. If you don't find them right away, come back here. I should be able to set up a tracking system to locate them relatively quickly, once Lucius brings me the hard drives. I had a hunch we'd need to find the lass again, so I inputted her specs in the emergency system."

Lucius grabbed his own bag. Hopefully, Derian's trip would be a simple retrieval. His nerves were strained since he'd seen the sheen of interest in Carlo's eyes on the ramparts. If the man knew she was a *tiresian*, he'd go to great lengths to acquire her for the conspiracy. Lucius didn't want her five-feet away from him, let alone across time. "We will meet back here shortly. We need everyone together again."

Derian's eyes focused inward as he faded from the room. Lucius followed soon after, determined to find a way to bring control back to the situation.

****

The three dark dots at the horizon drew closer and a deep rumble filled the air. Grace crawled out to get a better look. "Do you have any idea what year it is?"

Hailey joined her at the edge of the sandy beach. "No. I was more focused on just getting us out of there."

"How soon do you think we can jump again?"

"I don't know. I can jump pretty quickly by myself, but I've never tried to do it with a person more than once in a day. I don't know if I have it in me right now. If I try, I may end up leaving you here and not able to get back. Why?"

Grace shaded her eyes against the bright sunlight. The details on the approaching planes were finally coming into view. "Those are World War II bombers."

Hailey wrenched her gaze up toward the sky. "Are you sure? How do you know?"

"I had a book–"

"Right. Of course you did. Shit. This is so not happening again." She grabbed Grace by the arm and pulled her under the tree. Grace caught a glimpse of the bombers as they passed overhead. Suddenly, the sound of rapid gunfire filled the air. Birds scattered into the sky, adding their cries into the terrifying mix of noise. A minute passed then several large blasts shook the area.

Grace wracked her mind for a solution. With her talon-like fingers wrapped around Grace's arm, Hailey leaned in and whispered into her ear, "Those planes. Were those American?"

"Yes."

Hailey cursed under her breath and continued, "Then that means we're on the ground with the bad guys."

More rumbling from the direction of the sea had Grace ducking below the branches to look out at the beach again. Several more bombers followed behind the first. If Hailey couldn't get them out of there soon, they were in for big trouble. "Can you try jumping us again?"

"Then Derian really won't know where to find us and I have no idea where they went."

"What about another time on this island?" Grace said.

"With my luck we'll end up in the middle of a camp full of cannibals."

"We don't have many options."

Hailey rubbed her hands down her arms and looked out toward the beach as though scanning for someone to show up. Grace realized she needed to give the woman direction. She reached out, took her hand and focused inward, letting a vision take her. Adrenaline and fear sliced across her consciousness. No images, but the message was clear. They were not safe where they were. "We have to go now."

With wide eyes the *viator* wrapped her arms around Grace. "Ok, but I warned you. I'm terrible at this."

Grace felt a fuzzy sensation pool around her body and relief began to set in. Just as she was certain they would make a successful escape, the leaves beside them shook and three angry men in World War II Japanese uniforms stepped up beside them.

"Shit," Hailey said. One of the men wrenched her away from Grace. She struggled against his grip, shrieking in frustration. Grace held her hands out and plastered a glare on the two men pointing their rifles at her. They shouted in Japanese, but she shook her head to indicate she didn't comprehend. Japanese was a language she'd never studied. With hundreds of years of mind-numbing boredom she really should have taken advantage. But how was she to know she would face a moment like this?

They motioned for Grace to precede them deeper into the forest. Hailey was shoved into step beside her. She grumbled, "I am really getting tired of this. Just once I would like to land somewhere where they aren't trying to kill me."

One of the soldiers barked at them, threatening with the butt of his rifle. Hailey shut up.

Branches tore at their clothes and when she stumbled, Grace felt the barrel of a rifle pushed into her back. At some point, she realized she should have been terrified. Gods, she hoped Hailey's faith that Derian would find them held true. Ten minutes into the trek, more explosions shook the trees. These were much closer than the last. A heavy hand yanked her to a stop. She swung around to face their captors, as the three men searched the surrounding bush with nervous eyes.

Grace stepped closer to Hailey. Frightened men were significantly more dangerous than men in control of their emotions. She looked down at Hailey's fisted hand. Grace could see what would happen, just a touch and she would know. She snuck a glance at the men. Their attention directed elsewhere, she pushed away her fear and grabbed Hailey's wrist.

She sucked in a breath at the vision then tugged on Hailey's arm. "When I say so, run."

"What?" Hailey hissed.

One of the guards turned his attention back to the women. He gave a curt order and the three raised their rifles.

"Oh shit."

"Wait."

"Seriously?" Hailey rose onto the tips of her toes. Grace bent her knees and waited.

Suddenly, branches parted behind the three soldiers. Carlo stepped through and pointed a gun at the center man's head. Hailey gasped and the three soldiers swung around to discover the new threat.

"Now run!" Grace spun and took off through the forest. Hailey followed right behind. Three shots punched the air but the women kept going. One threat may have been dealt with, but it had been replaced by one far more sinister.

Branches snapped behind them and the crash of their pursuer through the brush sounded like the engine of an oncoming train. Her heart beat so hard she could feel it pressing against her ribs. Hailey shrieked as she plummeted to the ground, her foot twisted under an exposed root. Grace reached down to pull her up, but a hand grabbed her shoulder and threw her to the ground.

Carlo grinned down at them, his nostrils wide from drawing in air. The deviously handsome man, disheveled from the exertion, breathed heavily as he spoke, "I am not in the mood for the exercise."

Hailey struggled to sit up and he pushed a foot onto her chest. "Calm down, *cara mia*. There is no rush." He reached down and yanked Grace by the arm. She wrapped her fingers around his wrist and let the vision come. Fury and lethal frustration accompanied the sight of Hailey glaring daggers at him. A bright light flashed and she was brought back to the present.

"What did you see, my little seer?"

"Hailey is really angry with you."

"That is hardly interesting. She has always been angry with me." He cast a sleazy grin down at the prone woman, who responded with a nearly inhuman snarl. "Alright, *cara mia*. You may stand. We have a meeting to keep."

"We're not going anywhere with you," Hailey said.

Grace reached down to help Hailey up. A quick image flashed across her eyes. They were coming faster and with more control. Perhaps she could be useful after all. She turned and faced the smirking man, his confidence irritatingly evident in his stance.

He swiped his gun through the air in a nonchalant command. "It is time to go. We are going to the *Domus*. I trust you can find your way there, *cara mia*."

"I don't think I can do it right now. The last one took too much out of me. I've never done it twice in one day."

His smirk flickered. "Of course you can. You have, I have seen you. I am more concerned for the lovely Grace." He turned his attention to her. "You can jump again? I doubt you want to stay here where the Japanese will finish what they intended. They are not particularly understanding during these times."

"I cannot."

Hailey turned her lips down in confusion. "I don't get it. What does she have to do with it?"

Grace reached her hand behind Hailey and pinched her hip. The *viator* promptly clamped her mouth shut. She may be confused, but she paid attention at least. That was a blessing.

Carlo reached across and stroked a finger down Grace's cheek. She shivered beneath his touch. Hailey took a small step forward but his hand swung up and pointed a gun between her breasts. "Jealous, *cara mia*?"

"Dude, you're gross. Stop creeping out my friend."

Grace stepped away from his touch and asked, "What do you want from me?"

"Come now, do you not see the value of a woman with parentage such as yours?"

169

Erin Lausten

Hailey opened her mouth to ask a question, then thought better of it. She looked suspiciously at Grace, but kept her thoughts to herself. Grace reached over and gave her hand a reassuring squeeze, keeping the contact short to prevent the onset of another vision.

Gunfire erupted in the distance. Several birds crashed through the leaves above in a panic and Carlo swung his gaze to the trees. Grace pulled back her arm and aimed her fist at his nose. A sickening crunch announced the breaking of the bone and cartilage. Italian curses gurgled out as he stumbled back and put his hands to his bleeding nose.

Hailey recovered from her shock and said, "Why did you do that?"

"I knew you were not the person to do so. That left only me."

Hailey blinked several times then looked at the fuming Carlo. "At least he won't be so pretty."

19

Lucius stalked the sterile, white-walled room. Ten steps from one side of the room to the other did not give his long legs enough space to prowl. Why was he eternally cursed with rooms too small to accommodate him?

"Stop your pacing. You're making me nervous," Roderic growled from across the room.

"Is the tracking system up?" Lucius asked.

"Soon," Roderic answered, his head bent over the blue hued computer screen.

Three hours had passed and Derian had yet to reappear with the women. The clock on the wall ticked by, giving a false sense of security in its constancy. Each minute passed and the possibility of Grace being in grave danger increased. He considered following after Derian, but he would not know what he'd be jumping into. His patience was lacking, but he practiced restraint. Trust between him and his top *venator* was established long ago.

Roderic grunted as the screen changed. Tapping furiously on the small laptop, he pulled up a map similar to satellite imaging. The difference was this map could pinpoint a *viator*'s location in space *and* time.

Lucius stepped up beside Roderic's shoulder and asked, "How long before we can find Hailey."

Roderic swiveled around in the doctor's stool he'd pulled up to the stainless steel table. "An hour at least. The files need to transfer over from the other hard drive. Why don't you make yourself useful and find out what my crazy aunt has hidden in this room. I don't think she was working on *Domus* approved projects here."

Lucius bit back a retort about insubordinate scientists. Through years of service, Lucius commanded the respect of his colleagues and those under his command. Roderic was no exception, but he respected the Man not the position. They worked well together, but only because Roderic had no desire for a leadership position. He ran his lab his way and followed Lucius's orders only because they shared the same vision and goals for the *Domus*. Luckily the man was able to mask his disdain for authority when others were about– usually.

The room had been kept tidy and well organized. Stainless steel counters lined the walls. They were surprisingly clear of dust. Two large cabinets stood in one corner and when Lucius turned the knobs, they opened with well-maintained ease. The first cabinet contained various laboratory supplies. Beakers, test tubes, chemicals, and other items Lucius couldn't identify filled all the available space. Roderic would need to look through the items to determine if there was anything strange. To Lucius, it looked just like the now defunct lab at the *Domus*.

He opened the second cabinet and found stacks of notebooks, ranging from ancient leather bound volumes to the more modern pressed paper covered journals. Lucius pulled out one of the newer books and flipped it open. Graphs and symbols covered the pages. Unfortunately, the language was indecipherable. He walked it over to Roderic.

"Blasted woman had to take her notes in Minoan. It will take me forever to translate those books," Roderic said in a frustrated groan.

"Whatever she was doing, she didn't want others to know about it. How much do you think Lidiya knows?"

Roderic shrugged. "She never talked about Irene. I don't think they got along. But as soon as she shows up again, it will be the first thing I ask." He turned back to the computer screen and continued with another burst of commands.

Lucius returned to his investigation. A large refrigerator hummed in another corner. Hundreds of samples in test-tubes sat in the spotless interior, most labeled with numbers and letters that meant nothing to him. Hopefully, the answers to their identity could be found in the notebooks.

Footsteps scuffed on the concrete stairs. Lucius looked up as a frowning Derian entered the room. Lucius said, "No luck?"

"No," Derian answered and walked directly to Roderic. "Do you have them?"

"Half-an-hour," Roderic answered.

Derian clenched his fists. "We are running out of time."

"Patience. They will be fine for half-an-hour." Roderic waved the frustrated man away.

"You don't know Hailey. We need to find them as soon as possible," Derian said.

Lucius came up beside the two men. "Do you believe they have encountered trouble?"

"Every time Hailey jumps, she gets in trouble. I don't see why this instance would be any different."

Lucius frowned and looked at Roderic. He responded by lifting his hands into the air. "I can't make this happen any faster. It will take half-an-hour. Find something to do before I am forced to beat the both of you."

Derian swung around and stomped back up the stairs. Lucius decided not to follow him and returned to pacing. He could understand Derian's anxiety. At the moment Lucius would sell the sun to a madman if he could find a way to bring Grace back. An unfamiliar feeling of turbulence had him acting out of character and if he didn't maintain control of himself, he'd do something foolish. This undeniable desire to keep Grace safe and with him threatened to get in the way of his duty.

Roderic continued to type madly on the keyboard. Still pacing, Lucius replayed everything he knew about the conspiracy like a record in his head. Someone, or some group, had systematically established a hold on all of the *Domus'* facilities and supplies. They had grown a force large enough to both take over and hold those resources with little push back from those in the way. Carlo effectively cut the head off the snake when he'd shot Lucius. There were contingency plans in place should a crisis occur, but none of those had been enacted. The answer had to lay with the Council.

Only the Council could cancel the safeguards and effectively dismantle the entire system. But who had orchestrated the job? Marvin said the email sending all the non-essential staff home originated from Rusa's computer. Derian, however, stated that Rusa not only knew nothing of the conspiracy, but had essentially been railroaded out of the Council. Neither explanation made sense. Rusa was the loyal and steadfast leader of the *Domus* for over 1,500 years. Why would he turn traitor now? Lucius didn't believe it. But how could the man have had no idea what had simmered in the background?

Lucius stopped and clenched his eyes shut. Could both he and Rusa have been so blind? He felt the fool for not seeing this coming. A good strategist knew the players. A good strategist knew how to keep ten steps ahead of his opponents.

Roderic called to him from across the room and shouted for Derian to join them. The computer screen was populated with thousands of pin-prick sized dots. Most blinked red, meaning the *viator* had been located, but the identity was unknown.

Lucius asked, "Why are there so many unknowns?"

"I only uploaded the specs for a few *viator*s. This computer can't handle all the data we have and it would take too long. With you and Derian breathing down my neck I decided to speed up the process." Roderic clicked on several links, removing layer after layer, each representing a point in time.

"So where are they?" Derian asked from behind Roderic's shoulder.

"I have her pinned down to within a few decades. Seems she is on a beach. A small island in the South Pacific, to be exact." Roderic let out a breath in victory when he stopped on a layer with a bright blue blinking light. "There she is."

Lucius looked at the upper left corner of the screen for the exact time. Derian groaned, "I swear that woman should never be let out of my sight."

Hailey and Grace had landed on a Japanese-controlled island during World War II. Roderic looked up at the two men. "What is it with that woman? Did she not have enough fun with the Nazis?"

Derian gave him a disgusted look and pivoted away. Lucius looked closer at the screen. "There are two *viators* with her."

Derian swung back around and leaned in toward the screen. "Son of a bitch. How did they get to her so fast?"

"I don't know, but we need to get to them now." Lucius stalked to the door. The buffer in the room prevented them from jumping from the house. They would have to leave from the backyard. Derian followed close on his heels, his Glock already in hand.

They landed in a thick stand of trees. Both men scanned the brush, guns out and sweeping the area for threats. Derian moved to investigate beyond their spot but Lucius stopped him with a touch on the arm. Through the trees he could hear flowery Italian curses. Lucius motioned for Derian to follow and they slid through the trees toward the sound.

Between the branches, he made out three figures. Grace and Hailey stood together, their backs to where Lucius and Derian hid. Carlo was bent over, his fingers covered in blood. When the man looked up at the girls, a terrifying fury sputtered from his eyes. There was no sign of the other *viator*. Before he made his move, Lucius wanted to know exactly where all the players were. He directed Derian to circle around the group.

Lucius waited a few moments more. The additional *viator* still had not shown himself. Carlo reached out and grabbed Grace by the arm. She crumpled to the ground in a faint, pulling Carlo down as she went. Hailey sprung onto his back. "Get away from her!"

Carlo roared, dropping his arm from Grace to deal with the woman on his back. He flung Hailey several feet away onto the hard forest floor. Then he advanced on her, his gun held out with lethal intent. Lucius sprinted into action. Gun drawn and pointed at Carlo, he growled at the vicious man. "Leave her be, Benanati."

Carlo swung around with an evil sneer and shot at Lucius. The bullet flew past him, embedding itself into the nearest tree. He ducked to the side, drawing Carlo's attention away from the women. Hailey reached up and yanked on Carlo's leg, pulling him off balance. The gun now pointed at her blood-streaked face. "I had hoped to keep you around a little longer, *cara mia.*"

Hailey scrambled away from the gun and looked to Lucius for aid. Carlo glanced at him out of the corner of his eye. "I will kill her, *magister*, though I far prefer her alive. If she accompanies me, I will allow the rest of you to live."

Grace stirred from her spot on the forest floor, her eyes snapping open with sudden consciousness. She lay just out of Carlo's sight and Lucius saw comprehension flicker across her face. He flicked his wrist, hoping she would acknowledge his command to do nothing. She stilled.

"Enough of this, we must leave." Carlo reached his free hand down to pull Hailey to her feet. He lost his confident smile when Derian pressed the cool pistol into the back of his neck.

"Well played gentlemen," Carlo drawled then he faded from view.

"Damn it," Derain said. "I should have shot him."

Hailey and Grace struggled to their feet. Dirt and leaves clung to Grace's body. Tiny sticks stuck out from her frazzled black hair. Strain put permanent creases at the corners of her lips. The desire to reach out and gather her into his arms beckoned, but he held back, staring into the brush for any sign of threat. The other *viator* still had not made his presence known. Had he jumped at the first sign of threat?

Hailey ran to Derian and threw herself into his arms. Derian responded with a bone-crushing embrace. Hailey's whisper could be easily heard over the eerily quiet forest. "I knew you would show up. You always do."

Grace stared at them and wrapped her arms around her chest. Lucius walked over to her and pulled her into his arms. She sighed and melted into the embrace, shivers wracking her body. He looked down at the pixie of a woman in his arms and tucked a stray tendril of black hair behind her ear. Her eyes were tired and not quite as soft and innocent as the first time they'd met. But something flickered behind their depths, something that reflected strength and resolve. Was he to blame for her loss of innocence? How quickly life could change the eyes. Lucius said, "Did he hurt you?"

Grace shook her head then laid it against his chest.

"Him hurt her? Are you kidding? She knocked his nose right up into his head. You should have seen it. I've wanted to do that for so long." Hailey came over and grinned at them. Her shoulder-length blonde hair had wrapped around itself in a painful looking knot. She said to Grace, "I don't know if I can forgive you for taking the opportunity away from me, though. Maybe next time I can kick him in the balls."

Grace giggled into his shirt and then straightened, pushing herself away. "If the opportunity presents itself I will be sure to allow you the honor."

The sense of ease disappeared when all four of their heads swiveled at the sound of gunfire in the distance.

"What the hell is that?" Derian asked.

"The American's are bombing the island," Grace replied.

Derian glared at Hailey. "What is with you and this damn war? Can't you find a nice, peaceful place to land?"

Hailey continued to look worriedly toward the gunfire. "You know, I was wondering that myself." She turned back to him and flashed a giant grin. "I guess all I can do is practice."

Lucius grabbed Grace's hand. "We need to leave. Hailey, can you jump with Grace?"

"Sure."

Grace frowned and said, "You told him you weren't sure you could."

"Are you kidding? I lie to Carlo all the time. I feel great. I think I may be getting the hang of it actually."

Derian grunted, "I'll believe that when you stop landing in the middle of major world conflicts."

Hailey pointedly ignored him and turned to Lucius. "Where are we going? I could use some direction."

Derian pulled out the laminated map and handed it to Hailey. She scanned the image and handed it back. "I always wanted to visit San Jose."

"You did?" Lucius asked.

"Not really," Hailey said as she walked over and wrapped an arm around Grace. "So, we'll see you there in Original Time?"

Grace stared at Lucius with her big brown eyes. He couldn't tell if it was fear that reflected from their depths, but something was bothering her for certain. Something lay hidden in the depth of her silence. His intuition told him to trust her, but all the alarms of warning that made him an effective leader rang like sirens in a bomb raid.

Derian and he waited for the girls to disappear. Before they followed, Derian asked, "What about the other *viator*?"

"I am not certain. Perhaps they jumped prior to our arrival," Lucius said. Derian didn't look convinced and neither was he. With a wary eye on the overgrown brush he focused on returning to the northern California lab.

20

Grace sat with a plop on the back porch step. She didn't know if she could get used to jumping through time. Hailey joined her, cradling her head in her hands. Grace looked worriedly at the young woman. On the surface, they seemed about the same age, but in many ways Hailey seemed much older. It was hard to remember the woman had only been on this earth for thirty years. A *tiresian* took many more years to reach adulthood, at thirty Grace had still been a toddler. How strange a concept, to grow so quickly.

Grace stared into the lush green garden, the faint scent of mint and geranium wafting up with the breeze. Behind the sound of rustling trees was the muted rumble of human occupation. To Grace, the sound was deafening compared to the natural silence she'd grown so accustomed to. It seemed the odd one of the two must be her. Hailey at least lived comfortably in this modern world.

Lucius and Derian appeared beside them. Grace sucked in a breath at the unguarded intensity behind Lucius's expression. It faded behind the steel clamps of stoicism when he held out a hand to her. "We need to get inside the buffer. They have found it far too easy to find you."

Derian assisted Hailey up and had her through the door before Grace got her legs settled beneath her. Lucius put a hand to her elbow and ushered her up the pinewood steps. The thin screen door snapped shut behind them.

Hailey sat at a kitchen table, her thumbs pressed into her temples. "I don't think I can do that again for a while." Pain filled her eyes as she looked up at Lucius, "Where's Roderic? I need to talk to him."

"Downstairs. I will ask him to join us." Before he left, Lucius held out a chair for Grace and she accepted the gesture with a sigh of relief. She could use a very long nap and a shower. Gods, she hadn't had a shower in days. Her fingers looked yellowish-brown under the faint light peeking in from the partially covered windows. Black lines topped her fingernails and the skin had begun to crack. Perhaps she could ask to use the shower. They couldn't mind too terribly.

Roderic followed Lucius back into the room. When he caught sight of Hailey he said, "Lass, you look like crap."

"Don't beat around the bush. Tell me what you really think," Hailey replied, her voice monotone but accompanied with a slight catch of humor.

Grace shifted uncomfortably in her seat. All the space in the room seemed to have been swallowed by the three massive men. She felt like a mouse among elephants. Roderic swung his attention to her.

"You must be Grace." He held out a hand and she placed hers within it. When he pulled it up to place a kiss on her knuckles, Lucius took a step toward her and Roderic raised a brow at the move. "Christ, not you as well?"

Hailey snorted from across the table. "Don't even get involved with that. If you think Derian's bad, he's worse. He's all grumpy about it."

Grace looked from Roderic to Hailey. She had absolutely no idea what they were talking about. She glanced up at Lucius to see if he could give her a clue, but he just glared at Hailey. These people spent too much time speaking in riddles. She may never understand them.

"Move on to what matters." Lucius put a hand on the back of her chair, but addressed Hailey, "You wanted to speak to him."

"Right." Hailey shifted and dug her hand into her jeans pocket. She pulled out a thin vial, the clear liquid within shimmering in the pale light. Grace recognized it from the collection that was on the table when she'd first met them in Southern California. The same collection which disappeared with Hailey's great-grandmother at the most inopportune time.

"Where did you get that?" Lucius said. He did not sound happy.

"I found it before we left the apartment. I think Poppi dropped it before she jumped. It is the only one left, but I figured it would at least be something to start with." Hailey placed the vial into Roderic's palm.

"Why did you keep it a secret? What if it had gotten damaged in Carpathia or in your last misguided jump?" Lucius's deep voice rose, sending goose bumps across the back of Grace's neck.

Hailey held her hands up in surrender. "I get it. You don't like secrets." She cast a sidelong glance at Grace. "I promise to never keep anything from you again."

Roderic sniffed at the open vial. "So what is this that has our intrepid leader so irritated?"

"Well, it can be one of three things. Either its poison or something to prevent me from going nuts. The little adjustments Nikanuur made to my biology have some nasty side-effects. I may be going crazy. They had a medicine that was supposed to help."

"You said three things."

"Right, I did. They also came up with a way to negate the blood-tracking thing we can do. They gave it to me and now Derian can't find me in time anymore," Hailey said.

"Ah, I see."

"Actually, you don't. Well not completely. Since I am in a confessing kind of mood, I might as well come completely clean." Lucius and Derian both snapped their heads toward Hailey. Grace was glad the attention was focused on the spunky blonde instead of her. What would Lucius say if he found out she'd been keeping her own secrets?

"When I was held prisoner in Babylon they wanted me to do favors for them. I ended up helping Carlo retrieve a box off a plane. In order for him to follow me in time, they did the blood-tracking thing and now he can find me." She looked up sheepishly. "That's why he was able to find us on that island. I'm kind of glad he did, he saved us from the Japanese. But, I should have told you sooner. I know that."

Grace could feel the wood of the chair creak beneath Lucius's grip. She reached up and put her hand over his. Perhaps she would tell him what she'd discovered in her mother's journals. She wasn't keen on him finding out on his own. But she'd let the shocks of the day settle first. No point in making him more upset.

Hailey looked to Roderic. "So I am really hoping that what you have there is one that can help me. Please tell me it isn't the poison."

Roderic frowned down at the liquid. "I will do some tests. No matter what it is, I will want to be able to duplicate it."

"Even the poison?" Grace whispered.

He looked at her as though she'd gone daft. Perhaps there was a good use for poison, she just didn't know of any. A sudden need to get away overwhelmed her. "Do you mind if I use the shower?"

"Oh my god, what a wonderful idea. I got dibs after her." Hailey started to stand.

"Sit down," Lucius ordered. He addressed Derian, "Please show Grace the shower. I have some questions for Hailey."

Derian hesitated and Lucius looked up at the ceiling, "I am not going to hurt her. I want to know about this plane mission she mentioned. We are lacking clues at this point and I want to know what they were after."

Hailey rested her head on her arm and let out an aggrieved sigh. Derian took Grace by the elbow and hurried her from the room. They walked down a narrow hall and he pushed open a door. "There are towels in the cabinet. We'll see about finding replacement clothes. I think Lidiya's mother may have left some in the bedroom."

Grace had no idea who Lidiya was and thought to ask. She stopped herself with the words on the tip of her tongue. So much had gone on and they were all feeling the pressure. Frazzled thoughts plagued her. She could only imagine how Derian and the others felt. Their lives had essentially been thrown into an uproar with no warning.

"He means her no harm. He is a good man and only wants to make things right," Grace said.

185

Derian's expression didn't flicker. The depths of his eyes seemed to swim with ancient fatigue. "I do know that. He is my greatest friend and teacher." He looked down the hall and a smile lifted at the corner of his lip. "These reactions are new. I will learn to control them, but she has a way of getting under my skin."

With that he left her to her shower. Grace didn't move for several moments, staring into the cracked wallboard, her thoughts flying past with a vengeance. She doubted very much he would ever control the reactions he had toward Hailey.

The shower washed away much of the exhaustion and she walked out of the bathroom ready to take on the next challenge. She dug through the closet and found a button-up cotton shirt and pair of pressed khaki pants. Feeling significantly more comfortable, she sought out the others.

She found them down a narrow set of stairs hidden behind a partially open wood panel in the living room wall. As she stepped down into the bright white basement she wondered if Hailey had scoffed at the existence of another secret passage.

"There is no way you're cooping me up in this place," Hailey snapped.

"The minute you walk outdoors you will be a target for him and you know it," Derian answered.

Grace stepped onto the smooth concrete floor where she found Hailey pacing the room. Derian sat on a stool, leaning forward toward the agitated woman. Lucius rested with nonchalance against a stainless steel counter. When Hailey caught sight of Grace she waved the men off and headed toward the stairs. "My turn for a shower. You guys had better come up with a better plan than locking Grace and I up in this place forever."

"You want to lock us away?" Grace asked as she watched the irritated woman stormed up the stairs.

"Not forever," Lucius grumbled.

"I'm on their side. I don't think you should leave them here with me. Find another place to lock them away. I cannot get work done with all this whining," Roderic said.

"I don't whine!!" Hailey's voice carried down from the top of the stairs.

Roderic chuckled from his spot in front of a laptop set up on a far counter. "She is a firecracker, that one."

Lucius ran his hand over his hair and gripped the back of his neck. Roderic stood and walked to a machine sitting out of the way on one of the stainless steel counters. Grace stood a few feet away and curiosity distracting her from the plotting of the two men across the room.

Roderic pried the top off the vial and pulled out a small dish, then he placed a few drops of the liquid onto the dish and slid it into the machine. Sealing it, he pressed a few unmarked buttons and it began to hum, creating a slight rattling sound as it vibrated.

He turned, flashing an unrestrained grin, his eyes sparkling like soft blue mirrors. Grace blushed and looked away. The man was far too flirtatious. On the counter beside her sat three books, she flipped one open. "Oh! Minoan."

She picked the book up and brought it to a stool where she perched to allow for a more comfortable examination. The last time she'd seen Minoan was when she'd snuck into her grandmother's hidden stash of ancient texts. She'd stolen the book and spent decades deciphering its meaning. It would have been much easier if one of the elders had taught her the ancient script, but it was another one of the ways they meant to keep their secrets. At least the puzzle had provided a distraction from her mundane existence.

"You can read it?"

She looked up. Roderic leaned over her shoulder and peered into her eyes. He smelled of soap and smoke. His nearness made her feel warm, not quite the same as how she felt when Lucius held her close, but similar. She wondered what it would be like if he wrapped his arms around her. An eyebrow twitched and he speared a quick glance at Lucius. Grace swept her gaze back to the book. Gods help her from handsome *viators*.

"I do read it. A little."

"Can you translate it?" His voice rumbled in her ear like an oncoming winter storm.

"I believe so. Some of the words are unfamiliar. There appears to be a mix of Latin and other languages as well. Is it a medical text?" she asked and looked back up at him.

A chair scraped against the concrete floor. Lucius approached from across the room, his hard eyes plastered on the irreverent scientist. Grace handed him the book when he reached them.

"I changed my mind. The lass can stay. Her translating Irene's text will allow me to focus on analyzing Hailey's sample. And I imagine you will want me to produce more tracking serum."

Lucius placed the book on the counter and spoke to Grace, "Are you comfortable doing that? The man can be a rascal."

Roderic started to puff out his chest and Grace giggled. "I think I can handle it. He means nothing by his flirtations."

"You don't know that lass."

"Yes I do. You enjoy making others react by acting outrageously. I think that if you truly meant it, your approach would be more subtle. More genuine."

Roderic squirmed under her analysis and Derian laughed from across the room. "You cannot hide from a woman's intuition. And this one has it in spades."

Grace blushed under the compliment. Lucius said, "I think that she can handle you after all. I will leave her in your care."

He would be leaving again. Disappointment hit unexpectedly. There were many things to be done and in this game she was a small piece, yet she yearned for just a little more time. Unlike Roderic, whom she'd figured out relatively quickly, Lucius was still an enigma. One she desperately wanted to understand. She asked, "Where will you go?"

"Derian will be going after Rusa. With luck he will have established a force of *venator*," Lucius said.

Hailey stepped down onto the concrete, her hair hanging in wet strands and her cheeks glowing with a rosy sheen. "I want to go with him."

"No," Lucius didn't even blink when he answered. "I will be investigating the package Carlo retrieved from the plane in 2007. I have a hunch that may prove fruitful."

"You have no idea where that plane took off from or where it was going. I had no idea–all I got was a photograph and a date." Hailey slumped into a folding chair beside Derian.

"There was an incident in 2007. Do you remember it?" He directed his question to Derian.

"You mean the reports that the human government knew about our existence? I thought those had been determined false."

"I think this may be related. Each lead we followed at that time came up empty." He looked over at Roderic. "Were you collecting data of Hailey's whereabouts when she was at the Babylon facility?"

He shook his head. "No. I had a tracker on her prior to her capture, but they removed it."

"Wait, if you couldn't find me then, how did you find me and Grace this last time?"

Roderic grinned. "After you disappeared I figured we may need to find you again. I took a piece of your hair and pulled the markers that allow us to track you."

"Where did you get my hair? I don't remember giving it to you."

"Well now lass, your hair was all over Derian."

Both Derian and Hailey glared at Roderic. Grace looked away and rolled her eyes. He was at it again.

21

Grace rubbed her palms into her eyes and leaned back in the kitchen chair. Ten pages into the translation and she'd already developed a headache. Lucius and Derian left nearly five hours ago. Hailey spent the first three hours of that time taking a nap, still cranky about being left behind. Grace could understand her feelings, but this time the decision did seem to be the most prudent and so she hadn't put up a fight herself. The last two confrontations with Carlo were more than enough for a twenty-four hour period.

"Get out! Go find something to do or I'll tie you to a shower rod!"

"There's nothing to do! There's not even a T.V. here!"

Grace giggled. After waking from her nap, Hailey had thankfully taken to hovering over Roderic, leaving her to the focused translation work. She needed a break though, so Grace marked her place and joined the two *viators* in the basement. Perhaps she would be the needed distraction to give Roderic a moment of relief.

When he caught sight of her, he sighed and said, "How is the translation?"

"Dry. It is highly technical and I was correct, the Latin appears to be scientific terms. The one I am working on now seems to be experimentation notes. I am thinking of looking to see if she has notes on her conclusions. Those would be far more valuable to us."

Roderic pointed at two, floor-to-ceiling cabinets. "The collection is in the one on the right."

Grace opened the cabinet and her eyes widened at the sheer number of journals. Could these all be written in Minoan? It would take years to translate them all. Turning back to the room she sought out a chair, finding books with the result summaries and conclusions could take a while.

She pulled out a black and white pressed paper volume, flipped it open and found painstakingly recorded tables and charts. Page after page contained columns filled with equations, data, and unfamiliar symbols. Grace shut it and looked at the title. It simply read 'samples 5000- 6,550'. She returned it to the shelf and pulled out another similar volume. This one appeared to be records of samples 6,551-8,000. She placed it back where she found it and scanned the cabinet, ignoring the shelf that contained the data books. That left eight more shelves to choose from and she selected another book at random.

Hailey unfolded a chair, slumped onto the metal seat and said, "Can I help with anything?" Grace handed Hailey another of the books and the young woman flipped it open, the binding cracking from dry glue and disuse. Hailey continued, "What do you think she was doing?"

"I am not certain. It seems physiological, but on what I have no idea. She was experimenting on something but I don't know what the numbers and results correspond to." Grace sucked in her breath when she found a more promising book. Written in prose, the style appeared more like a journal entry than the precise recording of data. She flipped back to the first page.

"There are vials in the fridge. Do you think they mean something?" Hailey asked.

"Are there really?" Grace stood and ran to the fridge. The cool air rushed at her as she leaned in and pulled out a set of tubes. Labeled with numbers and symbols that corresponded with the tables she'd just seen a few moments before, they rattled as she held them up. "They are the samples. I wonder what they are." Light sparkled through a viscous liquid, clear with flecks of iridescent blue.

Roderic sidled up beside her, his smile warm and soft. A small shiver of pleasure ran down to her belly. His confidence and easy humor were an attractive mix, inspiring a smile to tug at her cheeks. But when she looked up at him from behind lowered lashes a shadow formed in the perimeter of her vision. There hovered an image of the staunch and handsome Lucius. Even when the man was gone she couldn't keep him out of her mind.

She sighed and handed the set of tubes to Roderic. "I have found the data tables that correspond to these. Perhaps you can make sense of it."

"Aye, perhaps." His expression changed to concern. "Are you feeling well, lass?"

Waving him off, she closed the fridge and returned to the cabinet. "Of course. It has just been a trying couple of days."

With one of the books cradled in her hands, Hailey hunched her body over, squinting at the hastily scrawled letters. "What is it with scientists and doctors? How hard is it to write something readable?"

Roderic grabbed the book and slid it back into place on the shelf. "There are more important things to worry about than legibility.

"Save me from self-important scientists." Hailey rolled her eyes and turned to Grace. "So are you going to take a nap or something? You haven't gotten any rest since we left Carpathia."

Grace shook her head and said, "I could not sleep if I tried. I suppose I am a bit over stimulated." And the moment she closed her eyes she would have visions of Lucius and not the sooth-saying type. Pressing her thumbs against her temple she let the pain focus her thoughts.

Roderic busied himself with analyzing the samples. Grace wanted to ask him about her new discovery. He would be the best to ask if she could indeed jump time, but something had her thinking twice about sharing her secret.

Yet, he had the knowledge she craved and no matter the answer, it would be more than she had previously. "Do you know much of the *tiresians*?"

He grunted, "Nay. Your people disappeared long before I came into existence."

Grace pressed her lips with disappointment. He continued, "But I know a little from others. Mostly hearsay."

"Do you know why we can see the visions?"

He didn't look up as he passed a rectangular glass plate under a scope. "Intuition is what I have heard. A highly developed predisposition toward intuition that evolved into something very near seeing the future."

Hailey piped up, "What do you mean very near?"

He leaned in and placed his eye to the lens, his voice a deep rumble in the room. "I don't think they see the future at all."

Grace cocked her head and sent Hailey a quizzical look. Not see the future? But she was living proof that *tiresians* could see the future. How could he think that? She replied, "I don't understand."

Silence met her response and a soft rattle echoed from a small ventilation grate in the side wall. A high-pitched creak accompanied the symphony of uncomfortable silence as Hailey shifted in the chair. Another moment passed as they faced Roderic's back, his shoulders bent over the apparatus, not even a muscle twitch to indicate he'd heard them. Grace cast a quick look at Hailey and was met with a cough from the antsy *viator*.

Roderic hummed a muffled tune and reached for a pen and pad of paper. His fingers scratched a hasty note, sending Hailey to her feet. "Did you find something? You found something didn't you?"

A raised brow in profile was the only reaction to her question. When he completed his notes, he turned back to them. Hailey breathed in to ask again, but he stopped her with a finger. "I don't believe you see the future, but I do believe you see something very like the future. As I said, *tiresian* capabilities appear tied to intuition. As we have found with the *viators*, whose skill comes from the fight or flight response, it is a development in a specific part of the brain."

"But what does that have to do with whether or not I can see the future?"

"You have been able to change the outcome of a vision, have you not?"

"Yes," Grace answered. Where was he going with this?

"If it is the future, how is it changeable?" he asked, his arms crossed against his chest as he leaned on the stainless steel table.

"It is the future should the intentions of the moment continue unchanged. I can see what *would* happen based on that moment."

"Aye, intuition." He smirked. "You have an ability to create a vision of a likely future based on information that goes unnoticed by those that are not *tiresian*."

Grace shook her head. "But if that were the case, then how can I know things about another's future that is impossible to know? If it is based on observation I should not be able to see a future location, one I have never been to before. And *tiresians* should also be able to see our own future clearly then, since that is the most easily observed information we do have."

"Aye, as for the last, I believe you cannot see your own future because of personal bias. No one can truly predict their own future. You are too close to the issue and charged with emotion. You have a personal stake in the outcome and cannot see it clearly."

Grace wondered at that. She had begun to see herself in visions. Had she learned to put away her own perspective to see things that pertained to her own future?

His grin tipped to the right and his eyes sparkled as he continued, "As for the other. That is the piece I am quite excited to discover."

Hailey coughed and wagged her finger at him. "No way. You have other projects first. Like figuring out what was in that vial I gave you. Now what did you write down in your chicken scratch over there?"

He rolled his eyes to the ceiling and pushed away from the table. "Hailey, you are the sister I never had and never wanted."

"Whatever," she snorted. "You're just butt-hurt over having to babysit me. Which, as you will remember, I wanted nothing to do with."

"Aye, that must be it." He pulled the slide out and placed it in a plastic rack. "I did find an answer, though I am not certain if you will be happy with it or not."

"Roderic," Grace whispered. If she didn't get this question out now she might never ask it and she would be stuck wondering. How could she sleep if she was constantly wondering? Both heads turned back toward her. Grace said, "I have just one more question, if you do not mind terribly, Hailey."

Hailey shrugged. "No, I get it. I was the same way when I first jumped time."

Grace released her bottom lip from the grip of her teeth and asked, "If a *tiresian* and *viator* were to have a child, would that child be able to foresee the future *and* jump time?"

Brows pulled together as he thought about her question. Hailey laughed and said, "Are you already planning a family?"

Grace tipped her head down and blushed. That hadn't even crossed her mind. Not at all. Roderic interrupted her thoughts with his answer, "I do not know. What *is* known is that a human-*viator* hybrid cannot jump time. But that does not mean that the same would be the case for a *viator* and *tiresian*. It is possible." He let his sentence drift, his eyes facing up as he thought. Then he shook his head, "I can't give you a good answer, lass."

A weak smile forced itself past her lips and she turned away. Perhaps she just was not meant to know. Their voices faded into the background as she drifted toward the stairs.

There had to be some way for her to discover if she could jump time. Roderic said the *viator* skill was tied to the fight or flight response. Perhaps if she put herself in a situation that forced the response...

How foolish would that be? She shook her head to banish the thought. It wasn't any more foolish than following Lucius and becoming mixed up with this whole situation. It was her life and she had every right to know all she could about herself. Even if that meant trying something foolish.

Grace climbed the stairs as Hailey whooped, "So my brain won't explode! That's awesome!"

****

Glass and metal met in a testament to modern sensibilities. The building he faced had the sleek lines and heavy concrete structure that so many favored in the early 21st century. Six carefully placed trees within immaculately maintained landscaping lined a long walkway. Solid glass doors reflected the scene with dark tinting evident only in buildings that had something to hide.

Lucius folded the newspaper and placed it to his side on the crumbly bus stop bench that faced the target. Five buses had already passed, each one pulling over to offer him a ride, each one met with a dismissive wave. His ruse had reached its expiration point.

The sixth bus creaked toward the curb, the tell-tale whine of brakes in need of replacement falling silent when the massive vehicle lurched to a complete stop. Lucius boarded, slipping a dollar into the machine before finding a seat near the rear doors. It would be a short ride.

Three minutes later he exited and strolled down a block, circling back to the building he'd been watching for over an hour. Four years ago, he'd received intelligence regarding a group of humans with evidence of *viator* existence. In general, humans cared very little about time travelers. Their science hadn't yet explained how it was possible, the physicists were stumped and the biologists completely ignorant of a traveler mutation. In addition, popular culture had a love affair with vampires, zombies, and secret agents. They couldn't care less if people could travel through time.

But one group seemed to take the possibility seriously and recognized both the advantages and the threat. Lucius knew careful management of the knowledge of *viator* existence was paramount to their survival. The minute the humans started wondering about them would be the beginning of a difficult period in *viator* history. It had never happened in the past and it would not happen while he stood at the helm.

In mid-July, 2007, Lucius had evidence compiled and a team ready to investigate. Then the Council had stepped in, leaving Lucius with the case closed and his hands tied. There had been little he could do beyond a cursory monitoring of the situation. And nothing came of that.

Now he was back where he'd started. This building had been central to the evidence. The black box had been another piece. Carlo's interest in the box suggested the humans were far deeper in the mix than even he had surmised. Intelligence had pointed to something important happening this day at this place and his intuition told him the two incidents were related.

Pulling a baseball cap from a messenger bag slung over his shoulder, he slapped it on his head. He stopped at a doorway and pulled off his jacket, tucking it into the bag. Leaving the bag behind, he returned to the building, slumping his shoulders and adding a hitch to his gait. It would not pass inspection by an experienced observer, but it would keep the mildly suspicious unaware.

He perched on the bus stop bench again, spread his arms across the back and crossed his legs. All the watchers would see was a man not afraid to be noticed. Hiding in plain sight provided a challenge he enjoyed tremendously.

An hour later, he hung his head back in feigned sleep. Several people joined him on the bench, only to leave with the bus. But the building across the street remained deserted. The lot to the left contained a guard shack and an entrance to an underground parking structure. He couldn't get a good idea of the number of people involved–not without going inside.

Stretching, he made a show of looking at his watch and stood to peer down the street for the next bus. He needed a new vantage point and eyed a coffee shop several buildings down. The view would not be as clear, but he couldn't spend the entire day seated at the bus stop.

A flash of movement caught his eye. The cat-like stride of his top *venator* would have been lost to anyone else watching the scene. But Lucius knew this man. They served the *Domus* together for nearly one thousand years. What was Derian doing sneaking up on the same building he had as a target?

22

Lucius ducked past a trash canister and slipped toward Derian. The dark-haired Anglo-Saxon had his back to Lucius's approach, but the slight scuff of a shoe against pavement made him turn his head to investigate. Derian's brows drew together when he recognized the *magister*.

Lucius hunkered down beside him, their bodies protected from view by a low-lying wall and a brightly flowered tree. It was the only blind spot on the building site.

"What are you doing here?" Derian asked, his voice a low whisper.

"I was about to ask the same." Through the leafy branches Lucius could see the double doors. Still no sign of movement.

"I'm following Rusa's trail. He disappeared after we last spoke. Roderic gave me a number of locations and I've hit negative on the last three."

"Interesting," Lucius murmured. What was the former head of the Council doing here? "I haven't seen him in the couple of hours I've been watching the building. But he could be inside."

Derian looked up at the roof. "Do you want to see about gaining entrance?"

A security camera hung on each corner of the building. It would be difficult to sneak in unnoticed. Lucius considered the wisdom of attempting a jump into the building. Without knowledge of the layout they could very well land in sight of the occupants. And that would put a giant kink in their plans.

Lucius glanced down the side of the building, a service door stood beside the trash canister. Probably locked and alarmed. "The roof perhaps?"

"I seem to have forgotten my climbing gear. Meet you at the top in five minutes?" Derian said.

Lucius grunted in response as Derian faded from view. Then he focused inward and let his body fade into time. Within seconds he stood on the roof. Derian had his hand on the doorknob of a stairwell leading into the building. When it didn't open he looked to Lucius. "I think I will just duck on inside and let you in."

With that, Derian faded away again. Lucius waited a few moments more and the door opened.

"Not too secure. But they never expect attack from above do they?" Derian tipped his lips up in humor. Then he started down the stairs.

The two men descended in a controlled hurry, pausing at each turn before proceeding down. Their feet echoed against the concrete despite their light steps. At each level they met a locked door. They stopped at the door to the second floor.

"It's a crap shoot. Which floor do you want to start with?" Derian said.

"Let's start with this one. I don't believe they will have anything of interest on the first floor."

"Do you know what day it is?"

"Saturday."

"Then hopefully things will be quiet on the inside."

Lucius agreed. Perhaps they would get lucky and meet with little resistance. But he didn't believe in luck. Only circumstance.

Rather than jump time again, Derian pulled a long pick from his pocket and set to jimmy open the lock. When a *viator* had no idea what he would face, it was always better to resort to old fashioned entry techniques. With a few deft twists, the door unlatched and Derian opened it. The rubber seal at the bottom brushed against the carpet covering a long hall.

Both men waited as they listened for sounds of life. Once satisfied that the hall would remain empty, they snuck in, closing the door with a quiet click. The hall extended twenty-feet to the right and turned sharply to the left. Derian led the way, his hand reaching toward his hip where he unsnapped the strap to his holster, the handle of his Colt 1911 within inches from his fingers. Lucius held the Walther PPK in his hands, ready for anything.

At the turn, both men glanced around the corner. Nothing. Their pace sped up as they canvassed the floor. Large rooms, filled with cubicles and run-of-the-mill office equipment were all they found. And not a soul haunted the halls. The lights were dim and they quickly concluded that this floor would bring them nothing.

Before returning to the stairs, Lucius stepped into one of the larger cubes. Thick spiral-bound reports lined the walls with titles that ranged from institutional policy to software instruction manuals. Whatever this was, they had found the middle management administrative floor. Whoever worked these cubes would have little knowledge of what really went on in the building. Anything related to the *viators* would not be found here.

They hustled back to the stairs. Derian leaned in to murmur into Lucius's ear before they entered into the echoing chamber, "All of the cameras are offline."

Lucius thinned his lips and pulled the door open. He had noticed. Why would all the security cameras be shut down on a weekend?

The next floor provided a similar experience. The only difference was the three, highly polished, state-of-the-art laboratories. Many of the machines looked the same as what Roderic used at the *Domus*. Lucius knew a little of what the man did, but the exact capability of each apparatus was beyond his knowledge.

They reached the fifth floor. When Derian pushed the door open, glaring light spilled in from the hall. This floor was not unoccupied. Derian popped his head into the hall and listened. His hand up, he motioned for Lucius to follow.

Lucius had little problem with Derian taking point. The man stayed as a *venator* long after Lucius had moved into a management position. Derian was the best operative he had. Long ago, their roles had been reversed, with Lucius leading the way, showing the young *viator* the ropes. It was an interesting turn of the tables.

They stayed to the wall and took the halls with stealth. The buzz of humanity heightened their senses and the white noise of electronics was easily heard when compared to the emptiness of the floors below. Derian motioned to the camera at the hall junction. It too lacked the red light that indicated it was in use. Someone did not want the moment recorded.

Muffled voices came from down the hall and Derian pulled his Colt from the holster. He and Derian slid down the hall until they reached a door sitting slightly ajar. They were exposed. With quick eye contact, understanding passed between them. If they were discovered both men would jump time.

A familiar voice rang out in agitation, "You said you had the facilities here to handle this! I am not giving this to you to just have it sent off to some scientists in Europe. If I had known that I would have dealt with them!"

Lucius recognized Rusa's voice. Another voice he did not recognize rumbled in response, the words too low to decipher.

"And how are you going to guarantee that?" Rusa said.

Derian pulled a small mirror from his utility belt and tilted it toward the crack. After a moment he looked up to Lucius and drew a square in the air then mouthed the word 'box'.

His nose flared at the information. Anger seethed within and Lucius gripped his pistol with a tight fist. Rusa had delivered the black box to the humans. No wonder the Council had stymied his investigation. They had known all along what was going on with these people. But did they all know or had Rusa gone rogue?

Lucius reminded himself not to jump to conclusions. Too many assumptions could lead to irreparable damage. If Rusa was in cahoots with the conspiracy, then Carlo would not have had to use Hailey to retrieve the black box from the humans. There was something deeper going on here.

Rusa grunted and whatever the man had said appeared to appease the ancient *viator*. Lucius motioned to Derian to follow as he turned back toward the exit. When they met at the stairwell he stopped. "We need to know what is in that box."

Derian kept an eye on the hall, his brows in a perplexed line. "That was not the Rusa from Original Time. It had to be him from a few years ago."

"How do you know?"

"He's put on a little weight since then."

"But you were following the Original Time Rusa."

"I know. It appears I missed him. Or he has not arrived yet. Do you think he knows the black box has been taken by Carlo?"

Lucius shook his head. That was a very good question. One he fully intended to ask the old man.

****

Grace looked down the forty-foot drop and reconsidered her intentions. The old wall in the municipal park rose above a concrete parking lot. When she'd approached, she'd seen several feet worth of graffiti covering the crumbly concrete face. A single car stood in the parking lot, the inch of dirt and slightly flattening tires gave the impression that it had been abandoned there for a while. She had the city park to herself.

She took a deep breath, closed her eyes and wrapped her fingers around the cold metal rail. After pulling herself together, she swung her legs over the top and positioned her body on the opposite side. Her heart flipped and stomach whirled as the reality of the drop struck her.

This was stupid. There was absolutely no evidence she could jump time. Not a single instance of a *viator* and *tiresian* child existed. If she continued with this insane plan she could seriously hurt herself. Or worse!

With a sudden intake of air, she let go of the rail and stepped out into the empty space before her. No point in arguing with herself when she'd already made the decision.

To say that the landing hurt would be an understatement. Pain lanced up her side when her knees buckled on impact and her right hip pounded into the pavement. Skin scraped away on the blacktop and she rolled to a stop. That had not gone well at all.

She lay on her back and looked up into the grey sky. A bird streaked across her field of vision, its wings pointed as it dove through the air, a sad reminder of her ungainly fall from forty-feet above. If that stupidity hadn't triggered a jump through time perhaps she really couldn't do it.

A well of disappointment opened within her belly, but the reason for the emotion remained elusive. Life was already difficult enough with the gift of visions. Why would she desire another obtrusive talent?

She closed her eyes and wiggled her toes. At least nothing appeared broken. That could have gone much worse. With a groan, she heaved her body up and brushed off the dirt and pebbles that dug into her skin during the roll.

Turning toward the road, she limped in the direction of the house. How would she explain her condition to Hailey and Roderic? An easy answer was not forthcoming. She sighed, knowing the truth would paint her as a fool. She *was* a fool, but it was a personal thing, something she did not intend to broadcast to the others.

Hailey might understand. The woman seemed to have tried her share of less than intelligent maneuvers, yet she never appeared ashamed. Grace envied her easy confidence.

She gave herself a shake. Of course she was down on herself. Things were new and confusing. She'd come from a quiet, uneventful life where her only problem lay in an autocratic and overbearing grandmother. In the last 48 hours she'd been through more excitement than she had ever seen.

Thoughts of home overwhelmed her. Had Tymion been able to pass off the ruse? He seemed quite adept at creating the kind of smoke screen Althea would believe. However, Grace still worried. The challenges the community of *tiresians* faced were far worse than a child being held back from freedom. Her troubles paled in comparison.

The realization that she'd never really known what was happening around her still tasted bitter. She'd always stayed out of politics, so much so that she didn't even realize when it was playing havoc on her life.

Now, because of some unexplained personal compulsion she was knee deep in *viator* politics. What was she doing here? What did she really think she could do to help?

The image of Lucius flashed into view. His frequent visits to her consciousness were becoming unwelcome. The handsome man may make her fluttery on the inside, but it did not mean she had any place in his world. What did the visions mean?

A soft growl emitted from her throat. Frustration had been building and she recognized its ugly signature.

Grace stopped and scanned the area. The neighborhood looked unfamiliar. With a giant sigh she glared up at the sky. Gods help her, she'd been so inwardly focused she'd completely lost her way in the strange city. Now she would have to backtrack.

It only took an extra ten minutes before she had herself back on the street leading to the house. She hadn't told Roderic and Hailey she'd intended to leave and for all she knew they could be scouring the area for her. It was inconsiderate and completely out of character. She quickened her pace.

What had gotten into her lately? Unfocused on the world around her and distracted by her thoughts was not an intelligent way to handle unknown situations.

She sent a cursory glance to her right and stepped into a crosswalk. The craftsman-style house stood across the street, quiet and unremarkable. Perhaps Roderic and Hailey hadn't even noticed she'd left.

A horn blared in her left ear. She swung to the side in time to see a glossy black pickup truck barreling toward her. Opening her mouth to scream, air wheezed between her vocal chords and no sound came out.

Tingles at the base of her neck sharpened her reflexes and she tried to step aside. Without warning a rush filled her ears and blackness poured into her mind. The asphalt road was the last thing she saw as she pitched down into another faint.

23

Something jabbed into her side. Grace groaned and lashed out with her hand. A startled cry responded, followed by a calm masculine crooning. She pulled back and focused on lifting the heavy lids stubbornly hovering over her eyes. Bright light pierced the crack between her lashes and she shut it out with a wince.

"Aye, come on now, lass. Open them up," Roderic said, his voice a rumble beside her ear.

Grace granted his request, but slowly, letting her eyes grow accustomed to the brightness a bit at a time. She groaned as the light brought both the world and her pain back into focus. The aches from her previous fall had intensified with stiffness from lying on the hard ground. Concern was written like a sad song along Roderic's brows.

"How do you feel? It can't be good, not by the looks of you." He ran a hand down her arm, tenderly checking her bones. She hissed when his fingers pushed into a flowering bruise. "No worry, we have the paramedics on the way."

Grace struggled to sit up. She did not need to be seen by paramedics. The bruises were minor and the most injury had been done to her pride, not her hide. "I am all right. Thank you."

Roderic put a hand to her shoulder. "Lass, you were hit by a truck. You are not all right."

Grace looked up at a stricken-faced man standing several feet away, his hands twisting a ball cap into a wretched mess. She looked to the black truck beside him. "I do not think he hit me."

The man stammered, "That's what I've been telling him! I stopped before I hit you. I know I did."

Roderic speared him with a glare. "You look like someone that has been run through a press and beaten with a block of wood. He hit you."

She pushed up onto her knees and gave a wobbly smile before standing. "No. These injuries are not from him. I promise you. These I acquired all on my own." With her hand outstretched, she wobbled toward the distraught man. "I am terribly sorry for the fright. It seems I fainted in the walkway. I am so grateful you were able to stop."

The man looked down at her hand, his faced scrunched in confusion. When he went to accept her offering of peace Roderic growled, "Lass, I do not think–"

"Roderic, I am fine," Grace said, her patience low. "This man did not hit me. Now please can we all go on our way, I am certain he has somewhere else he needs to be."

"Well I do, but…"

Sirens blared around the corner and she rolled her eyes to the heavens. Gods, she did not want to have to explain how she'd acquired the patchwork of bruises, but it seemed she would not easily avoid the issue.

An hour later, the paramedics had left, satisfied that her injuries were easily mended. The police left a little less convinced of the truth of her story, but when she refused to press charges or even acknowledge that the accident occurred, they left, shaking their heads as they went. The grateful driver waved with enthusiasm as he swung around the corner, destined to never again encounter the crazy lady that had somehow just fallen in front of his truck.

Grace gave a dramatic sigh and allowed Roderic to help her up the steps into the house. "Really, I am not hurt so badly that I require your assistance."

"Humor me." He led her to one of the vacant bedrooms and tucked her into the four-poster bed. He hastened from the room and Grace allowed her body to sink into the spring mattress. It was certainly more considerate to her aches than the blacktop road had been.

She knew for a fact truck did not hit her. So the only explanation was that she fainted–again. Her hand slapped the duvet in an explosion of pent-up frustration. Nothing good comes from blackouts. And with the frequency with which they were occurring, she had to be getting worse. Perhaps it was time to speak to someone about it.

Roderic returned to the room, a bowl in one hand and a terrycloth towel in the other. Grace scooted to the side when he eased onto the bed. "You have scrapes and bruises everywhere, lass. Let me help clean you up."

He dipped the towel into the water and raised it to her cheek. Pain seared for a moment as he dabbed away the blood and dirt. She grimaced. Something told her she did not want to see how she looked in the mirror.

His eyes held concern and something deeper. Something that had been hidden each time she'd looked into his blue eyes previously. What did the wall this man hid behind protect from the rest of the world? He blinked when he caught her intent gaze and the wall slid solidly back into place.

He held the towel out to her and said, "Here. I am sure you would rather."

Grace wrapped her hand around his wrist and stopped him. "You are a strange man. You have more secrets than anyone knows, don't you?"

Roderic lifted a brow. "Secrets? I do not think you should be speaking of secrets, lass."

She dropped his hand and leaned back against the pillow, casting her gaze away. "What secrets do you think I am hiding?"

He dropped the towel into the water and braced his arm on the bed. "Well, I do not believe for one minute you tripped and fell down a hill." He waited, but Grace didn't respond. He continued, "And you are lying about what happened in front of the house."

"I am not lying. The man did not hit me."

"Then why were you unconscious?"

Grace pulled her bottom lip between her teeth. Would it matter if she told him the truth? She did not know who to trust. Lucius seemed to consider this man trustworthy, otherwise he would never have left her with him. Yet, he held so many secrets. Secrets, just like her.

"I..." Grace stopped, searching his face for an answer. But he did not give her one. Unlike Lucius, whose face bespoke centuries of goodness and strength, Roderic was a blank mask. She wrapped her fingers around the duvet and took the plunge. "I do not know why, but I have been passing out lately. It happens at the most inopportune times as well. First when we faced Carlo, then again when Hailey and I were on the island and just now as I crossed the street."

He frowned. "And it has never happened before this?"

"No, not ever."

"Not even related to your visions?"

Grace stopped. When she was taken by a massive vision she did lose conscious awareness of her surroundings. But she never lost herself in blackness. Instead, she would be overwhelmed with imagery and sensation. "No, the experiences are vastly different."

He grunted and reached into the water. A stream poured from the cloth as he wrung the excess water into the bowl. Silence thickened in the room.

She worried that her usefulness here would be called into question. If Lucius knew she could faint at any moment, then he would insist on keeping her away from dangerous situations. While the logic was sound, she knew she could not bear letting him go without her. Not if she could be a help. Not if there were even a possibility something terrible could happen to him.

She looked up at Roderic. "Do you think you could keep this a secret between us?"

Roderic raised a brow. "Now what would you want me to do that for?"

"I just...I just think it would be better for all if it were that way. I do not want anyone to worry."

"You do not want Lucius to worry, you mean."

Grace lost her next thought and gaped at Roderic. He chuckled, "Well, if I hadn't seen it your eyes before, I would know now that he'd had you."

"Had me?" Grace stuttered, "What do you mean had me? He does not have me at all."

Roderic lifted his head and laughed until the room rang from the noise. "Well, than you will not mind if I do this."

Water splashed as he dropped the towel into the bowl and leaned toward her. Grace's eyes widened as his face loomed in front of hers. His lashes lowered as his gaze fell to her lips. A hitch caught in her throat and her heart thudded. What was he doing?

As he came closer, she lifted her hands and grabbed at his shoulders, stopping him before his lips could meet hers. With the resistance he stopped, tipping his lip up, his eyes sparkled as he said, "See, you are taken with him."

She opened her mouth to respond, but was interrupted by a growl from across the room, "What exactly are you doing, Roderic?"

Her eyes peeked over Roderic's shoulders at a stern and fuming Lucius. From behind him Derian glared at the audacious Roderic's back. Grace blanched and pushed him away, wanting to pull the blankets over her head and pretend the moment never happened.

Roderic stood slowly and turned toward the two men at the door. "Well, now, I was just taking care of the lass like you asked me to."

Lucius fisted his hands and color rose along his neck. Grace held herself still, not trusting herself to stay on the bed. If Lucius were to lunge at Roderic, would she let it happen?

But the question did not matter. Lucius promptly swung around on his heels and strode from the room. Derian met Roderic with furious eyes. After a moment, Roderic threw up his hands and said, "What is the matter with the man? He should have hit me."

Grace's mouth dropped open. Roderic was clearly out of his mind.

****

Lucius stormed out the front door and turned the corner onto the narrow drive. His hands clenched as he battled with this unfamiliar emotion. Rarely did he let anger surge to the surface and never had he felt the desire to turn on a colleague. A man he considered a friend.

Pushing open the weather-beaten wood gate, he entered the miniscule backyard, willing the cool breeze and domestic surroundings to soothe his ire. Never had he let emotion rule his reactions. And certainly never over a woman. What was wrong with him? He had no claim on Grace. If she wanted to entertain a rascal like Roderic, she had every right.

The smack of the front door screen hitting the jamb heralded company. Lucius turned his back and prayed for patience.

"Are you out of your mind?"

"Leave, Roderic. I am in no mood to deal with you."

"No mood? You are in the perfect mood to deal with me. Does the lass mean so little to you?"

Lucius swung around to pierce a glare at the fuming Scot. What right did Roderic have to be angry with him? What game was the man playing? "She is not here for my gratification."

"Aye? Then why is she here?" Roderic narrowed his eyes and continued, "Do you know the risk you have put us under, bringing a *tiresian* into our midst now? Do we not have enough to worry about without a woman filled with secrets watching everything we do?"

"Grace is no threat."

"Oh? And how do you know that? And even so, to what purpose does she serve? A translator and pretty piece to look at?"

An overwhelming desire to grab his friend by the throat came over him, but he straightened his frame and flared his nostrils as Roderic paced before him. Grace was with them purely by circumstance, nothing more. He knew she posed no threat. He knew this with utter certainty.

However, Roderic might be correct that she should be sent away. Their situation was tenuous at best and she had already been exposed to Carlo's dangerous hand. He could not be worried about her safety and leaving her with Roderic again was out of the question. The man clearly doubted her trustworthiness. Although, it obviously hadn't been enough to prevent him from trying to kiss her. Lucius glared at the nearest tree.

Roderic quit his prowl and leaned against the clapboard wall. Lucius pulled himself together and said, "You are correct. This is not a place for her." He moved to pass the man, but Roderic put out a hand to stop him.

"You truly have no idea do you?"

Lucius felt his self-control pitch and his anger flew back to the surface. In a flash he had his forearm against Roderic's chest, his arms pinned beneath the vise of all his strength. "I fail to see why you play games. Or perhaps the trust I have had in you is misplaced."

Roderic chuckled and his eyes flashed with humor. "It is about time you let some of that frustration out, old man. Your self-control was beginning to piss me off."

Lucius pushed away and glared. Roderic rubbed absently at his arm and said, "Perhaps your trust in me is misplaced, but then that has never been a secret. But no, I am not an agent against you in this. I am as invested in determining the force behind this conspiracy as you are."

Roderic looked toward the front of the house then lowered his voice. "I do not believe the lass is part of the conspiracy, but she has deep secrets behind that innocent façade. Secrets that you could discover if you would stop hiding behind your self-control and get close to her."

"Everyone has secrets."

"Aye, but not everyone is a *tiresian*."

"I won't feign affection to pull secrets from her. That is a skill you possess, not I."

Roderic's jaw tightened. "I will forget that jab and consider it a symptom of the strain you have been under. I said nothing about pretending you like the lass. You are as hot for her as she is for you. I am merely telling you that she has secrets. And secrets are the last thing we need right now."

The man was mistaken. Grace was not 'hot' for him. Had he not just interrupted her with Roderic? He stalked away. He needed to clear his mind and determine the best place to send Grace. If Roderic were correct and she was hiding something from them, it would be best if she were gone. He may trust her by instinct, but lies and disinformation were dangerous.

Roderic called out to him just as he passed the front gate, "She pushed me away you idiot. She clearly wants only you."

24

Someone was at the door. Grace huddled under the covers and willed them to leave. A soft knock sounded and Hailey cleared her throat. "Are you Ok?"

Grace murmured a response and dug deeper into the duvet, listening for the sound of Hailey's retreating feet. A moment passed and Grace took a tentative look at the door. The doorway was empty and she let out a sigh of relief.

"Are you sure?"

Grace jumped at the sound of Hailey's voice coming from the opposite side of the bed. The mattress depressed as Hailey joined her among the folds of fluffy cotton. "Because it sounded like Roderic went a little ballistic on Lucius. Do you know what's going on?"

"Not really. I think Lucius believes he walked in on a personal moment between Roderic and me. But I am not certain why Roderic is so angry."

"A personal moment?" Hailey continued when Grace didn't offer more, "Why exactly would he think that he walked in on a personal moment?"

With a sigh Grace answered, "Because Roderic tried to kiss me just as Lucius walked in."

"Get out! No he didn't!"

Grace giggled. "He did."

"Did you kiss him back?" Hailey asked. Her voice was lowered but couldn't mask her avid interest.

"No, I did not."

"Oh good. Because I think Lucius is much more your style. And I wouldn't trust Roderic as far as I could throw him. Considering he's a big guy, that wouldn't be very far at all."

Grace stifled another giggle at the thought of Hailey throwing the large Scot across the room. "I do not know what the fuss is all about. There is nothing between Lucius and me."

Hailey snorted in disagreement, but a deep voice interrupted her response. "Indeed nothing? It seems that we are the only ones unaware of what is between us."

Grace pulled the blanket away from her face and stared at Lucius standing at the door. She blushed and quickly looked away.

"Dude. Ok, so I will leave you two alone." Hailey stood and scrambled to the door. Leaning in as she passed, she whispered something in Lucius's ear, then pushed him inside and shut the door behind her.

Silence permeated the room and Grace considered pulling the covers back over her head. Suddenly, Lucius stood at her side. He placed his fingers to her face and turned her eyes to him. "What happened?"

She reached up to touch the scrape on her cheekbone. That one had probably occurred when she fainted before the truck. It was the only one she did not remember from her ill-conceived jump from the park wall. Embarrassment flared at the thought of her foolishness. "It is only a scrape. I fell while crossing the street."

His eyes flashed with heat. "What were you doing away from the house?

"Am I a prisoner here?"

He dropped his hand, his answer short and crisp, "No. You are not."

An unexplainable well of tears built behind her eyes. Was it stress or disappointment making her feel weepy? She struggled to keep the tears from spilling. With her palms pressed into her eyes, she called upon an inner strength. "I do not know why I am even here."

"Why are you here?" he asked, his voice strained.

Grace didn't look up. How could she explain? Lucius made it clear from the start that she was not needed nor wanted. While her visions may have provided some assistance, did it really warrant her continued presence? Perhaps it was time for her to return to Oregon. Phillip had undoubtedly discovered her missing from their scheduled meeting point. He must be terribly worried.

Lucius sat beside her and put his hand to her face again. She raised her eyes to his and saw a tempest of fire blazing within them. For once the steel resolve had melted behind something far more palpable. Pulling her lip between her teeth she waited. The movement pulled his hungry gaze to her mouth.

"Lucius?" Her lip throbbed when she released it to speak. He did not respond, but threaded his hand into the hair at the back of her head, her scalp tingling at the pressure. He pulled down on her hair, lifting her face up and exposing her throat. A growl rumbled from his chest and she answered with a tiny moan.

"I need to kiss you," he said.

"Yes," she breathed, unsure how she found the air to respond. The descent was slow, his lips a feather against her own. He tested her offering, a taste only. Chest heaving, she felt the thunder of blood passing through her heart. A tiny whimper passed through her lips. His hand tightened in her hair and a wall of passion erupted.

The kiss deepened and filled the space that sat like a roiling mass of confusion and desire swirling between them. Their tongues clashed together in a storm of unfulfilled desire held captive too long by circumstance and self-control. Grace wrapped her arms around his neck and pushed closer, pulling the warmth and strength of his passion toward her body.

Lucius hauled her across his lap, his arm snaking beneath her shirt to splay against her bare back. Arching at the touch, she pulled away from the kiss and stared at him with passion-glazed eyes.

He ripped her shirt over her head and slid his hands down her side, brushing his thumbs against her breasts. She gasped and her cheeks heated at the contact. A seductive smile spread across his lips as his gaze took in the taut peaks. He lifted his hand and brushed them across the aroused buds.

A feeling unlike any she had ever felt flared and stars crossed before her eyes. Moist lips took one of her breasts as his hand kneaded the other. Grace cried out at the sensation, her body straining for something new and altogether unexpected.

His hand touched the warmth between her legs and she nearly jumped from his lap. The intensity fought to overwhelm her. She wanted to pull him completely into her, to find a release from the chaos flowing through her senses. He lifted his head from her breast and placed his hand against her cheek.

"I am going to make love to you. If this is not something that you want, you need to tell me now. I do not know that I can stop if we go much further."

"Stop?" Grace whispered, but he misunderstood and began to withdraw.

"You are hurt, it is unthinking of me to even–"

She grabbed his face and pulled it to hers. "I do not think I will be responsible for my actions if you were to stop now. Please." She pressed her lips against his and reached to pull his shirt over his chest. His enthusiasm returned with full force, as he stilled her hands on his shirt and completed the task for her.

He threw the shirt aside as she ran her hands across his chest. The hairs tickled her fingers and she leaned down to place a kiss against his warm skin. Lucius caught his breath and froze as she continued to run kisses across his chest and along his collar bone.

Grace looked up into his eyes, hoping he could see all that she felt within her. His nose flared and he lifted her from his lap, laying her against the pillows. With quick and efficient movement, he removed his pants and rejoined her on the bed. Her eyes widened at the sight of him, but he did not give her much time to consider the implications of his size.

With long strokes he ran his hands up her torso then pressed his body against hers. Skin against skin stoked the fire between them to levels unknown. Grace let the tide of desire crash through her until she shook from the intensity. His hand dipped between her wet folds and she cried out a pleasure.

Leaning in, he kissed her with a furious passion then slowly pressed against the entrance to her desire. Full and foreign, the feeling had her catching her breath. The ache was unlike anything she had ever known. Grace called his name as he passed through her barrier and settled deep within her welcoming heat. He lifted his head and looked into her eyes, concern playing across his brows. "Did I hurt you?"

"No, please," she gasped. "Please don't stop."

He leaned down and pressed a soft, heartrending kiss against her cheek bone, creating an ache within her heart that threatened to overwhelm her with feeling. Then he began to move within her.

Slow stroke upon stroke called against her passion, building a fire within her that seemed to know no pinnacle. She looked into his eyes and begged him to lead her to her release. His pace quickened and the ecstasy of sensation roared to the surface, sending her to the peak of her passion, she clenched and called his name. He stiffened above her and through the fog of her descent from climax she heard him roar.

****

Grace trailed her finger lazily along his side, teasing away the last of his mindlessness. He pushed against the mattress to relieve her of his heaviness and slid to her side. Wrapping an arm around her back, he pulled her into a tight embrace. His heart still raced from the passion they'd shared. Never in his life had he expected a moment like this to be quite so intense. So much beauty held in such a small package. He'd spent so much time focused on the survival of the *Domus* and the needs of the *viators* he had convinced himself that moments in the arms of a woman could only be momentary releases, with emotions held quietly at bay and non-committed. But there was nothing superficial or non-committal about how he felt at that moment.

Her glazed eyes sought his and she smiled in a slow, well-satisfied air. Suddenly her expression changed and she let out a short laugh.

"What?" he asked.

"It is nothing." She buried her head into his chest.

"It is not nothing. Why do you laugh?"

Her lips buzzed against his chest in a muffled response and he pushed away to draw her head back out into the open. He stared down at her and waited. Her cheeks blushed as she toyed with her lips pulled between her teeth. Lifting a finger to her abused smile, he teased her lips from her mouth. She giggled again.

With a growl he rolled on top of her and held her down in the soft, downy covers. Leaning in he whispered into her ear, "Tell me your secret, Grace."

A fleeting flash of trepidation crossed her eyes, but she recovered the teasing glint in half a breath. "There is no secret. I am just slightly shy of speaking my thoughts." He raised a brow to encourage her to continue. "Oh, all right. I found it humorous when I realized my worry was for nothing."

He lifted his hand and brushed his fingers along her cheek. "What was it that had you worried?"

Despite her rising flush, she answered, "I had worried that I would not be the one to enact that particular vision with you."

"What vision?"

"The vision of you making passionate love."

"You had a vision of us making love?"

She wiggled beneath him, trying to free herself from his hold. He held her tight. The woman beneath him had already captured him. It was only fair that he repay the favor. When she realized she could make no progress, she stopped and made eye contact. "I had a vision of you," she coughed and sent him a pleading look. He gave her no quarter and she finally let it all free. "I had a vision of you making love, but I could not see who you were with."

"And you worried that it would not be you?"

She let a slight, embarrassed smile touch her lips and he rewarded her with a tender kiss. His passion stirred and he ended the kiss before he was tempted to show her again how truly she had captured him. Rolling to the side, he stared into the white, popcorn ceiling.

Reality began to sink its fingers back into the room and the warmth he felt in her arms seeped away. He grabbed her hand in an attempt to keep a little of it with them.

"Something worries you," she said, lifting her body to lean over his, concern written across her features.

He let the quiet return, thinking of his response, unsure how to proceed. Normally he would be ten steps ahead of the opponent. But lately he felt three steps behind. With Grace, there were pieces to the puzzle that had been left unrevealed. He could not continue to fight against a hidden enemy and have to decipher the secrets held by those he trusted, those he kept close to his side. What kinds of secrets had Roderic seen in Grace? What piece had he missed?

"Lucius?"

"Roderic believes you are withholding something."

"He told you that?" she said, her voice sharp. He turned his head and looked at her. Irritation flared from her tense shoulders as she shook her head. "I told him... I did not want to concern you. I know that you already have so much to worry about."

"Secrets are far more dangerous than an overabundance of worry."

"I can understand that." She frowned then sighed in resignation. "I had another blackout. This is the third time since I have met you and it worries me. I do not know why it is happening."

Lucius propped himself on an elbow. "Have you been ill?"

"No. I do not believe it has anything to do with that. It seems to happen when I am in a stressful situation. It is so strange. I did not have any trouble when we were running from the sniper at my home or when we were inside Carpathia. Yet, it happened on the island with Hailey and at the apartment."

"What made you pass out this time?"

"I was nearly hit by a truck."

"Damn it woman!" Lucius sat up and seethed. What had she been thinking? "This is why you were to stay at the house. You cannot be protected if you continue to be foolish."

"Foolish?" Grace whispered, hurt reflected in her eyes. She rolled off the bed and walked toward her clothing. Keeping her head away from him, she tugged her shirt over her head. Fabric brushing over skin was the only sound in the room.

When she finished pulling on her slacks she faced him, fire flashing in her eyes. "I am not here for you to protect. I am here to help you. If I wanted that kind of life I could have stayed in Oregon." She turned away and he took the opportunity to retrieve his own clothing.

When she turned back to him, she stood with her hands on her hips and a hint of steel in her eyes. Strength radiated from her and he admired it. But a strong will and best intentions could not negate the fact that she was vulnerable to whatever the conspiracy intended. She did not have the training or the knowledge to handle whatever lay ahead.

"I cannot allow you to put yourself at risk. If you do not know what is causing these blackouts how can you know when they will happen? What if you had been hit by that truck? What if it happens where we cannot come to your aid?" He stopped himself before he continued. What had him truly worried was the possibility Carlo and the conspiracy knew what she was. What lengths would they go to in order to acquire a *tiresian* to exploit for their own cause?

Grace threw up her arms. "I cannot know. Does that mean I need to be locked away? Does that mean I am of no use to you? Shall I just return to Oregon and pretend that you," she gestured to the door, "and everyone here means nothing to me when I can do so much to help you?"

Lucius flexed his hands. "Perhaps."

A short cry fell from her lips. "You want me to leave?" Her voice barely carried over the bed to where he stood. Pain rippled between them and he did not know how to prevent it.

"Grace," he pleaded.

A voice bellowed from the other side of the bedroom door. "This is no time for romance! The man is the *magister*. He has responsibilities!"

The door burst open and Rusa stood at the entrance, a display of fury gripping his frame as could only be done by the giant Minoan. He threw a scathing glare at Lucius then looked toward Grace and his mouth fell open. "Damn it man! What are you doing with my niece?"

25

The giant *viator* chugged through the front room like a freight train stuck in an endless loop. Derian stood against the far wall, his gun held loosely in his hand, but his eyes intent on the prowling man. Lucius stood across from both men, his arms crossed and his glare stony and hot. The man's arrival was a convenient interruption from the stalemate between Grace and Lucius, but she did not welcome this new confusion. Not another piece to a puzzle she never knew existed. It was too much.

"Tell your man to put away his weapon," the giant ordered.

"No," Lucius responded.

"This is no time to be a child. Put down your weapon." The man stopped in front of Derian and they stared at each other. A rustle from the stairs drew Grace's attention.

Roderic tipped his head into the room, a flash of shock quickly replaced with a broad grin. "Grandfather, I see you have decided to join us. Fortuitous, as I believe we have a few questions for you."

The man rounded on Roderic. He moved so fast for a man of size, Grace flinched. "Questions? You have questions for me, you insolent boy?"

Roderic laughed and Grace stared at him in fascination. He must truly be mad. He slowed his speech to an exaggerated version of his Scottish brogue. "Ye really are a blustering old man. Now, do ye want to be reasonable about this, or shall I encourage Derian to shoot ye? I am sure Lucius would be more than happy to turn his eye the other way, considering all we have discovered."

"Discovered? What the hell are you talking about?" He turned his eye to Grace, "and what are you doing with Aru's girl."

Roderic and Lucius both cut their gaze toward Grace. Derian kept his eyes pierced on his grumbling target. Grace blushed under the attention and looked to the giant of a man for an answer. Any answer at this point. Aru was a name she knew. Short for Arudara, it was the name her mother wrote in her journals. The name of her father.

"Who are you?" she asked.

His eyes softened and he took a step toward her, but a warning grunt from Lucius stopped his advance. "Really man? What have I done to earn your distrust?"

"Perhaps you could explain about the black box you delivered to the humans in 2007," Lucius answered.

The man snorted and waved the comment off. "That is old business and means nothing."

"Nothing?" Derian growled, "That nothing nearly got Hailey killed."

Grace decided she was out of her league and moved toward a loveseat in the corner. They may eventually come around to discussing her parentage, but at the moment, they were far too concerned with other business. Business she had no connection to. The gorge that stood between her and Lucius only seemed to grow deeper. Again, she wondered at her decision to join him on this adventure. Perhaps it would be better for her to be elsewhere. Except, she thought, for the giant stranger that seethed across the room. His promise of knowledge of her family was far too tempting to disregard.

That and a piece of her still reeled from the incredible lovemaking she and Lucius shared. To go from such an incredible moment to frustrated bickering had her tied up in knots. But she could do nothing about it now. Things seemed to always get in the way between them.

"What do you mean Carlo has it?" the man bellowed.

"How the hell could you not know?" Roderic answered.

"What was in the box?" Lucius asked.

The cushion beside Grace depressed and Hailey smiled at her. "So much for my nap. Who's the big dude?"

"Roderic's grandfather is all I have gleaned so far."

"Rusa? Really? I expected him to have an accent like his grandson." Hailey leaned back against the pillows and pulled her legs up onto the cushion. "Well, I guess that was a dumb idea since he's probably old as dirt. I bet Scotland didn't even exist when that guy was born."

Grace looked to Rusa. A strange name, but it was vaguely familiar and had the sound of the ancients. How old could he be?

"What are they talking about?" Hailey asked.

"A black box. They appear pretty upset about it."

"Oh, that box," Hailey replied, then grew thoughtful. Again, Grace felt woefully out of the loop.

Suddenly, the room fell silent as all four men stared at each other. Whatever answer the men had expected from Rusa, he had surprised them with something altogether different. Hailey broke the silence, "So, feel like filling us in?"

Rusa murmured, "It's confidential–"

232

"They gave the humans the *viator* genome," Derian said as Rusa glared in retaliation.

"Um, OK. And that's bad?" Hailey said.

"Aye, in Carlo's hands it can be," Roderic answered.

Grace watched Lucius. His expression tense and steely, but a slight tic at the corner of his jaw indicated his level of irritation. He finally spoke, his voice low and directed at Hailey. "What Nikanuur was able to accomplish was high school chemistry compared to what they can do with the knowledge they now have. With a skilled and talented scientist, they could do unspeakable things. Hundreds of times worse than what you saw in Babylon.

Hailey blanched. "Well I guess we had better do something about it then."

Grace turned her attention back to Lucius and found him staring hard at her. Anger seemed to flow between them and she grabbed the pillow at her side. Why was he angry? Then he turned his eye to Rusa and she knew. Secrets were dangerous. And he had just learned of hers. One she did not mean to keep from him. At least, not for as long as she had.

Grace stood to approach him. He couldn't think she meant to deceive him. There just hadn't been a right time. He couldn't think that she held it back from him intentionally. A shadow hit the corner of her eye and Rusa moved to stand before her. "Are you all right girl?"

Putting her hand out to prevent from falling against the man, she wrapped her fingers around his wrist. And the world spun. Lights popped like flash bulbs and her head pounded. The vision threw everything around her into oblivion until all she saw were two sightless eyes staring back at her.

Grace shrieked and pain lanced through her knees as they connected with something hard. Then she was flying through the air. Light and darkness fought over her and the deathly eyes continued to stare. Then they blinked, slow and surreal like a child's dolly. Her ears rang with her own screams until the darkness rescued her from her terror.

****

Grace woke to more screams, only these were most certainly not her own.

"Lady, you had better run, because when I get my hands around your neck you're gonna wish you'd never been born." That was definitely Hailey.

"Baby doll, please. Just listen for a moment."

"Like hell!"

A loud thump sounded from across the room and bodies rustled against each other. Grace opened her eyes and lifted her torso to see what was going on. Lucius put a hand to her shoulder and pushed her back onto the couch.

Grace caught a quick glimpse of Hailey as she passed by the couch, a ceramic lamp in her hand and fury flying off her like smoke off a grease fire. Grace pushed herself up again, only to have Lucius shove her back down onto the couch again. "Please," she said.

He glared at her, then turned his attention back to the room. Frustration billowed. She tried again. "Let me up."

He leaned down and placed his lips beside her ear and said, "No."

Then he lifted himself away to continue watching what she could not. "Gods forsake you, Lucius Gratius Cossus. If you do not let me up I shall curse you until the heavens open and Hades builds a bridge to hell."

Lucius turned a shocked eye toward her and rewarded her with a slight smile. "Curses Grace? Perhaps you do have a bit of your grandmother in you."

Grace glowered at him. "There is nothing of that woman in me."

Shattering glass drew her attention away from him.

"A lamp? A lamp? You just threw a lamp at me!"

"Damn straight I did. If they would give me my gun I wouldn't have to!"

A snicker escaped from Grace's lips. Hailey might be bent on destroying her adversary, but she always had a way about her that teetered on the ridiculous. The sparkle in Lucius's eye suggested he shared her opinion. She took the opportunity to speak to him while he was slightly amused. "I did not mean to deceive you. I did not know I was half-*viator* until most recently. And I did not know what the implications might be. I should have told you sooner."

He gave a quick nod. Grace waited a moment for more, but his attention had returned to the fiasco playing out in the front room. "Lucius, please let me up."

"Not until I know you are well."

"I am well enough."

"Not good enough."

"I am not a fragile doll. I am well enough and you will allow me to sit up!"

Lucius looked down at her, only this time the hard edge seemed far less combative. Something worrisome lurked behind his expression. "What did you see?" he asked.

Grace sucked in a breath and looked away. It had been the kind of vision a *tiresian* dreads. The kind that marked

235

you and could never bring good to those involved. But Lucius would be unlikely to allow her this secret. Not now. "Death. I saw death."

"Whose?"

Rusa walked across her field of vision. He cast a quick glance at his grandson then returned his attention to Hailey and Poppi. The strength of animosity between he and his grandson seemed palpable, but the vision had shown a much different story. As Roderic lay unmoving, his eyes glassy with the advent of death, a very real grief-filled fury had reflected from Rusa. Grace looked to Roderic, lounging in a chair, sporting an unaffected and bored expression. Lucius said something she didn't quite hear, but she answered his original question, her finger pointing toward Roderic, "His."

****

"Reena! Sit down. Derian, get a handle on your woman," Rusa bellowed. The room grew still for half a moment and Lucius waited for more sparks to fly. The old Minoan may have led battalions into war and manipulated several centuries' worth of political opponents, but he quite obviously had no idea how to deal with angry women.

Hailey proceeded to give him a verbal lashing that unfortunately would teach the man nothing. Grace shifted beneath his hand again. Nothing had prepared him for the sheer look of terror that had washed across her face when she touched Rusa half an hour before. The screams had lasted only a few seconds, but her skin was still bleached with fright and her eyes held a haunted depth that worried him.

Grace put a hand to his arm. Despite it all, she didn't have the sense to stay still when her body quite obviously needed it. He didn't let her up. She would just have to deal with it.

"Who is Reena?" she whispered.

"Poppi. Reena is her ancient name. The blasted woman decided to change it to that ridiculous name only recently."

Grace's eyebrows formed a 'v' as she processed the information. "I suppose that makes sense."

"What does?"

"Why Hailey is so angry."

Angry was not exactly how he would describe Hailey. But Grace had a talent for understatement. "I suppose she is."

"Damn it, Lucius. We do not have time for this!" Rusa shouted from across the room. The truth was Lucius envied Hailey's ability to focus her fury and release it against her target. At the moment, he craved his sword and wished for a battlefield to release his own. But those were years that had passed and the time was not ripe to repeat them. Knowledge would provide a better salve to their wounds now. It was time to rein Hailey in.

He stood, knowing that Grace would take the opportunity to rise as well. With one eye on her progress, he approached Hailey and Poppi. Rusa stood between them, his hand gripped around Hailey's arm. Derian was swooping in to engage the ancient man. Allowing Hailey to fight her own battles was one thing Derian understood, however, it appeared he drew the line when someone got physical.

Lucius held up a hand and stayed his top *venator*. Derian paused before standing down. Then Lucius placed his hand on Hailey's shoulder and murmured into her ear. "This is not the time."

"Come on. You know what she did! She left us to die."

A muffled response rolled from Poppi's lips, but a subtle movement by Rusa had her lips sealed. Rusa released his hand from around Hailey's arm and said, "We have much to discuss."

Lucius gestured to the chairs around the room.

"I am so not sitting in the same room as her," Hailey said.

"Then you will learn of what is discussed here by second hand," Lucius replied.

Hailey clenched her fists and glared at him, then stared back at Poppi. "This sucks."

Grace shifted and made room for Hailey to join her on the couch. Derian perched on the arm of the loveseat beside Hailey, clearly marking the line where his protection extended. Lucius moved to stand to the side, between the two factions, while Roderic lounged across the room in an easy chair that had grown far more easy through the years than the manufacturers could have ever intended.

Rusa settled into a stiff metal kitchen chair while Poppi remained standing, putting the big man between her and the others in the room. Her glances continued to shift uneasily toward Hailey, an unexpected vulnerability apparent in her movement. Rusa folded his hands and directed his comment to Lucius, "We have come to request your assistance."

A derisive snort erupted across the room, but Lucius's glare sent a silent command to keep Roderic silent. Lucius said, "Tell me."

"You have, until this time, been kept unapprised of certain developments in *viator* politics. We have known for some time of a potential threat, but had not fully anticipated the extent or the imminence. We had intended to deal with the problem internally, but unfortunately, that opportunity was lost and we now find ourselves in the current crisis."

"The Council?" Lucius asked.

Rusa shook his head. "You know as well as I that the Council lost its effectiveness centuries ago. It more or less existed for a few *viators* to feel they sat in a seat of prominence, when all they really did was vote over idiotic notions that meant nothing."

Lucius buried a grin. Despite the man having been the leader of the Council, he accurately described Lucius's own feelings. But if it were not the Council... "Then who?"

The only signal to Rusa's agitation was a slight flexing of his hands. Poppi gripped the top of his chair with tensed fingers. Whatever they had to say, they did not expect him to take it well. Lucius only wished they would quit dancing around the subject and get it over with.

"It has been no secret that the Council was no longer effective in managing the needs of the *viator* community. The *Domus* itself has grown into a bureaucratic monster stagnating under lack of direction."

Lucius stiffened, but Rusa raised a finger. "That is no criticism of your leadership. You were given a ship with unpatchable holes. Your efforts prevented it from going under centuries ago and allowed us to deflect any attempt at it being commandeered by the other group."

Patience growing thin, Lucius narrowed his eyes and spoke in sharp, even tones, "You have yet to tell me who you are aligned with. Quit the bullshit and tell me."

Poppi replied before Rusa could gather his words, "We are led by Donas."

Shock should have lasted longer, but after the initial declaration, fury settled in. Lucius snapped, "You are out of your mind."

Hailey piped up from the couch, "Wait, what? I thought he was dead."

26

After Poppi's declaration, the room erupted into chaos again, sending Roderic to his feet, Hailey into stuttering confusion and breaking Derian from his usual stoic demeanor. But, what had Grace most concerned were the fists Lucius had clenched at his hips. Even when she'd pushed him to frustration's end, Lucius had never reached the limit of his control. That limit appeared to be dangerously close and it frightened her.

Focusing within, she drew upon the patience built through years of dealing with her grandmother and the other hot-blooded *tiresians* in the community. She chose to turn the tide. Grace stood and walked toward Rusa. As she passed, each *viator* ceased their outbursts and watched as she stopped a foot from his chair. "Tell me about my father."

"This isn't the time."

Grace threw her hand up to prevent Lucius from continuing his objection without removing her gaze from Rusa. "You said I was your niece, that you know Arudara. As I am uncertain whether you will walk out of this room alive with the current attitude toward you, I will have my answers now."

"You have Althea's eyes," Rusa said and tilted his lip up in a half-smile, "and her temperament it seems."

Grace snarled and leaned toward him, her nose inches from his. "I grow tired of being compared to my grand-mother. I know enough of that side of my family. Tell me of my father."

"He's dead. Your mother killed him a century ago."

Grace gasped at his emotionless response.

"Aye, but he deserved it. As much as Donas did. But you keep bringing that bastard back to life don't you?" Roderic drawled.

"Donas is a hero. The strongest *viator* and the only man that can lead us now! Who else has sacrificed so much for our people?" Poppi lashed back, pointing a finger at Lucius. "You would not even be alive if it weren't for him!"

"You keep saving him, don't you?" Hailey said from beside Grace, her voice uncharacteristically measured. "You told me you stopped going back in time to save his life each time he died, but you lied. You never stopped. How many times has he died?"

Tears trickled down Poppi's cheeks that were red and swollen with emotion. "I can't count the number." She looked at Grace. "But it doesn't have to be that way."

A growl reverberated from behind her and Grace felt a strong hand grab her wrist. Lucius pulled her toward the door. "You did not come here for assistance. You came here for Grace."

"That is not the truth," Rusa called and Grace looked back to see him towering over Hailey as he pushed past the mob in front of him.

"It is the only way we can ensure the stability of his leadership," Poppi pleaded.

"Shut up woman," Rusa shouted.

Lucius propelled Grace from the room into the kitchen just as Rusa reached the door.

"Listen to me."

Lucius ignored the giant *viator* and grabbed his Walther from the counter. He checked the ammunition and slid the magazine into position.

Rusa tempered his bellowing and quietly shut the door. "Reena is understandably sympathetic toward Donas. You know that. If we were only concerned with the *tiresian*, we would have taken her from you."

Lucius bristled at the implied threat and Grace tightened her fingers in his hand. She asked, "What would they have me do? Why would a *tiresian* be of any benefit?"

"Each time Donas dies, someone must go back and prevent the circumstances that led to his death. Death, however, is a stubborn mistress. Every time we bring him back, death finds a way to reach him," Rusa answered and Grace shivered. They were playing with something unnatural and frightening. He continued, "But if death could be averted, it is possible that eventually they could break out of the cycle. This is what she wants from you. A warning system to prevent his death."

Grace frowned and replied, "But that would require almost a constant attendance on him."

Rusa laughed, "Yes. It would be a full time position. Not one I would wish on anyone."

She completely agreed. Lucius had a slightly stronger position. "It isn't going to happen. Donas can fight his own battles with death. What does he have over all of you that you have stooped to following a madman?"

"He wasn't always mad. He was a strong leader once. Even saved your life, if I recall."

Lucius flared his nostrils at the statement, and Grace wondered at the history that existed between Lucius and the mysterious Donas. What must the man have done to create such animosity?

"I won't deny that his actions saved the lives of me and my men. But it is a small consolation to the numbers that died in that entire campaign."

Rusa leaned against the counter, casting a quick eye at the door that led to the front room then said, "It is for this very attitude that we need you to be on our side. We are afraid that the circumstances have taken their toll. We need an even hand to mitigate the influence."

"You mean you want someone around that isn't afraid to shoot him when he goes mad."

Confused, Grace stepped a little closer to Lucius.

Rusa answered, "That would be a benefit, yes. But not entirely that. His temperament hasn't changed much in the two thousand years since you knew him. The man is still an asshole. And with the current crisis, we cannot afford any possibility of instability in the leadership."

Lucius tucked Grace against his side and warmth spread from where his arm wrapped around her back. She felt protected at that moment, not stifled and that made her stop to think. Three hundred years of suffocating protectiveness sent her running from her home, right into the arms of someone that did the exact same thing to her. She should be terrified of this; yet, she just wanted to put her head against his chest and let him protect her. Why?

The rumble of his voice broke through her thoughts. "Does Reena know you intend to remove Donas from power?"

"There are no plans to do that. The idea is to be prepared should there be a need."

Lucius didn't reply. He kept his gaze hooded and unimpressed, but Grace could tell he was processing the angles by the way he absently stroked his finger against her elbow. Impatience rippled across Rusa's frame, clearly uncomfortable with silence. "We need you. And now with the conspiracy having the genome, the threat can only escalate. We have the resources you need to fight this battle and you have the skills we need to ensure victory."

"Then you will be content if Grace is not part of the package?" Lucius replied. She snapped her head to the side and glared at him. The barest hint of movement at the corner of his eye told her he was very aware of her appraisal.

Rusa frowned at Grace, but gave his assent. Lucius straightened and said, "Then I will consider it. I will need a little time to make arrangements."

The frown remained, but the relaxing of Rusa's shoulders indicated that even the minor acquiescence removed a heavy weight from his mind. Grace hoped the man enjoyed it, because she certainly couldn't. Lucius was going to push her away–again. It was one thing to wait for him while he went on a mission; it was an altogether different thing for him to shut her out completely.

"The leadership will be meeting in Original Time tomorrow evening. I will provide directions to the location."

"Derian and Roderic will be accompanying me."

"No. Leave my grandson here, he will cause more harm than good."

"He is one of my most trusted advisers. He comes or I do not."

"Do you honestly believe he would be able to hold his tongue around Donas?"

"No. And I don't particularly care that he does. He comes with me or there is no deal."

Red flowered across Rusa's neck but he kept his lips pressed together. When he turned to walk back into the living room, Grace let out a breath that had somehow been held back during the exchange.

When she looked up at Lucius, his expression told her exactly what he had on his mind. He was about to do something he would regret and it had everything to do with her.

****

Hailey grimaced and leaned in to wrap her arms around Grace's shoulder. "I'm sorry."

Grace didn't respond, keeping her eyes on the wall across the room. There wasn't a thing she could say to change the situation. Hailey may have become something of a friend, but her loyalty lay with Derian and his lay with the *viators*. Which meant Grace was out of luck.

The room faded from view and a slight shiver of anticipation ran up her back, settling into a subtle warmth at the spot where her head met her spine. In another situation, she would have assumed a vision was impending, but none came and the room was replaced by a landscape of tall shrubs and rocky desert.

A cough beside them had Hailey quickly removing her hands and stuffing them into her pockets. Refusing to make eye contact, she turned to check their surroundings. Lucius met Grace's gaze head on, regret still evident, but the certainty of purpose continued to shine strong. "You won't be here long, just until we can make better arrangements."

Grace stared at him hard, but kept her thoughts to herself. If she opened her mouth now she would not be able to hold the reins on her anger. He was doing what he thought was right and she respected that. Unfortunately, he was dead wrong.

Convincing him of that had been irritatingly impossible. Things were said she wished she could take back. Not because she didn't mean them, but because of the way she uttered them. Pain pierced her heart. Control had been wrenched away from her again and it didn't hurt any less. He turned his eyes away from hers at the creak of an opening door and her heart plummeted to her knees. Sadly, it seemed to hurt more because he thought he was doing the best thing for her.

Grace followed him toward a clapboard house. A narrow porch ran across the front of the building and two windows with gingham curtains stood on either side of a screen door. Hailey waited at the bottom of the steps as Lucius continued toward the door.

Hailey grabbed her hand just as she was about to follow him up the stairs. "I would stay with you." Hailey let out a heavy sigh then continued, "This really sucks. The only reason they aren't making me stay here too is because Carlo can track me. He cares about you though. You know that's why he's doing this, right?"

Grace squeezed her hand and said, "Yes. I know. But, that does not make it right."

A big boned, blonde woman with her hair pinned up in a tight crown atop her head opened the door at Lucius's knock. An easy smile touched her lips and crinkles at the corner of her eyes bespoke years of laughter lined with hard work. Lucius visibly relaxed at the sight, perking Grace's interest. He turned and held a hand out to Grace.

"Louisa, this is Grace."

Sliding her hand down her hips, Grace felt suddenly conspicuous in her slacks. A hundred and fifty years ago she'd had a dress very similar to the one Louisa wore. What must the woman think of the two women in men's clothing?

Louisa turned her smile to Grace and Hailey. "Well now Mr. Luke, you have never brought a woman by before."

Grace blushed and held back, but Hailey gave her a shove toward the stairs. After a polite greeting, Louisa herded the two of them into the house while Hailey waited outside. She showed them to a sitting room with worn but well maintained furniture and clean hardwood floors.

"I have a favor to ask you," Lucius said as he declined the offered seat.

Grace settled into a sturdy upholstered chair. Bringing in something so lovely from the east coast would have been costly, but it created a warmth which seeped into her tense bones. Memories of the era swamped her. She'd been barely out of her adolescence during the late 1800's, just beginning to understand the nature of adulthood.

Louisa sat in a chair opposite Grace, her smile never faltering. "You know I'd do just about anything for you. But stop with the dithering. What do you need? I've never known you to hold your tongue when you meant to say something, so you have gotten into trouble of some sort. Do you mean to be bringing trouble here?"

Lucius answered with a quick shake to his head, "No. Nothing like that. But yes, we have run into a challenge. I need a safe place for Grace to be while I take care of things."

"I see," Louisa paused and considered Grace for a moment. When she continued her voice was measured, "I see. Well, if you don't mind her being in your room, it won't be a problem for me. The rooms have been full up since spring, so I can't put her in any of the others."

Grace kept her glare on Lucius. Why did he have a room here? The easy relationship between the two had her curious and perhaps a little jealous. She clamped down on that thought trail and focused on the issue. Jealousy had no place in her current frame of mind. He was a controlling bastard and who cared if he had a lady friend in every decade.

He shifted uncomfortably under her gaze and within five minutes he walked out the front door. Louisa left her in the sitting room to close the door behind Lucius. Grace ran a finger below her eye, trying desperately to withhold tears. Gods help her, she didn't want to cry.

Louisa returned, her hands on her hips as she stood at the door. "Well now, we can't have you in those clothes for much longer. All my boarders are out and about, but they'll be coming back for supper pretty soon. We don't want them getting the wrong idea. Mr. Luke didn't prepare you for this, did he?"

Grace looked up, confused by the woman's direct appraisal. "No, we did not have much time."

"Well, now I am sure that was the case, but believe me, I am certain he could have done better." Louisa turned away and stalked toward the stairs. "Come on now. I have a dress I think will fit you just fine. We'll get you settled then you can help me in the kitchen and tell me what he did to get you all bothered. He's a good man, but is just about as dense as any of them."

Grace stood and followed the woman as she shuffled up the stairs, suddenly feeling the weight of the last day's frustrations lift enough to think positively. She'd never had a chance to really talk to someone about her frustrations. Perhaps it was just the thing she needed.

27

Lucius hadn't seen Donas in nearly two thousand years. Arrogance still clung to the ancient *viator*, but a harsh hint of malice existed which hadn't been there previously. Lucius kept his expression bland, but his trepidation increased. Rusa and the others had deceived themselves if they thought Donas hadn't already succumbed to the madness. He scanned the rest of the occupants of the room, but then again, perhaps they were all a bit mad.

Fifty *viators* filled the warehouse room, split into minor groups of affiliation. Several members of the defunct Council hovered around Donas, their faces impassive. A contingent of the *venators* had shifted upon the arrival of Lucius. Derian kept a wary guard while Roderic settled into his customary sardonic pose. Rusa stood alone at a spot between them all.

"Please do not mistake me for rudeness, Lucius, but you have never shown interest in the brotherhood," Donas said, his voice popping across the metal ceiling.

"I have never had an interest in politics."

"We both know that is not true. You were quite adept at the game in Rome. Perhaps you are still unhappy I stole your glory?"

"There was never glory to be had in Rome. Only death. All because of a lust for power. I only care to protect the welfare of the *viators*, not seek to rule them."

Donas lifted his brows with derisive intent. "So arrogant in your professed selflessness. You have always been short-sighted to the impacts of power and politics. But then, it could explain your ineffectual handling of Domas and the crisis at hand."

Derian stiffened, but Lucius remained unmoved. He wielded his control of silence as a weapon he knew Donas would be unable to withstand. As expected, the ancient *viator* shifted his direction. "Where is my great-granddaughter? I had expected her to join you."

Again, Derian shifted in response, but Lucius replied, "Hailey has been compromised. The conspiracy is able to track her movements. Perhaps you would have preferred we lead them to you?"

Donas frowned as Poppi leaned in to whisper into his ear. Then he turned his attention to Roderic to say, "That is unfortunate. Her talents would serve us well. Have you had any success in removing the link Carlo has to her?"

"I would have more luck if the blasted interruptions would stop. I can't get a damn thing done with all your manipulations. Can we just get to the point so I can get back to work?" Roderic answered.

Rusa's jaw tightened in response, but Donas dismissed the surly answer and looked to a man at his left. He had the hunched shoulders and shifty eyes of a lackey. Donas continued, "We may be able to provide some assistance. We were able to retrieve several volumes of notes from the ruins of Nikanuur's lab. We believe they may also provide a key to the other projects he had been working on prior to his-" he paused to look at Derian, "demise."

Information was the greatest of weapons and Donas excelled at wielding it to his advantage. Lucius knew this conversation was simply to establish the man's dominance in the game. What Donas did not realize was each piece he revealed provided Lucius the tools he needed to complete the puzzle. Poppi had proved to be a highly effective spy for her husband. What remained to be seen was how much information they would spill regarding the conspiracy.

Donas continued, "If I can be assured of your loyalty, we will provide you the volumes in exchange for services."

Roderic jumped in before Lucius could speak. "Services? Would you be looking for whores then? I know a few that may be interested, but ye would have to pay a pretty penny."

"Damn it boy, mind your tongue," Rusa bellowed.

Donas held up a hand. "Prove to me I can trust you, and we will discuss what we can do for each other."

Roderic bristled, but Lucius knew the comment had not been for the irritable scientist. Rusa had a purpose for insisting Lucius infiltrate the brotherhood. But it appeared, Donas had one as well. Lucius said, "I don't trust you and you sure as hell can't trust me. We both know that. But I will stop the conspiracy from whatever it is they intend to do. If what you provide allows me to do this, then you have your answer. If not, then we are wasting each other's time."

Silence descended and Donas steepled his fingers beneath his chin. The man's eyes flicked toward the contingent of *venator* that slowly moved closer to Lucius during the deliberations. The remaining *viator*s in the room stood quietly, clearly watching to see how the conversation would play, holding their cards close to their chests. Lucius wondered how many of them shared Rusa's concern over the stability of Donas' mental faculties. Would they support a sudden shift in leadership?

Lucius had no intention of wresting power from Donas, if that was what they were waiting for. He had a single goal in mind, and being leader of a power-hungry conglomerate was far from it.

"The conspiracy has branched away from political power plays. They have established a strong following and collected enough resources to make a real push toward their ultimate goals." Donas stood and began to pace. "As you have seen, they have begun to make moves toward establishing unnatural advances in *viator* abilities. If unchecked, they will take this fight outside current *viator* realms."

"What the hell do you mean by that?" Roderic asked.

Donas stopped and lowered his voice for effect, "We have determined that they intend to bring about war not just between *viators* but to the humans as well."

Lucius was not surprised, he gathered as much from Hailey's accounts of her conversation with members of the conspiracy in Babylon. Any *viator* that reached a point of power naturally looked toward the advantages of a *viator*-run world. Preventing such a thing was one of the principle reasons for establishing the *Domus*.

"They have already established control over the *herculians*, next they will focus on the *tiresians*. With the talents of the three groups, they believe they will be unstoppable in controlling the world."

"Where the hell did they find *herculians*?" Roderic asked.

"We have always been here, *viator*." A giant of a man responded from the shadows. "We have just been better at hiding ourselves than you have."

****

Grace pulled her lip between her teeth. A sudden pain testified to the fact that she fell to the bad habit far too much lately. The swollen tip of her lip had worn down to a sensitive nub and if she wasn't careful she'd make it bleed. She sighed. Phillip would have given her hell if he'd seen it.

Metal banged as Louisa slammed the cast-iron stove shut and locked the door. Inside a pan of biscuits baked and Grace's mouth watered at the thought of dinner. She couldn't remember the last time she'd had a filling meal. Too much had happened over the last couple of weeks, exhaustion seeped in and the strain made her far too weepy.

"He's a good man. I can tell you that. But he's a man and that means he don't have half a brain at times." Louisa turned to face Grace, wiping her hands on a faded blue towel. "Go ahead and tell me. Keeping it all bottled up inside will only give you an ache in the belly and a pain in the head."

A smile touched her face and Grace let the easy camaraderie in Louisa's comments soothe her frustrations. Grace said, "It is not just Lucius. Although, I am angry with him."

Louisa murmured with compassion as she lifted the lid off a pot that had been simmering on the stove top. Grace continued, "Honestly, I think the problem may be with me. I have been protected my whole life. Someone has always decided my fate and I have been powerless in preventing that. By leaving me here, he has done the same."

When Louisa remained silent, Grace felt encouraged. She hadn't actually had anyone to talk to like this before. Not even Phillip had the attention span necessary to really listen, especially about feelings and emotions. "My family is incredibly insular. They have isolated themselves from the rest of the world for decades and they wield control like a weapon."

Grace looked down at her fingers. "I have strong feelings for Lucius, that is no question. But I do not know if the anger I feel at being left here without a choice in the matter is due to his actions or left over feelings of helplessness from being a captive of my family for so long."

Louisa stopped working at the kitchen to look squarely at her, a worried crease above her brows. "Seems you got a whole lot of hurt bottled up inside you."

Perhaps she did. She'd never looked at it that way. But the frustration seemed an awful lot like sadness, pain and resentment.

A rustle at the door announced the entrance of a small boy, his hair sticking up like spines on a prickly pear cactus. With one look at Grace, he swung back around and ran out the door he'd just entered. Louisa shook her head and continued fussing with dinner. "He's shy like his daddy was. Took the man near three years before he got up the nerve to say five words to me."

Grace stared at the empty door. What would Lucius's boy be like, she wondered? Would he be stoic and strong like his father? An image of a dark-haired boy with wide brown eyes and a cautious smile popped into her head. She gasped, but relaxed when she realized the sight was from her own imagination and not a vision. She couldn't possibly foresee a child by her and Lucius. That would be far too presumptuous.

"Well now, Mr. Luke, he's a protector and I reckon that's a good thing in a man. It makes a man a good daddy and I figure every woman needs a little protecting in her life. But that don't mean it stops you from living your life as you please." Louisa frowned as she looked at Grace and continued, "There's a big difference between protecting and controlling. And Mr. Luke ain't a controller."

Grace furrowed her brows and let the statement settle into her mind. Was there really a difference? How did Louisa know for sure? Grace asked, "How did you meet Lucius?"

With a cautious smile Louisa started, "Well now, he did a bit of rescuing of me when I needed it bad. My husband had just died and we didn't have a lick of money to help us get through the year. Arthur, my boy you just saw, was still jest a baby and it looked like I would be needing to go back to Oklahoma, where my family is."

A dark memory clouded Louisa's eyes and Grace figured a striking pain lay behind the words. "You didn't want to go back home?"

"Lord no. They'd have me locked up tighter than a fine lady's corset. I suppose it's a might like your predicament. My family likes to keep things the way they see it should be and if you don't like it, they make you walk that line. At the end of a shotgun barrel if they got to." Louisa sighed and leaned against the table, the darkness in her thoughts passing as she continued with her story, "I didn't want to raise Arthur in that. His father was a western man with a free spirit and his boy is going to be the same way. I jest didn't have any idea how to make sure that would happen."

"Then you met Lucius?"

"I was in the mercantile begging Mr. Higgins for a job for the tenth time and Mr. Luke just walked into the building. Said he needed someone to keep watch over his house he'd just bought. Would be happy to have someone run it as a boarding house."

Grace looked around the kitchen and finally began to understand. She hadn't been dropped off at a friend's house, he'd taken her home to the family. "This is his house?"

"Sure, but don't be sayin that around him. He says it may be in his name, but it's my house all the same. The money that comes in from the boarders takes care of me and Arthur, and what's leftover is going into savings. I'm going to buy this place from him outright one of these days, even if he says he's gonna just give it to me."

Grace sighed. He really was a good man and she did understand that what he'd done was what he felt was right. And she couldn't say being protective of others was a bad thing. Truth was she would probably feel the same in his situation. She couldn't take a lifetime of frustration out on one man. It was certainly not his fault.

"Y'all are in a heap of trouble, aren't you?"

The comment startled Grace. "I suppose. Though I am not sure how much and from what quarter. Lucius is concerned but I think he is overreacting a little."

"Yes, well, men can do that. They get that heat up in their belly about a fight and they think many things be bigger than they are. But I've never known Mr. Luke to be like that." Louisa turned back to the stove, lifted the lid off the beans and began to stir vigorously. "Heavens, they're getting a might hot on the bottom. Can't never seem to get this right."

The scent of beans and brown sugar filled the room, with a slight lingering undertone of scorched sauce. Grace propped her head on her hand. It looked like she would have to come to terms with her situation. There wasn't much she could do but wait for Lucius and Hailey to return. Any bit of crying wouldn't do a thing since she had no way to travel time and even if she could, she'd have no idea where they'd gone or how to help. She'd spent her whole life waiting for something to happen, what would a little longer matter?

28

The *herculians* had once been a strong and vibrant community. With similar lifespans, they assimilated easily into the human culture, carving a successful niche of safety in obscurity. In all things, the *herculians* were essentially humans, except in one. When their adrenaline was tapped they could accomplish the most astounding feats. Extreme strength and remarkable speed were only a few of the talents a *herculian* could exhibit.

Unfortunately, the use of their talents created adverse effects which significantly decreased their life expectancy. Each time they accessed their talents they took a giant step closer to death. This necessitated a quiet and serene lifestyle in order to live to a respectable age. However, serenity was not a common character trait found in the *herculians*. Many died early. Many before they could reproduce.

The man who stood before them had to be in his early thirties. The look of health and stamina suggested he maintained a strict control over his talents, but a ripple of unreleased power and strength seemed to wait just beneath the surface.

"Gentlemen, I would like to introduce you to Cade. His assistance has provided significant access to the mind and purpose of the conspiracy. Without him, we would be quite at a loss regarding the direction they have taken."

Roderic snorted with impatience. "You want to tell us why a *herculian* would have any idea what is going on with the conspiracy?"

Cade responded before Donas could begin. A slight frown marred the face of the ancient *viator* and Lucius took note. It seemed Donas faced a struggle for power on various sides. Not a man or woman in the room appeared to buy into the current leadership. The question remained, what purpose did they all have in joining together? Should that purpose fail, there would be little left to keep the faction together. It posed an interesting problem for Donas and gave Lucius an edge.

"This group you all call the conspiracy approached our people several years ago. It'd been centuries since we last had contact with a *viator*. Your people were just myths and tall-tales. When they showed up, they awed us with their capabilities and promises. And now they have us as an army. An army too young in this world to know better." Cade spat out the last in a frustrated west-American drawl.

"What promises were made?" Lucius asked.

"Long life and the free use of our talents." The two men's eyes met and an understanding was quickly reached. The *herculians* had been given the promise of something for which few could say no. That the man standing before Lucius had declined said much of his character.

"And why have you not accepted their offer?" Lucius asked.

A confident grin lit up on Cade's face when he said, "Well, I know enough that when someone starts talking about taking over the world, the odds are always on them failing. Ain't never seen the world taken over yet. Not even Rome could do that."

"Then why have you joined with this group? They surely are no better than the conspiracy," said Derian.

Cade laughed and followed Lucius's eye to Donas. "Well, he's only talking about taking over the *viators*. I figure if that's all he wants I can work with him. As long as I get my people set back straight, I can work with a lesser devil."

Fire flashed in Donas' eyes and Rusa sputtered at the irreverent *herculian*. Roderic took the opportunity to grab the cat's tail and said to Donas, "Well it seems you have yourselves a crack team ready to follow you into battle. What is it you'll need from us?"

Lucius maintained a steady eye on Donas. Others in the room may feel that little threat lurked behind his lack of control. That no one deferred to him said much, except for why the man still held control of the room.

Donas stood and walked toward Lucius. "Join me in the other room?"

Lucius acquiesced and followed the man through a solid metal door into a sparse office. The warehouse clearly sat empty and unused for quite some time. Did the owner know it had been commandeered today to house a meeting that could impact all *viators* if not all of humanity?

Donas shut the door behind them with a murmured command at Poppi to stay behind. "That blasted woman won't let me walk three feet without grabbing onto my arm."

"How many times have you died?"

For a moment Donas looked tired. "Too many to count."

Poppi had to be exhausted. Each time Donas died, she went back in time to ensure his survival. Unfortunately, death and fate do not give up their quarry easily. Each time his past was changed through her direct interference a black mark would be placed on his soul. Each time would push him closer to madness. In Lucius's opinion, the man had begun to teeter on the brink of insanity long before his death. So the threat he posed now had only been compounded.

"Tell me, Lucius, do you grow tired of hiding? Do you not wish for a chance to walk this earth as equals with all that live here?"

Lucius crossed his arms over his chest. "I do not see that we are unequal. We live the life that is required of us."

Donas shook his head, clearly feeling pity at Lucius's inability to see. "To have to police our own from interacting in any meaningful way with humanity is not living a free life. For centuries we have been forced to withhold our natures and activities on the chance that it could adversely affect the time line. So what if we change something in the past and it impacts the lives of those that come later? Does the same thing not happen in Original Time with humans? Do their actions not impact the lives of a future person?"

"True, but that future does not yet exist. When we go back in time and make changes, it impacts something that has already happened." And people that already had souls. It was the responsibility of all *viators* to limit their impact on the people of Original Time. Morality demanded it. Lucius had seen far too often the ill effects of an irresponsible *viator*. Families lost loved ones, people ceased to exist. It became a piece no one quite knew was missing, but was noticed nonetheless. It was why he ran the *Domus* as he did. It gave him purpose.

Donas snorted, "And who are you to say the changes we make in the past were not meant to be? Does the high and mighty Lucius have free knowledge of the morality of creation? Do the gods speak through you to determine what the future holds?"

Lucius declined to comment. The *viators* had debated the purpose and philosophy behind the same argument since the day they first jumped time. He had little patience for it. "If this is what concerns you, why do you not join with the conspiracy? It seems your desires are aligned."

"No. You have always seen the issue of goodness and evil as black and white. I am a good man. I have no desire to rule over all the people of the world. Only to be free among them as we are. As we were meant to be."

Lucius bit back a comment. Many a tyrant spouted nonsense about freedom when seeking power. Donas may not want power over humanity, but he certainly desired dominion over the *viators*. "Who is leading the conspiracy?"

Donas accepted the shift in topic with grace and answered, "I do not know. We know of many that have joined with them. Claudia for one. Possibly Osric. But we know they do not lead the movement. Someone has created a strong network that hides the identities of the leaders effectively. For all we know, any number of their spies could be in the room behind us."

Claudia was a familiar name. She'd jumped for the first time during the Roman era, around the same time Lucius had. Hailey's description of the woman that had approached her at Nikanuur's laboratory fit Claudia perfectly. A giant mouth and a sense of entitlement, she would be ripe for this kind of movement. Osric was a surprise, but not a big one. He'd never taken much interest in the *Domus* or in the fate of the *viators* at large. Whatever the conspiracy offered him, it would have been personal.

"And the notes from Nikanuur's lab. What have you learned from those?"

The response took a few moments as the man weighed his intentions. Lucius was pushing for information and that was the only thing Donas had to offer him. Give too much, and any hold he might have on Lucius would disappear. Donas clearly understood this. However, Lucius had no intention of agreeing to anything, without a little more. Too much was at stake.

"They are seeking to increase the capabilities of *viators* to levels never seen before." Donas picked his words carefully. "But it is not limited to just that. They are not deceiving the *herculians* in their offer to increase their lifespan and protect them from the effects of their talents. They can, and they are doing it through the combination of *viator* and *herculian* genetics."

That was definitely a problem. Lucius queried further, "The results?"

"Conclusive. The changes are even more stable than what has been done to increase *viator* capabilities. In addition, they have been able to give *viators* access to the traits of a *herculian*."

Trepidation filled him. A *viator* with access to super strength and speed would be a formidable enemy. Difficult for human or *viator* to defeat. "That is a significant advance."

"Yes, one apparently made possible by Rusa's fumbling of the genome issue."

"About that..."

"Water under the bridge. We have bigger issues at hand."

Lucius stilled and clenched his hands. What could possibly be a more important issue?

"You heard that they are attempting to gain an alliance with the *tiresians* much as they have with the *herculians*. To this point, they have been unsuccessful. However, in light of what has been discovered regarding their physiological advances, it seems apparent they wish to include the *tiresian* traits in their bag of tricks."

A *viator* with the strength of a *herculian* and the ability to see the future of possibility like a *tiresian* would be nearly unstoppable. Even if they were able to only create a few with those capabilities, a reality of world domination might actually be attainable.

He did not trust Donas, or his intentions. But it appeared they would be fighting together–again. But Lucius knew the man now and he would not let him destroy a thousand men's lives this time. Not like he did on a bloody battlefield fighting for the Roman Empire. History would not repeat itself.

"What do you want from me?"

For the first time, Donas visibly relaxed. "I need a commander. The *venators* need a leader they respect and they respect you."

Lucius inclined his head in the closest thing to a salute he would give the man. The elite forces of the *viator* were still his. With command of the *venators* in hand, he could make significant inroads toward squashing the threat of the conspiracy.

"From what we gathered from Cade and others with connections, Althea has rejected any attempts at negotiation with the conspiracy. We fear they are done with asking."

Lucius looked at Donas, his back turned and head down as though his thoughts weighed heavily. When Donas swung around, a glint of speculation entered his eyes. "They know of Grace. They know of her mixed heritage. If they have her, there is no need for the acceptance of the *tiresians* and no need for their continued existence. When they have Grace, they will eradicate her people."

****

Fire and screams. Heat burned her eyelids and pain crashed through her belly. Grace reached out and clawed against her assailant, desperate to be free of the threat. Her shout caught in her throat and her hands ripped through cloth. She opened her eyes and saw yellow.

Relief plummeted through her at the sight of the floral wallpaper and the single-paned window. Hands still shaking, she looked down at her bed sheets to find a giant tear where she had ripped it apart with her hands. Immediate guilt over the destruction helped to lessen her fear of the dream. She'd have to find a needle and thread to mend it. Louisa couldn't afford to have her guests making a mess of the linens.

Grace stood to dress, determined to push the vision away with physical industry. After all, it was a dream. Not a vision. It couldn't possibly be a vision. Fear and exhaustion could create images very similar to visions in depth and character. And she had plenty of both.

Sneaking down the hall, she entered Louisa's room, hoping to find the sewing supplies in the open. Sunny and bright, the room quickly gave up her prey. Found tucked in a small box, Grace pulled out a needle and a spool of coarse thread. It would do for mending and hopefully she could deliver the sheet with the damage already repaired. Louisa had been so kind already, Grace couldn't do anything less.

Back in her room, Grace jumped onto the bed. Pulling her legs beneath her, she began to mend. After a few stitches, memories of the last time she sewed swamped her. It had only been a year ago when she'd taken a needle to her cousin's socks. Despite being the one who could replace goods from the outside, he still managed to wear his clothing until they fell off of him.

She smiled at the memory of Phillip, but quickly became overcome with fear. The image from her dream crashed back into her mind. Phillip covered in blood, sightless eyes staring back at her and his hands stretching toward her in helplessness. Grace stifled a whimper. He hadn't been the only one.

Then there had been Tymion, standing tall in all his masculine glory, commanding his people in a battle they never truly believed would occur. A battle between *tiresian* and *viator*. A battle where Lucius stood on the opposite side.

Her hands began to shake and she lost purchase on the needle. Tears welled up in her eyes as she relived the dream. Could it be more than a dream? Could it be the fate of her people? Could it be her fault?

29

Lucius peered out across the field. The *tiresian* compound looked about the same as it had when he'd been there several weeks prior. Whatever the conspiracy intended for the group appeared to be on hold. Grace safely ensconced in Louisa's boarding house over a hundred years in the past might give them the time they needed to prepare for the oncoming threat. It might give them the time, but it wouldn't make the process easier.

"You said they weren't exactly friendly the last time you spoke," Derian said in a hush.

"That is correct."

"Don't mean to put a wash on your optimism, but how do you know we'll be able to get them to see reason this time around?"

Lucius kept his head down and counted the number of *tiresians* walking the lane that led toward the main building. That was where they gathered before, when Althea had sentenced him to death. A three story building stood to the left. Based on the curtains and number of children playing outside the entrance, it had to be a domicile for many of the *tiresian* families. It was possible Tymion lived in those quarters, but he doubted it. The man seemed more prone to living alone. It was easier to hide duplicity when privacy could be had easily.

A second lane branched off from the main one and led into the trees. Over the top of the canopy, Lucius spotted a gabled roof and whitewashed walls. He pointed toward the house and Derian said, "Do you think that's Althea's?"

"Don't know. We'll find out." Lucius scooted backward into the bushes and Derian followed suit. They would duck through the trees to avoid detection and hopefully be able to find a vantage point to watch the house. Lucius would prefer to avoid Althea if at all possible. Tymion seemed to have a more sympathetic and straight-forward ear. But if they had to tie the old woman to a chair to get her to listen, he'd consider it as an option.

"Hey guys, what are you doing?"

Derian rolled onto his back, his gun out and pointed just as Lucius reached for his.

"Dude, seriously, it's me. Chill." Hailey dropped to her knees beside Derian, her eyes wide and uncertain.

"I told you to stay at Jason's place," Lucius growled, one eye pointed toward the lane in case they were heard.

"Yeh, well, that didn't work out all that great. Carlo stopped by. Again."

Derian sat up, his hands reaching for her immediately. "What happened? Is Jason all right? Were you hurt?" He ran fingers over her arms looking for injury.

Hailey grinned and shrugged. "I took Jason for a ride to work and told him to take a vacation. Then I booked it here."

"You jumped a human?" Lucius asked.

"I jumped my friend. Don't get all self-righteous with me. I wasn't about to leave him for Carlo to mess with. I figured you'd be done with your meeting by now. Didn't expect you to be playing in the dirt."

Lucius frowned, but he was out maneuvered. Who knew, perhaps Hailey would be useful this time around. She'd certainly held plenty of surprises for the enemy in the past. Unfortunately, the conspiracy appeared as eager to have Hailey as they were to get a hold of Grace. He'd known leaving Grace in New Mexico would have her fuming, but it was the right thing to do. He'd seen the look of speculation in Carlo's eye when he'd spotted Grace in Carpathia. She was a target. There was no way in hell they'd get their hands on her—not on his watch.

Lucius led them through the trees as Derian quietly filled Hailey in on the necessary details. She pulled out her own pistol and grinned. "You know I'm always up for another adventure and I'm dying to meet Grace's grandmother. I have a few things I'd like to say to her."

Lucius brought them to a halt a hundred feet from the house. Victorian in style, it had two stories, a porch that ran across the front and a quaint swing rocking in the wind beside a window. A shadow passed in front of the window and Lucius crouched down to watch.

"You saw something? What did you see? Was it her?"

"Hailey, shut up."

He felt the young woman settle down beside him in a pout. She had far too much energy. When this was all over and the conspiracy dealt with, he'd have to find a decent job for her or bar her from ever stepping foot in the *Domus*. She'd drive him nuts. That is, if there were a *Domus* to return to. Lucius shook it off. The future would become what it needed to be. If the purpose for the *Domus* had run its course, then it would be time to move on and find a new direction in life.

The quiet and resourceful Grace returned to his thoughts. She had a strength within even she didn't recognize. As different from Hailey as much as two women could be, her unique blend of naiveté and wisdom made him trust her more than he'd trusted anyone. Beyond even Derian, and that was something to think on.

She may be angry with him, but he was doing everything he could to ensure she had a life to live where she could revel in her freedom. He may not be welcome in her life when all this was done, but he sure as hell was going to make certain she survived what lay ahead so she could reject him later.

"Wait, I think I see something," Hailey said in a hush as she strained over a branch, peering between a break in the leaves. "Wow, that's one well built man. Is that Tymion? Dude, you have some serious competition if that's the dude that was going to marry Grace."

Lucius looked to where Hailey pointed. Tymion walked with another, lankier *tiresian*. Phillip. They needed to follow the two men and catch them alone. It would be the best way to warn the community of the impending danger.

He turned to give direction to Derian and Hailey, but found them staring up at three armed men. Lucius lifted his hands in surrender, prompting the other two to do the same.

"Didn't you have enough of us last time?" one of the men asked. Lucius didn't bother to answer. It seemed they were going to have to do this the hard way.

****

"The train don't come through town for another couple days," Louisa said from behind a slightly yellowed sheet hanging from a line in the breeze. She threw another cloth under the line into the basket Grace held. "And even so, I told Mr. Luke I would be lookin after you, and I can't do that if you run off on a train to who knows where."

Grace stared into the distance at the few buildings she could see of town. She'd not had a chance to investigate the local area, things had happened too fast. But now she wished she had a better idea of what the land had to offer. "If not a passenger train, then perhaps a supply train?"

Louisa peeked around the linen. "What on earth would you want to be goin' on a supply train for?"

"I would just need to stand in front of it," Grace mumbled. An oncoming train might be the only thing terrifying enough to force a jump through time. If she could do it at all. If not... well that didn't bear thinking of. Louisa continued to stare and Grace dug for an explanation. "I know that my family is in terrible danger. I cannot tell you how I know this. I just do. I must get back to them."

"Mr. Luke wouldn't like it if I let you run off."

"Well it is not Mr. Luke's life we are discussing right now, is it?" Grace retorted, the words significantly more waspish than intended. She quickly recanted, "I apologize, Louisa. Worry has me acting out of sorts."

"It happens to us all. Well, come on now. If you intend to be leavin', you may as well go prepared." Louisa dropped the last sun-dried sheet into the basket and walked back to the house.

Directing Grace to leave the basket in the kitchen, she continued toward the front of the house and then up the stairs without pause. When they reached Lucius's room,

Grace began to wonder at her purpose. What could Louisa mean by preparation? There wasn't a thing in Lucius's sparse room. She'd spent enough time in it to know.

Louisa pushed open the door and approached the corner of the room. Three fingers pressed against the corner wainscoting, initiating a soft click and the small panel of wood loosened. With a twist, Louisa pulled the wood panel forward and another click sounded before a piece of the wall opened to reveal a small hideaway along one side of the room. "Mr. Luke told me that one day he may not come back. I didn't want to hear it then anymore than I want to hear what you have going on now. I know you both live lives pretty darn different from mine."

The door opened a little more and Grace spied a small armament lining the wall of the hideaway. Modern weapons hung beside more period arms, including some be far more familiar in eras where bronze was the dominant metal. Wide-eyed, Grace held out a hand to brush a finger along a tall wooden spear. A flash of intuition hit, not quite a vision, but a certainty instead. This had been Lucius's. And it had been used in battle. Steel strength and reserved emotion emanated from somewhere within.

Louisa opened a drawer in a compact dresser that sat beneath the hanging weapons. Cardboard boxes from various eras filled the inside, each with a description of the weapon above that the ammunition correlated to. Louisa pulled a few of the boxes out. "I figure since he told me to use this whenever I felt I needed it, that he would be thinking to offer the same to you."

"I do not know."

"Of course you do. He wouldn't want nothing bad to happen to you, even if he did disagree with what you were planning to do."

"Yes, but I do not know that I can bring them with me." Grace knew that Lucius and Derian could both bring weapons through time. And Hailey had developed the ability to teleport objects independently through time. But she'd heard stories of *viator* taking years to learn how to transfer anything more than the clothes on their backs. Even if she could travel through time in this instance, there was no telling if she could bring anything with her. "I do not even know that I can do what I need to do."

Louisa stopped and stared at Grace, and for a moment, she felt like the woman thought she'd left her brain at the door. Finally, the silence passed and Louisa spoke, "Well now, if there is one thing I learned through livin' life out here, than it's this. If the Good Lord has decided you need to be doing something, then he will make for darn sure it happens."

"But what if I am not supposed to do this thing?" Grace asked.

The woman rolled her eyes, grabbed a revolver from the wall and dropped it into Grace's hands. Immediately, Grace was swamped with visions. Several angry faces fell in and out of focus. The walls of her family's home grew in stark solidity, and the very gun that she held in her hand skidded across the floor to land at Phillip's feet.

Shock and realization hit between her shoulder blades. This weapon would play a part in the battle which lay ahead. And there was only one person that could bring this weapon to the field. It meant that... "I will be doing it."

275

Louisa slapped her on the shoulder. "Of course you will. Now come along, I have your clothing still from when you first got here. I imagine you don't want to be leavin' in that dress. Besides, I want to be keepin it for myself. Sherriff Randolf promised me a picnic this Sunday after church and that's my prettiest dress."

30

The metal of the pistol had warmed to her touch, taking away some of the frightening quality. She still had no idea how to use the thing. If pressed, she'd be able to figure it out, but the thought of that much killer power in her hand had her avoiding the issue. Of course, *when pressed* would be the last moment she would want to be figuring out the weapon.

Grace weighed the gun in her hand, looking at the hard lines of steel and finger smudges from her handling. She'd never done anything more than shoot rock salt out of her shotgun. That had been nearly thirty years ago. Violence was seen in limited quantities within the community and rarely had she been involved enough to see the aftereffects, let alone the action itself. She stared hard at the pistol. Three hundred years with the same group of people, and she had no meaningful friendships. What did that say about her?

She tightened her fingers. Her life may have a lack of relationships, but she had family. And if her visions were correct, then Phillip's life was threatened. He was the closest thing to a friend she had and the only real family she knew. Nothing could stand between her and being there for him. Not an enemy bent on control and domination. Not unexpected blackouts. Not even time itself.

The wind whipped across the New Mexico desert, taunting her with its constancy. All the resolve in the world wasn't helping. She still had not discovered how to jump. The tiniest hint of doubt crept toward her confidence. If she let it take control she might as well run back to the house and huddle beneath the sheets until time ended. Or at least until the modern age when she could discover what happened on this day in the future.

A rustle of feet crushing the brush rustled beside her. Grace looked down to find young Arthur gazing up at her. He took a quick step back before she could remove the intense desperation from her eyes. "Please don't run. I am sorry. I did not mean to frighten you. I have just been thinking."

He did not lose the cautiousness, but remained beside her nonetheless. "Why haven't you dis-peared yet?" he asked.

"Disappeared?"

His disheveled hair shook as he nodded his head with vigorous seriousness. "When Mr. Luke comes out here, he always dis-pears."

"You have seen Mr. Luke disappear?"

At her question he stopped bobbing his head to look her square in the eyes. After a short pause he replied, "But he don't take as long as you do."

Grace couldn't help the small laugh that escaped at his statement. "No. I imagine he does not. He is much better at it than I am, you see."

Arthur pursed his lips and lowered his brows in a concerted effort to appear solemn. The two of them settled into an agreeable silence. After a few minutes, his patience reached a pinnacle. Kicking his toes into the dirt, he said, "I think you are doing it wrong."

"I am quite certain that I am. But I do not know how to do it."

"You look like you want to fight someone. Kind of like how Billy gets when his Pappa smacks him around."

"Oh my. Do I?" Grace sighed. That was assuredly not the way to jump time. She'd never seen that look on the face of any *viator* as they faded from view.

"When Mr. Luke does it he looks like he's tryin' to find somethin' he lost. Only it looks like he's looking in his brain."

Grace cocked her head toward the boy and considered his comment. She knew just the look he'd referred to. She'd seen it on Hailey's face more than once prior to a jump. It was the kind of look people had when they grew lost in thought, grabbing at memories or tendrils of thought that proved elusive. Could that be the answer?

Grace looked inward, letting her body relax and her mind ease. Was there something within that could point her the way?

A slight tingle began at the base of her neck, building a little at a time. Fright made her clamp down on the familiar feeling. It was far too much like what she experienced prior to passing out. She didn't need to do that in front of the poor boy. Imagine what he would have to say to his mother?

"Why did you stop? That was the look. Just like Mr. Luke! You even dis-peared a little," he said, showing the first bit of excitement she'd seen all afternoon.

"I–well, it never worked that way for me before."

He gave her a look very similar to one his mother had given only hours before. It was like she'd left her brain behind and her words rattled out of an empty head. "But that's why you keep tryin'. If you can't do it the first time, you keep on tryin' 'til you get it to work."

Grace opened her mouth to respond, thinking something along the lines of only a fool tries the same thing expecting a different outcome, but flapped her lips shut. There was no need to get snappy with the child. And what could it hurt? She had no other insights to help her along. "All right, but if I fall down and do not wake immediately, please do not tell your mother. I would not want to worry her."

Again he gave her a derisive glare, bordering on rudeness. How odd children were, not hiding behind false politeness. With a weak smile, she tried again. Her thoughts turned within and when no indication of a blackout appeared she let her body relax. The tingle intensified and the feel of blood pulsing through her veins suddenly became identifiable. Allowing the sensations to take over, she focused on her home in the Oregon woods.

Suddenly, she felt as though a wall stood between her and her destination. Confused she began to retreat.

"You almost got it! Don't stop."

Arthur's words goaded her forward, but still she struggled against the wall. Then she remembered the buffer field that protected the community from *viators*. She'd never be able to jump home.

But she could get close. Focusing on the road several miles from the community, she let herself go completely.

The first thing she felt was the stark difference in the air. She opened her eyes to lush greenness and felt her body nearly put in shock by the humidity. Pores soaked in the watery air like a man dying of thirst, but then the cold seeped in and she thought fondly of the dry desert warmth.

Elation had her heart skipping every other beat. She'd done it! She'd actually done it! But why now when every other time she'd end up laid out in a faint?

Grace looked down the road. The community waited down that road, and with it, an impending confrontation with the conspiracy that plagued Lucius. Now they were bringing the fight to the *tiresians* and Grace had every intention of preventing their success.

But first she had to figure out which direction to start running.

****

"What kind of fool returns to a death sentence?" Althea stood before them, much like she had only weeks prior. Now the room stood empty but for a few guards, the three *viator* and the ever commanding Althea.

"I have no animosity toward you, Althea," Lucius said.

"That speaks well for your soul, but does nothing for the animosity we feel toward you," she replied. "My sentence still stands. You will be immediately executed. What remains is a determination for your companions. As you have brought them with you, I can only assume they intend to aid you in whatever nefarious scheme you have concocted. In addition, you have kidnapped my granddaughter, and so I am not feeling lenient to your concerns. Therefore, they too will join you in Hades."

Hailey snorted as the woman turned to leave, stopping the ancient *tiresian* in her retreat. Althea said, "You are a bit insolent for one about to meet death."

"Oh please, I've faced scarier bad guys in the last month. If you're done performing, we have some serious business to talk about. You're about to have a shit ton of nasty *viator* and *herculian* baddies up your butt and we're the only ones that can help you."

Althea's mouth dropped open and Lucius wondered if it were the first time anyone dared speak to her so frankly. Perhaps it was just the thing to swing the tide back in their favor. "That which has essentially disabled the *Domus* has now targeted the *tiresian* community."

"You told them of us?"

"It seems your secret is less secure than you anticipated. No, I did not tell them of you. They already knew. The conspiracy has grown in power and influence. Gaining a hold on the *herculians* was their first step. Now they aim to gain power over you."

"Impossible. We are well defended. No *viator* can jump within the boundaries of the community. We would see them coming from miles away with the sentries and security cameras." Althea's stance relaxed and her eyes filled with dismissal.

"Right. 'Cause you saw us coming? We got within feet of your house before you picked us up," Hailey said. Lucius could see the frustration building within the young *viator*. Derian and he had significantly more experience dealing with stubborn and foolish leaders unwilling to see the facts that lay before them. Hailey just might shake the ancient *tiresian* if she continued to be blind to the issue. Lucius might even allow it.

"Even if they brought an entire army, we would withstand the attack. With our stores of weapons, they have no chance of success. I have ensured our safety for over 800 years. Your measly attempt at uprising will not be more than a minor disturbance for us. I guarantee it."

Hailey rolled her eyes and opened her mouth to respond just as the door to the room flew open. A man, his eyes wild with fear, held onto the door, blood pouring from a wound at his temple. He scanned the room. When he found Althea, he stumbled toward her, rambling a stream of incoherent words.

"What is it Chryses?" Althea walked toward the bleeding man, concern replacing the cool arrogance.

"*Viators*. In the town center. They just appeared. Thirty of them. And more in the forest," the man managed to reply.

"Impossible."

"Seriously? Even your own guy tells you and you still won't believe us?"

Lucius put a hand on Hailey's arm and addressed Althea. "Your store of weapons? Where are they?"

Althea swung to confront Lucius. "I would never betray my people to you. This is a ruse. An attempt to gain knowledge of our capabilities. These men that have found their way into our community are clearly yours."

With a look from Althea, the guards moved to take control of the three *viators*. As one reached for Hailey, Derian dove toward him. Lucius pivoted around another guard to avoid capture.

"As you resist you only reveal more of your guilt," Althea stated as she moved toward the door. "Take them to the detention cells until we have dealt with their compatriots. Chryses, come with me. We must find Tymion."

Althea slammed the door behind her, leaving the guards to deal with the uncooperative *viators*, not bothering to wait until they had the situation under control.

Hailey smashed her foot into the back of her attacker's knee. He shouted as he dropped to the ground. Derian wrestled with another as Lucius and his guard circled each other, their expressions a mirror of wary resolve. A fourth guard moved to assist in disabling Hailey.

Derian barked a warning and Hailey hit the ground and rolled into the legs of the approaching man. Surprised by her move, he fell, leaving both in a tangle of limbs that wiggled about in a desperate fight for purchase.

Momentarily distracted by his friend's plight, the guard that faced Lucius provided an opening. Lucius took it. With a swift jab he disoriented the man then shifted his weight to throw him to the ground. In seconds the guard lay unconscious.

The guard with the twisted knee took his place in front of Lucius, but his mind was clearly not in the moment. These men were not used to fighting. They may have trained together in anticipation of a day like today, but the reflexes gained through practice were limited and the discipline from experience was decidedly absent. Lucius decided to try a new tact.

"She is a strong leader, with only the best intentions for her people." The guard looked up sharply as Lucius continued, "I have nothing but respect for her and your people. What was done to you in the past was inexcusable and I do not blame you for your reaction to our appearance here."

Lucius intentionally let down his guard and provided the perfect opportunity to strike. But the man did not take it. Heartened, Lucius finished his words, "But today she is wrong. These men in the town center are not ours. They are the force we have come to aid you against. They threaten the vitality of the *viator* as much as they do the *tiresian*. If you continue this fight, then you face them alone."

"What advantage would three *viators* truly give us in a fight against so many?" the man asked.

"Well, this for one." Hailey said, her hands holding two pistols with each pointed at an assailant. She threw one to Lucius then waited as another materialized in her empty hand. The guards all stared in consternation.

Hailey grinned like a cat caught with a mouse. "Surprise. I got super powers."

Derian rolled his eyes and said, "Can you take anything seriously?"

31

Tymion and Phillip emerged from the security building. Each held a rifle and had a look of determined purpose. With a deep breath Grace stepped from her place of hiding behind a tree, waiting for them to notice her beside the lane.

Phillip caught sight of her first. He stopped, shooting a quick look at Tymion, before trotting toward her. "What are you doing here?" his voice an unfamiliar growl.

"I came to warn you."

"Curse it, Grace. This is not the place for you right now."

Tymion joined them, his expression as unwelcome as her cousin's. "You need to leave."

"Have they arrived yet?" she asked.

"How do you know?" Phillip replied as Tymion reached out to wrap his hand around her wrist.

"I saw it."

Tymion tugged her toward the security building, slamming the door shut after the three of them entered. "You do not know what you saw."

Grace yanked her hand from his grasp. "I know perfectly well what I saw. There will be a battle here. And you are fighting on the wrong side."

"Grace, you don't understand," Phillip pleaded.

Tymion pushed her toward a door. "You will stay here until it is done."

As he propelled her into another room Grace answered, "Damn you to Hades! Stop pushing me away. There are bigger things at hand here than you know!"

A movement across a security screen caught her attention. Thirty men swarmed around the town center. They each held a long pole weapon and wore the same black uniforms she'd seen in Carpathia. "They're already here." She turned her eye to the black box that controlled the buffer preventing *viators* from landing in the community. It was quite obviously turned off.

Realization struck and she swung back to the two men. "You let them in. What have you done?"

Phillip quickly looked down, but Tymion held her gaze with confidence. "It is what is right for our people. We have lived too long under Althea's tyranny and this was the only way."

"No!" Grace snapped her hand out and wrapped it around Tymion's wrist. The vision hit hard. Flashes of pain and flurries of activity filled her sight. Across the dust and smoke of battle she watched as her people fell in blood and violence. The buildings crumpled into piles of rubble. "No. Many will die. Please. Please stop this!"

Tymion pulled away, disengaging the vision and bringing her back to the present. He moved to shut the door. Grace pleaded, "Tymion please. This is not the way to win our freedom. The men you have joined with, they only seek to use and destroy us."

He squelched the fleeting moment of uncertainty with a stony resolve which tightened his jaw and Grace knew she had lost. The door shut behind them and she was trapped.

Phillip's voice echoed across the room which led to the exit, the sound barely penetrating the solid wall between them. "But her vision."

Tymion answered, "She is not the only one with visions, Phillip. I have seen our victory. All will be well."

Then the door slammed shut a second time, blanketing the building in silence. Grace flipped the light switch on. The room had one exit and that was now locked. Two windows on the back wall stood seven feet from the floor.

Grace grabbed a desk chair and rolled it to the windows. Her hands barely reached the bottom of the sill. Paint ran around the edges, sealing the window shut. She scanned the room. There might be something that could assist in scraping away the paint, but in truth, time was running away from her.

People crossed the security screens and she watched in horror as one man engaged his pole weapon. A red glow emanated from a bulbous top, creating a focused wave of heat toward an opponent. She couldn't see the target, but the man continued on in a new direction. Whoever was hit had not fought back. Had they survived the attack or were they now laying in agony, unable to reach help?

Frustration sent her jumping from the chair. There had to be a way she could escape. There had to be something she could do to help. Another five *viators* appeared on the screen, weapons ready. They were sending in reinforcements. Grace wondered if Tymion yet realized the error he made. He could not possibly have intended the death and destruction she was witnessing through the security cameras. Another two materialized in another section of town.

She cut her gaze to the black box which controlled the buffer. She could at least stem the tide. Her finger punched the button that engaged the system. The red light beside the button blinked twice before it changed to green. Satisfied, she crossed her arms. Perhaps it would give the community a brief respite.

Of course, it also sealed her within the security hut completely. Now that she reengaged the buffer she realized her one opportunity to escape had been another jump through time. She had a choice. Leave the buffer alone to prevent more of the enemy from materializing into a larger force or turn it off and attempt another jump.

Pulling her bottom lip between her teeth she stared at the box. Gods this was frustrating. She had few options and none of them were good.

One of the women from the community dashed across the screen, her infant son held tight in her arms. She glanced back and Grace got a good look at the expression of fear that spurred her on. The woman ducked into the thick cover of a bush. Only moments later, one of the black-clad *viators* appeared, his pole weapon held up in wait for a target. Thankfully, the man appeared unaware of his quarry's hiding spot.

Another screen showed the main community building. Behind it, she could see her people huddled around the windows of the three story apartment complex where most of the community lived. The glint of metal showed the stockpiled weapons had been reached and they were making a concerted effort at defense.

A large force of the enemy swarmed toward the main community hall. One of the men approached the front door with caution, then with swift movements, yanked open the door and threw in two small objects. He retreated toward the group of *viators* huddled behind a dumpster.

Several of the building's windows blew out in a rain of shattered glass. Men entered through the front door, now hanging askew from the force of the explosions. Grace wondered if her grandmother found another place from which to lead their people during the battle.

She braced her arms on the desk, unable to tear her gaze away from the disaster playing out before her. She had to get out of the security shed and do something. There was little she had to offer, but she couldn't sit here and do nothing.

Straightening her back, she looked to the door. There had to be a way out. As she brushed her hands down her hips, she felt the hard lines of the revolver pressed against her back where she'd tucked it into the waistband. How had she not noticed the bulk of the weapon against her skin? Grace slid it out and examined the features.

A vague memory of Lucius using a similar weapon encouraged her to open the cylinder. Five bullets sat flush in their holes, one was left empty. She snapped the cylinder back in place. Nerves had her hand shaking in anticipation.

Lifting the revolver, she pointed at the door and squeezed the trigger. Reflexes closed her eyes and when they opened she saw light through the small hole she'd put in the center of the door. She frowned. She'd been aiming at the lock mechanism. This was going to be a little harder than anticipated.

Wasting her ammunition on an escape had significant disadvantages. But she was officially out of options. Grace lifted her arm, determined to keep her eyes open this time.

She pulled the trigger and again her reflexes squeezed her eyes shut. When they opened, another hole had been punched through the door six inches up and to the left of the first. Not even close to where she wanted it.

Raising her arm a third time, Grace prepared for another shot. Three times the charm. She didn't bother to worry about her eyes.

"Grace?"

The sound of a voice calling from the front room startled her, sending the gun up and the shot wild.

"Gods Grace, what are you trying to do?"

"Phillip?"

"Are you done shooting?"

Grace ran to the door and put her eye to one of the holes. A flash of color across her line of sight had her gripping her fingers tight around the revolver handle. "Phillip, is that you?"

The door knob rattled and she heard the metal key being inserted into the lock. Grace stepped back and raised the gun a fourth time. The chance that the man on the other side of the door was anyone but Phillip was slim. The voice sounded right, but distorted by the door. She just couldn't trust it. If only her hand would stop shaking.

The door opened. Phillip's blond hair and gangly frame sent a sigh of relief through her body. He said, "What were you trying to do? Air condition the room?"

Grace grimaced at her cousin. "Do not be a smart-aleck. There is not enough time."

"I am sorry, Grace. We thought we were doing the right thing. We were terribly wrong." He turned and strode to the building's front entrance. "All we can do is try to stop the situation from getting any worse."

Grace looked around him as he opened the door. Shots echoed through the forest and screams sounded from the direction of town center. "Where is Tymion?"

"When we realized what was happening he sent me to you and made his way toward our people barricaded in the apartment complex."

It was the best place for him to be. Tymion may have made an irreversible mistake, but his dedication to their people was unquestionable. He may just be able to find a way to stem the tide of disaster. Grace turned her attention to Phillip and the memory of the horrific visions crashed back to her consciousness. Could she prevent his death? Had the circumstances already changed so he no longer faced an untimely trip to Hades?

Reaching out a hand, she wrapped her fingers around his wrist and let the vision swallow her. When it receded a new feeling of resolve had settled within her belly. The future was not set in certainty. She could change what she had seen. She had to."We need to find Lucius. We must hurry."

****

The explosion rocked the building on its foundation. Derian and Lucius stood on either side of the back room door. When the dust cleared, Lucius cracked the door and watched for the invasion.

"Don't you have to pass fire code or something? How can you not have a back door to this place?" Hailey berated one of the guards.

Five *viators* in black slunk through the front door, their weapons up and movements cautious. Lucius let the door shut and he pointed the others toward a far wall where they could set up a barricade to repel the attack. Derian moved several chairs and a table together to form a barrier. He said, "Don't think these will do much against those pole weapons."

"It is better than nothing. We need to find a way to a safer location, get to the others, and consolidate a defense plan," Lucius said.

The guards clearly had no idea where to start. If they were an example of Althea's best and brightest, they were in serious trouble.

Hailey sighed and ran up to Derian. She wrapped her arms around his neck and gave him a quick kiss. "I will be right back, don't get shot again."

"Wait!" Lucius called out, but she'd already faded from view. "Damn it, Derian, that woman doesn't listen to anyone."

"No. She doesn't. But neither does yours."

"What do you mean mine?" Lucius asked, but didn't wait for an answer. The door crashed open and the first of the attackers rushed into the room.

Derian took him down with a shot to the shoulder. The man grabbed his arm and fell to the ground. Lucius reached for the dropped pole weapon and threw it to one of the guards. "Figure this thing out. We'll need it to get us out of here."

Another burst of heat pulsed into the room. Lucius put up his hand to protect his face from the pole weapon's fury. Had he been directly in the way of the force of energy, he'd be writhing in agony on the ground. A man entered in the wake of the receding heat. Lucius floored him with a hit to the back of the head with the butt of his pistol.

Derian pulled the man out of the way of the door in time to duck from the heat of the next blast. Lucius met Derian's eye across the door. The enemy was unlikely to continue sending in one man at a time. They needed another plan. Both waited for the next assailant to enter the room.

Suddenly a rush of heat from the far side of the room blasted past toward the door. A scream came from the man about to enter. Lucius turned his attention to the guard across the room, his eyes wide and the pole weapon trembling in his hands. The man beside him gave a derisive glare and grabbed the weapon from his compatriot's hand.

Striding to the door the man pressed a button on the side of the pole, stuck the end out the door and pulled a thin metal lever. Shouts accompanied the heat wave. Lucius followed the man's lead and sent several shot's over the guard's shoulder into the fray of the enemy.

Men dove in every direction as Derian added to the cacophony by firing several rounds from his Colt 1911. The main hall had very little cover and the enemy combatants scrambled toward the exit for their only chance at escape. Soon the room stood empty.

"Not exactly a victory, but better than nothing," Derian said.

Lucius agreed as he retrieved a number of abandoned pole weapons left in the main hall. "They are not well trained."

A shriek preceded a body flying through the front door. He hit the opposite wall and slunk to the floor unconscious. Lucius and Derian had their guns on the door just as a Cade entered with a giant grin. "I've been needing to do that for a while. Thank you for the opportunity gentleman."

Hailey ducked in behind the *herculian*. "Dude. You should totally check out what he left you out here. I thought *viator*s were cool, but this guy is unreal!"

32

Five men rushed out from the forest, their hands devoid of weaponry. Grace tugged Phillip to the ground and peered through the trees.

"Friends of yours?" he asked.

"I do not know. Perhaps."

Three of the men picked up speed, hitting an inhuman pace then jumped up the side of the main apartment wall, scaling it like a squirrel up a tree. One reached the first open window on the second story and dove in. Soon after a *tiresian* flew out the same window and landed with a sickening thud on the ground.

Grace gasped. "My gods. I do not believe they are on our side at all, Phillip. We must hurry."

The two of them skirted the lane, keeping low to avoid detection. The main contingent of enemy was focused on the *tiresians* shooting from the towering apartments. Grace whispered, "Who could those people be? Not *viators* surely."

"No. Never heard of a *viator* being able to do that," Phillip answered.

Grace stopped, putting a hand out to her cousin. "*Herculians.*"

Phillip snorted and said, "There haven't been *herculians* since before you and I were born."

Beyond the trees, bodies littered the ground outside the grand council hall. A man wrestled with another. One wore the solid black uniform of the enemy, the other was a giant in a simple pair of jeans and a t-shirt, fitted snug about his chest. Grace raised a brow, he was definitely not a *tiresian*. In truth, she'd never seen a man built like that.

The giant man lifted the other above his head and threw the body against the wall. Grace squeezed her eyes shut as Phillip let out a rush of air directly into her ear.

"That was not pleasant," Phillip said. "But he appears to be fighting the same men we are. Who's the girl with him?"

Grace opened her eyes and looked up. "Hailey," she shouted. Then she jumped up to follow her friend entering the hall. What luck to find them with such ease! She would have to thank the gods. But later, when there was more time and less violence surrounding them.

The familiar frame of Lucius ducked through the front door just as Grace made to enter. She put out a hand and a familiar warmth sizzled through her arm as her fingers touched his chest. "Lucius. You are all right."

He frowned down at her. But she stepped away to prevent his questioning eyes from initiating a scolding. Her heart did a slight stutter at the sight of him and the lack of welcome prompted feelings of disappointment. But she knew better than to read anything into it. Of course he was unhappy with her arrival. As Louisa said, he was a very protective man.

Her mind understood all that, so why didn't her heart?

Several more people joined the party in front of the hall. The giant of a man stood beside four *tiresians*. Each of those men had spent several years serving her grandmother during ceremonies. They looked out of place beside the battle-tested *viators* and the buff stranger.

Derian grinned at Grace then looked to Lucius. "See. Yours doesn't either."

Lucius cut his man a glare and reached for Grace. He propelled her toward the trees and motioned for the others to follow. The stern set to his lips had her fumbling for an explanation. "I know you are angry. But I had to come. I saw what would happen. Would you deny me the chance to intervene for the safety of my people?"

The foliage provided some cover, but soon the mass of disabled *viators* left strewn about the hall would be noticed. Their current location would be the first investigated. Even Grace, with her significant lack of battle experience knew that. Lucius met eyes with Derian and an unspoken conversation occurred before the men led the group through the forest.

After ten minutes they stopped and waited, listening to the distant sounds of battle. How much longer could her people hold off the attacking force? "Lucius? Please tell me you understand."

His eyes softened when he looked down, giving her a breath of hope. With a quick glance to Derian, he took Grace's elbow and guided her away from the group behind a set of trees. When they were out of sight, Grace continued, "Lucius I know that–"

He grabbed her by the shoulders and hauled her up into a heavily heated kiss. The suddenness of the embrace rocked her off balance and pushed all thoughts of fear and conspiracy from her mind. The kiss felt like a clear day after months of rain. A relief which felt so right. It was something she'd missed for hundreds of years without knowing it. And it ended far too quickly.

Pulling back, he tucked a strand of hair behind her ear. She raised her hand to find a large chunk had pulled loose from her hastily made ponytail. With a quick twist she restrained the long lengths. It gave her the time to pull herself together. When she looked back up at him, an uncommon smile touched his lips.

"You cannot blame me for wanting to do all I can to protect you. As long as I live I will continue to do so." He raised his finger and brushed it down her cheek. "But I cannot blame you for needing to be a part of this. When it began, it was my fight. My people's fight. Now, it belongs to us all."

Grace responded with a tentative smile. His own expression intensified and he continued, "So I will simply have to stay by your side to ensure that nothing happens to you."

"Oh for the gods' sake Lucius. You will not need to be by my side all the time."

He leaned in and said, "I will consider it an absolute pleasure to try."

Grace blushed and looked away just as Hailey pulled back a branch. "Ok lovebirds, we got to move. Derian is pretty sure they've discovered the mess we left at the hall, and this guy Cade is itching to get back in the fight."

Lucius grabbed Grace's hand and they rejoined the group. Cade paced the small clearing as the *tiresians* milled about impatiently. Derian addressed Lucius when he caught his attention, "Do we have a plan?"

"We find the leaders and put a stop to the attack."

The men all nodded, but Grace wondered if any of them had an idea how to accomplish the plan. Lucius started toward the edge of town, but she stopped him with a hand clenched around his elbow.

Letting the vision clear she shook her head. "You will not find them there."

"Then we will try this way," he said as he changed direction to lead them toward the old Victorian house which had been her family's home for years.

The vision she saw this time was both encouraging and frightening. "Yes, they are there."

The group hustled through the trees until they reached a small ridge just above the house. Ten *viators* patrolled the perimeter of the building. Two men dressed in less conspicuous clothing leaned against the wood pillars that held up the porch roof.

"Are those two yours?" Derian asked Cade.

The man frowned, his glare vicious as it pierced the two men blocking the door to the house. "Frank and Jon joined up with the conspiracy three years ago. Some of the first to go."

"Scary strong like you?" Hailey asked him.

"Yes. And fast."

"Well crap," she replied.

Cade grinned and answered, "No matter. I'm faster." He stood and looked to Lucius. "If you gentlemen would handle yours, I will remove mine from the equation."

He ducked through the trees and sped past the porch, flipping his middle finger up as he passed. Startled by the unexpected sight, the two men on the porch watched him fly past with mouths slightly open. Finally, they realized what they'd just seen and jumped off the porch in single leaps, dust billowing from their feet pounding on the dirt lane.

"Dude, what next? Guys in capes flying in the sky?" Hailey asked.

One of the *tiresians* gave a derisive snort. "No one can fly. That is just modern fantasy."

"Daedalus did it," another replied.

"That does not count. He had mechanical wings."

Grace sent a caustic glare at the two men. "This is not the time gentlemen." They averted their eyes and Grace looked to Lucius and Derian. "Shall we?"

Hailey giggled and pulled her gun from her waistband. "I think that's Grace's way of saying let's get moving."

Lucius had a sparkle in his eye as he leaned in to give everyone direction. With a quick hand to Lucius's wrist, Grace checked the success of the plan and then they were off. It wasn't a complicated plan, but it would serve to get them into the building with relative ease. Unfortunately, what lay ahead would be far more complicated. Grace glanced at her cousin, tempted to send him into hiding in the forest. But she knew better. He would run from this fight no sooner than she would.

****

The odds were terrible, but the *tiresian* guards accepted the challenge with calm reserve. On the outside. Inside they must have been a roiling tempest of nerves and terror. Any man who had never faced adversaries in battle might. But Lucius respected their ability to maintain dignity at a time when it was most needed.

The men crawled away through the brush to set up a number of locations within the wood. There they would distract the force watching the house with sporadic fire. Once the distractions were in place, Lucius, Derian, Phillip and the two women would circle around the back. They would enter the building through an old cellar window Grace said always remained unlocked.

A low whistle pierced the air, letting them know the men were in position. Lucius led the group toward the old building just as gunfire across the yard drew the attention away from their location. Additional guards were expected at the back of the house, but with the commandeered pole weapons, Lucius intended to make quick work of removing that threat.

They reached the cellar window and Grace fell to her knees, hooked her fingers under the wood frame and slid it up. For Grace and Hailey the entrance would be easy to slip through. For the men, it would be a tight fit. Derian gave Lucius a skeptical glance. He didn't have time to complain about the plan before two guards jogged around the corner.

Neither appeared to have expected a party of intruders, giving Lucius and Derian the time to swing the pole weapons against the men, striking before the others could fire. Both landed hard, unconscious from solid hits to the skull. They would wake with terrible headaches and hopefully only minor damage to their mental faculties. Lucius could only muster a minor amount of sympathy. They had chosen a terrible master.

Lucius looked down in time to see Grace's feet disappear into the cellar. Hailey closed the window and stood. Lucius grabbed her arm and said, "What are you doing?"

"Come on now, we know you can't fit in there. I would have loved to see you try though." Hailey smirked and ducked past him. Stopping at a narrow door, she waved the men over in time for it to swing open and reveal a wary Grace.

"Hurry. I can hear them in the first floor rooms. We may already be too late."

They joined her in the damp darkness and closed the door with quick efficiency. Phillip led Derian to the cellar stairs. With ease from experience, Derian scouted the way, leaving the others to wait for his signal.

Lucius took Grace by the arm and leaned in to whisper into her ear. "What do you mean too late? What have you seen?"

She pulled her bottom lip with her teeth and refused to make eye contact. "More secrets, Grace?"

"No." Her eyes snapped to his when she answered. Then she looked away again. "I just do not want to speak of what I do not wish to see again."

"How can I help if I do not know what you expect?"

"I–" Grace stopped then let a rush of air leave her lungs. "I saw my grandmother dead. And Phillip as well. Both here, in the rooms upstairs."

Lucius lightened his grasp on her arm and ran his hand up to her shoulder. "You have said your visions are not set in certainty. They are only based on the moment's intentions. You don't know that nothing has changed that could impact that outcome."

Grace looked up into his eyes, the slightest bit of sunlight from the cellar window reflecting the gloss of tears along her lashes. "Yes, but they have not changed yet."

He pulled her into an embrace. The gift of sight was often portrayed as a curse. Never had it seemed so true. To be able to see the future allowed for a kind of control men would kill for, but it also could torture the soul with knowledge of things that could never be changed. "Have you told him?"

"Phillip? No. Would it make a difference if I did?"

Lucius considered the question and came up with no answer. Should a man know the moment of his death? What kind of impact would that have on the decisions made?

"The forces of destiny have always played a sadistic game with my people. We see enough to change a little, but the grand plan is never revealed. What seems at one moment a future that must be avoided at all cost could be the key to a future that is intended to be." Grace turned her head up to him and a strength and wisdom shone from her eyes unlike any he had seen. "I can only do with what the gods have chosen to show me, and so I can do nothing less than try to influence a different outcome. Fate has given me a glimpse of a future I cannot change and I can do nothing but play this out to the end."

Lucius ran his finger down her cheek and said, "The fates are fickle women with little to do with their lives beyond meddling in mortal affairs. Whatever they have set before you, know this. You do not face them alone."

Grace blinked and a piece of the bleakness chipped away. She cocked her head and a slight smile tugged at the corner of her lips. "I think you might love me a little bit, Lucius."

He leaned down and framed her face with his hands. "Grace, I love you significantly more than a little bit."

A sharp laugh erupted from her lips and she covered her mouth to quell the sound. With a quick glance toward the others, she leaned in to say, "That I did not see coming. I do love being surprised by things."

Warmth spread from her smile to his chest and for a moment, he lost himself in the wonder that in over two thousand years, it had been *this* woman he'd waited to love.

Derian's deep voice cut through the moment, bringing them all back to the present. "It's clear. Two guards crossed into the room just left of the stairs. They seem distracted by our friends out front. We need to move fast."

Lucius gave Grace's shoulders a quick squeeze then hurried up the stairs to join Derian. Whatever the fates had in store for them, they would discover very soon.

33

The guards were easy enough to dispatch. Both men were focused on the fighting outside and unaware of the two *viators* sneaking up behind them. Derian removed the unconscious men to the corner as Phillip waved Hailey and Grace into the room, leaving the door open a crack behind them to keep watch on the hall.

"Now what?" Hailey whispered, her shoulders tense.

Lucius rolled his eyes with impatience. Would the woman never stop talking? Grace stood beside her cousin, straining to see beyond Phillip's shoulder. Lucius frowned. What had he been thinking bringing this fragile and untrained group into this situation? He considered taking Derian and sealing the other three in the room until everything was handled. But one look at the determined set to Grace's mouth and the intensity in her cousin's stance told him he would meet fierce resistance–a fight he wouldn't win.

With a quick nod to Derian, he slid between Phillip and the door. The hall was quiet, but a soft rumble of voices could be heard a few doors down. Narrow and carpeted with a threadbare runner, sneaking up on the room would be relatively easy. Provided the wood beneath their feet didn't creak like so many old homes tended to do.

Lucius motioned for the others to follow. In one hand he held his Walther, ready for whatever they would find. The others had their weapon handy as well. Grace and Hailey held pistols, while Phillip and Derian brought up the rear with the unwieldy pole weapons.

A raised hand stalled the others as they reached the door where the voices emanated. A heated discussion echoed into the hall, betraying frustration and lack of control. Lucius waited a moment to listen.

"Will you let more of your people die? Are you truly so arrogant to believe they wish to die for your adherence to an ancient feud?"

Hailey squeaked beside him. When he turned to her she mouthed the word, "Babylon."

He narrowed his eyes. Whoever was in the next room, was in Babylon when Hailey had been captured. No simple underling, they were higher representatives of the conspiracy. Which made whoever it was extremely valuable to him.

"You were as eager to enslave us then as you are now, Claudia. Do not attempt to present this as anything different. My people will never be *viator* chattel. And they will die to prove it."

Grace's nose flared and she shifted forward. Lucius held out an arm to prevent her from running past him into the room. From the sound of shifting feet and muffled coughs, he'd counted at least three more people in the room with Claudia and Althea. Which were *viator* and which were *tiresians* would be undetermined until they saw who shot first. Lucius needed Derian to go in with him to take control of the situation.

A click and a high-pitched ignition heralded the engaging of one of the pole weapons. Believing Derian read his mind about entering the room first, he turned and discovered a grim-faced Phillip holding the weapon to the startled group.

"Phillip," Grace whispered in alarm.

"I am so sorry, Grace. Please know that there is no other way." Phillip cast a quick glance at the weapons Derian and Lucius held. "Please place those on the table before we enter the room. They would be furious if I let you walk in armed."

Derian scowled and leaned his pole weapon against the wall as Hailey, Grace and Lucius placed their guns on a small side table standing just outside the door. Then Phillip motioned toward the entrance, his fingers hovering over the thin lever that with the slightest pressure would send a roar of heat and agonizing pain over the tightly spaced group.

Grace stared at her cousin, intense and clear-eyed she refused to move. "I have seen the outcome to this, Phillip. You must change your mind."

The man shook his head and replied, "Tymion said it most aptly. You are not the only one that has visions. I have seen it as well, and this is the only way for our people to truly be free."

"You are a fool if you believe that."

"Perhaps, but only the gods will determine the cast of this die."

Hailey placed her hands on her hips and scowled. "Are you fricking serious? Can you get any more melodramatic?"

Grace swung her attention from Phillip to glance at Hailey, providing Phillip the opening to shove Grace toward the door. Lucius reached out and pulled her toward him before she stumbled to the floor. The eyes that met his were filled with a quiet fury. "The fates have dealt me a dangerous card, Lucius."

He clasped her hands in his, hoping her words did not portend a reckless action. When they crossed the threshold, five heads swung toward them, quickly followed by a number of weapons being shifted toward the newly recognized threat. Phillip entered and realizations dawned across several brows.

"Phillip, you have brought us a gift," Claudia said, a sick delight dripping from her expression.

"What have you done you stupid boy?" Althea quickly jumped in. The flash of fear in her eyes a most unexpected reaction. The woman had never shown fear in her entire life.

Claudia slithered toward them, stopping a foot from Hailey and sneered. "It is too bad that Carlo could not join us for this. He would be terribly disappointed to discover a *tiresian* had found a way to do what he could not."

"You didn't have to go through all this trouble just for me," Hailey snarled.

Claudia lifted her head to the ceiling and let loose a terrible laugh. "You think so well of yourself. I suppose some of it is warranted. You truly do have some fascinating talents. But no," she turned her gaze to Grace, "You are not nearly the most interesting one here."

Grace stiffened beside him and Lucius tightened his grip on her hand. The truth of Claudia's desire confirmed the conspiracy had pegged Grace as a valuable commodity. It was clear they would go to great lengths to take from her what they wanted.

"No. She is not yours," Althea shouted as she charged forward, her hands outstretched and fingers spread like an eagle's talons. Shots hit the woman seconds after she posed a threat to Claudia, sending her to the ground in a sudden, bloody fall.

Grace cried out and lunged toward her mortally injured grandmother, but Claudia intercepted her, wrapping her hands around Grace's forearms.

Suddenly, the entire room stilled as Grace stopped mid-motion. Her eyes glazed and skin took on the pallor of marble. Claudia dropped her hands in terror as Lucius leaned forward to pull Grace behind him. Before he could, Grace revived from her vision. She faced Claudia and the tone of her words could have frozen an ocean. "I have seen your death and by the gods on high, this is a fate you cannot escape."

****

The woman's lips trembled and Grace felt satisfaction at the fear that came from her prediction. Moments slowed to an aching degree and the room sharpened in perspective. Her grandmother lay still on the old aubusson carpet, the slight inflation of her chest the only indication she still lived. Three unfamiliar *viators* stood before her, weapons drawn, uncertainty clear in their stance. Phillip moved to the side of the room, shock in his eyes as he stared at Althea's body.

Grace stalked Claudia, her movements slow and methodical. A powerful sense of purpose had taken root within her belly and this woman would pay for the pain she'd inflicted. The only piece that kept her tied to reality was the three *viator* friends who stood behind her, supporting her through everything that happened. Otherwise, she would very well let loose the tempest of fury and claw the woman's eyes out, ensuring her own death as well as Claudia's.

"What do you think you can do to me? You see the future, but you cannot do more than that," Claudia said, her

310

confident words conflicted with her retreat from the advancing Grace.

"The biggest fools believe we sit idly by in a world determined by the fates. The agent of the future is the intent and actions of the moment," Grace said, shifting her direction to corral Claudia toward her colleagues.

"Phillip's visions have already guaranteed my success. Are you saying your visions of the future are more accurate than his?" Claudia forced a laugh, "What value are predictions of the future if you all give different answers? Perhaps your powers are less useful than we thought."

Grace let a slight smile tug at her lips as the woman stopped in front of the single-paned window. Through the glass a scene of battle played out, but one which leaned toward the *tiresian's* favor. Tymion had brought his people to a stand, the opposing force weakening before them. She returned her focus to Claudia. "Time does not follow a line of predictive destiny. The fates may influence the outcome, but they cannot control free will. Have you never read philosophy?"

Claudia showed no spark of understanding and Grace knew it ultimately did not matter. A shuffle of movement behind her drew the attention of the men beside Claudia. Guns came up and the moment from her vision crashed into the present. Grace dropped to the ground as shots fired.

Rolling she ended up along the far wall before finding her feet again. Two of the *viator* men lay unmoving on the ground while the other held his weapon on the upright Hailey, the pistol in her hand pointed back at him.

Lucius and Derian both stood, ready to pounce and cautiously wary. Claudia screamed at Phillip, "Use your weapon!"

He shook his head. Eyes unfocused, he dropped the pole. Everyone watched as it hit the floor. With a cry Claudia dove, wrapping her fingers around the long metal pole and swinging it up to point it at Hailey.

"Oh hell no," Hailey said, her finger moving to pull the trigger on her pistol. Before she could fire, the unnamed *viator* shot at Hailey. Derian was already diving for Hailey's knees, sending her to the ground and the bullet passed, ineffective.

Lucius lunged at the man as Hailey's gun flew from her hands toward Phillip. Grace watched the surreal sight of her vision coming true. Hailey had done it again, transporting a weapon from thin air into her hands, only this time it was Grace's weapon. The one she'd brought from New Mexico. Her cousin leaned down and grabbed the gun, his eyes rising to meet Grace's.

She shook her head and her breath caught in her throat. It didn't have to be this way. She could stop it. Reaching her hand out she cried, "Phillip stop."

"Too late," Claudia growled and engaged the pole weapon. A roar of blinding heat rushed toward Grace. Phillip pulled the trigger and shot Claudia in the chest. With a gurgled cry, she stumbled, shifting the merciless weapon's intensity to her cousin. The flash heat struck Phillip direct, forcing him to his knees. Grace watched in horror as flames ignited on his chest, the scent of scorched hair filling the room, his skin blackening within seconds.

And then it stopped. Grace spun to see Lucius wresting the pole from Claudia's grasp. The other *viator* lay at his feet, his head twisted at an unnatural angle. Claudia landed in a heap, blood beginning to pool beneath her. Lucius threw the pole across the room and kneeled beside the dying woman.

He pushed his hands onto her wound and shouted at Derian to help the others.

A fog of unreality filled Grace's senses. Turning her head to the side she saw the charred body of her cousin, unmoving, his eyes sightless. She hadn't stopped it. What purpose did she serve if she couldn't stop a tragedy from occurring?

With a tentative step, she moved toward Phillip, but a quiet cough stalled her approach. She looked down into her grandmother's glassy eyes. "Grace."

Falling to her knees she grabbed at the woman. "Grandmother. Oh gods, please help us." Rifling over her clothing, Grace tried desperately to find the wounds. Sticky blood covered most of her body, making it difficult to locate the source.

A strong hand stilled one of hers and Grace looked up into her grandmother's ashen face. "I am done, Grace. I have seen it, as have you."

"No."

A slight smile from her grandmother came as a surprise. Then she continued, "Do you believe that I have loved you?"

"Grandmother..." Grace whispered, her voice scratchy with emotion.

"I have, though I know it never seemed that way. I loved your mother as well. We have all made mistakes, my dear. And my greatest was never telling you the truth." Althea coughed, the sound wretched to the ear. "Your mother was not banished from the community. She left on her own, to save you. To protect our people from your father."

"My father?"

"A *viator*."

"I know," Grace turned her eye to Lucius then said, "they are not all evil, grandmother."

"Oh course they aren't." At the clipped tone, Grace returned her eyes to Althea. The woman held her gaze with a depth of intensity that was difficult to return. She continued, "But I could not afford to think otherwise."

The last words came breathy and Grace looked up, frantic and at a loss for what to do. The community had limited health services, being rarely needed and therefore underutilized. And even the minor first aid supplies available would be unattainable through the current battle being fought beyond the house.

She looked down, the realization that there truly was nothing left she could do hitting like a punch to the gut. "Grandmother, I..."

"We cannot try to heal centuries of wounds in a few moments, I know this." Althea gripped Grace's hand tight, the color of her skin grey and her lips flaxen. "These are your people. They need you to lead them. You have the long sight and hold the blood of Tiresias in your veins. Go to my home, find the journals beneath the floor boards. You will see your answers there."

Grace pulled her lip between her teeth and tears threatened to overwhelm her eyes. This was not how she wanted to say goodbye to her grandmother. And the answers Althea promised would only create more questions. Grace was no leader to her people. She'd never been a part of the community, always sitting on the fringes. Never engaged, never a part of anything. She had none of the qualities of a leader, not like Tymion. Not like Lucius.

"Grandmother, I cannot be that person."

Althea closed her eyes, her chest rising with a shallow breath. Through her lips the barest sound was breathed and the words struck like bells from an angel. "Yes you are."

34

Roderic emerged from the makeshift hospital room, shutting the door behind him, his expression tense. Lucius pushed off from the wall where he'd been leaning, waiting to hear what was to become of the woman inside.

"Endymion is a decent physician. He's got her settled and the worst of it cleaned up. But I don't believe we'll be hearing from her anytime soon," Roderic said, blowing out a breath of frustrated air.

Lucius frowned. Claudia was the only tie they had to the conspiracy. If she died from the gunshot wound, they would lose a valuable advantage against the enemy. "We will have to wait and see."

"Aye, but do you really believe she will talk even when she gains consciousness?" Roderic wiped his hands on his pants and walked down the hall toward the narrow stairs.

Lucius didn't answer. Both men knew she would be unlikely to betray her superiors unless they had something to offer. And what she wanted was power. Lucius would go to great lengths to prevent the woman from succeeding in her aspirations. But the conspiracy did not necessarily know that. With Claudia in their hands, the other side would be sweating, waiting to see what came of the campaign's failure.

At the bottom of the stairs, the two men turned the corner and entered a small parlor. Furniture filled the room, leaving little space for meeting, but it was the least cluttered of the house. Rusa stood uncomfortably across the room, his immense frame tense as he stared out the window.

Roderic found a reasonably dust-free settee and slumped against the ancient upholstery. Despite his apparent exhaustion, he couldn't help baiting his grandfather. "Are you Donas' errand boy now, old man? He has you hopping between here and there like a page from the dark ages."

Rusa didn't budge and not a flick of movement betrayed his customary irritation with his grandson. Lucius watched as the ancient man turned, his expression tired and wan. He directed his gaze at Lucius. "We had no idea they had grown this strong."

"Strong? Certainly not strong enough if the *tiresian*s were able to fend off the attack," Roderic answered. Lucius kept his thoughts quiet, waiting for what the man had to say.

Rusa turned his tired eyes back to the window. "That was no army. It was a test. According to Cade, there are over 300 *herculian*s at their disposal, yet we only have evidence of seven being here. If they intended to annihilate these people, why hold back?"

"Perhaps they underestimated the strength of the *tiresian*'s defenses. It would not be the first time arrogance got in the way of a successful campaign," Roderic said.

Lucius followed Rusa's gaze out the window. The man had a point, despite Roderic's suggestions. Everything the conspiracy had thrown at them so far was minor. Each scuffle had been small groups on very specific missions. What had their goal been during this particular fight? If it was a complete destruction of the community, or even the subjugation of the people, they could have thrown many more resources at the situation. The game, it seemed, had only begun.

A cough at the door drew their attention. Cade leaned against the jamb, his arms folded across his chest. "It seems to me they're collecting."

"Collecting what?" Rusa asked.

Cade shrugged, but Lucius already knew. He finally broke his silence, "Grace. Hailey."

Rusa and Roderic raised identical skeptical brows but Lucius continued, "The genome. The *herculians* and the *tiresians*. It's clear they are experimenting with combining the traits of each of the people, even gaining traction in some of the areas. But it is also clear they haven't reached their goal. Otherwise we would be facing those with augmented powers already."

Roderic said, "They haven't figured it out yet then. And they're looking for answers."

Lucius ran a hand over his hair, warming up to his theory. "With Nikanuur gone, they would have to find a new brilliant mind to continue his work. It would have been a step back in their research and they know they are vulnerable."

"Then they will be looking for another Nikanuur. Someone that could take up where he left off." Barely restrained energy pulsed around Roderic as he spoke, "And they are looking for shortcuts. Grace with her mixed genetics would be one. So would Hailey and her mutations."

Rusa tapped a finger against his jaw and said, "We know what they want. The women and a replacement. Who, other than Nikanuur, has the knowledge of science and physiology to accomplish what they desire?"

Rusa and Lucius met eyes then they both turned to Roderic. He threw up his hands. "Don't look at me like that. I haven't had any new job offers. And they couldn't give me what I want, even if they did."

"Yes. But they don't know that," Lucius said.

Roderic tightened his jaw and gave Lucius a stony glare. "I am no spy."

Rusa rippled with enthusiasm as his laughter rang through the room. "Well boy, you are now."

****

"Grace?"

She looked up at the sound of Roderic's voice, her hand holding open one of the various books she'd pulled from her grandmother's library. Rubbing the edge of her palm into her dried out eyes, she closed the cover. Aristo lifted his head from where it lay on the desk, his expression less inquisitive than irritated by the interruption from his nap. Grace smiled and ran a hand down her good friend's fur, thankful the old cat found a way to avoid being brought down in the violence.

She arched and kneaded her fingers into the muscles of her lower back. Far too much of her time had been spent reading over the last few days. While Lucius and Tymion led the cleanup after the attack, Grace dove into her grandmother's writings, determined to understand the past and perhaps gain insight in how to proceed for the future.

Unfortunately, she still had no clear idea how to move forward. A council meeting, just that morning, put even more pressure on her to take a permanent place of leadership in the community. Althea's hand of control extended even beyond death.

"You look exhausted. You need to rest." Roderic moved into the room and took a seat across the table. He flipped open one of the books but quickly lost interest.

"You look as tired as I am."

He placed his chin on his arm and looked so much like a forlorn puppy that Grace gave a sad smile. She'd lost two family members, only to gain a new cousin. Memories of the near kiss earlier that week made her blush with embarrassment. With a quick prayer of gratitude to the fates, she let the past lie. "Did you know my father?"

"No. He'd broken ties with my grandfather and his sister centuries before I came along. You'll discover we have quite a prolific family."

Grace tempered her disappointment. So many mysteries remained and perhaps the story between her mother and father was lost in time. There were so many other things she needed to focus on; it really seemed to matter little. Though for one moment it would be nice to see her mother in a light not shrouded in tragedy.

They sat quietly together, both lost in their thoughts. After the battle, Tymion had taken the news of Althea and Phillip's deaths incredibly hard, pulling away and vowing to make amends for his mistake. Darkness settled over the community and Grace wondered if they would ever recover. The elders looked to her as Althea's heir, demanding she claim her place as the matriarch and lead their people into a new future. And she still had no idea how to proceed.

From outsider to leader. How would she cope? How could she possibly be the person they needed? She looked down at her grandmother's story. Althea told her she had the long sight. At the time it meant nothing, but now... now she understood. The strength and accuracy of her visions was hereditary and as she grew older, the images would become more vivid, the implications more far reaching, the responsibility greater.

Her eyes rose to her *viator* cousin. His sightless eyes still haunted her. How many deaths would she predict? Would foreknowledge prevent the inevitable? "Roderic, I saw something."

"About me?" He raised a sardonic brow and let a smile erase the reflection of deep thought from his face. He was so charming when he looked like that. Grace imagined he knew it. She lowered her head and pulled her lip between her teeth. Roderic said, "I don't want to know."

"But–"

"Lass, I prefer the surprises."

"Roderic, please–"

"No." He waved a hand at her and said, "Now, do you want to know why you have been having the blackouts?"

"You discovered something? How could you possibly know?" Grace had only mentioned the issue, and never submitted to an examination. Yet, he sat so confidently with his knowledge.

"Critical thinking, lass. It is a lost art. I may not have the strategic mind of Lucius, but this," he said as he patted the side of his head, "works just fine."

Grace laughed, letting the lightness of his comment remove the fear and intensity that had welled within her. He continued, "When you have blacked out, it has been at times of extreme stress or danger, correct?"

She nodded.

"For a new *viator*, those would be times when a jump would initiate. We have learned to control the response, choosing when and where. But when the skill first manifests, it is usually instinctual."

"But then why would I blackout and not jump time?"

He held up a finger. "Ah, but you are not all *viator* are you? And your *tiresian* capabilities are far more developed." He waited, letting the implications settle, but Grace still did not understand. She scrunched her face and he released an aggrieved sigh. "When you would have jumped in those situations, your mind knew that jumping was not the optimum choice, based on your intuitive sense of the future. So the one talent prevented the other from engaging, but it shorted out the system, and you passed out."

"Oh my." She stared at him, eyes wide. It made sense, but what were the implications? Could she control it? There were so few things that she understood, this just added another piece to the overabundant pile of puzzle pieces that had been thrown at her. "I do not know if that is good or bad."

He shrugged.

"Do you think I will be able to control it? I do not like passing out. Perhaps if I–"

A cough at the door interrupted Grace's words and Lucius looked in. Roderic stood abruptly. "Well, I think the implications remain to be seen. You'll figure it out, lass. Now I have to be leaving. There's a world to be saving."

Grace stood as well, anxiety filling a pit in her stomach. She wasn't sure she could handle losing another member of family so soon, even if he was newly realized. "Roderic?"

He turned back as he was about to leave the room. She said, "Please be cautious."

Flashing a grin he turned to Lucius. "Take care of my cousin. She and Lidiya may be the only family I care to keep around."

Lucius shook his head at Roderic's back as he disappeared around the corner then entered the room, his gaze focused with steely intent on Grace. Anticipatory shivers ran up her spine and she looked away. After everything, those eyes still caused the most unexplainable reactions inside her.

"You are tired," he said, his voice a breath away from her ear.

"Yes, that has been pointed out. Tell me, Lucius. You have been a leader for so long, how do you do it? How do you take the responsibility for so many and not fail?"

He leaned a hip on the heavy desk, encouraging Aristo to find a new place to perch. For years, Grace had seen this desk as her grandfathers, left precisely as he had it for the decades. Apparently, her grandmother missed him far more than she ever let it be known. She ran a finger over the time-glossed finish.

"Leadership is a gift given by those that wish to be led. The greatest responsibility lies with those that have chosen to follow. They must choose someone worthy of the office. After that, it is respecting the gift that has been given, staying true to those needs of your people that mean the most to them." He let a soft smile rise and grabbed her hand. "They have chosen well. You will do fine. And you are not alone."

Grace looked down at his hands, strong and rugged. They reminded her of what a solid pillar of strength he had been for her. "What my people need the most–I am not certain any of us truly knows what that is right now. They are torn. Some wish to run, just as we did 800 years ago."

He ducked his head to make eye contact with her. "Will you be running again?"

"No." Her answer was fast, instinctual. "No. We have run for long enough."

"It will take time and work on our end to mend the ties between the *viators* and *tiresians*. But I believe we can." Lucius pulled her into his arms and continued, "Together, if you will allow me."

Grace smiled and let her head lay against his chest. Perhaps leading her people through the current crisis would be easier if the two groups united. It would certainly be more enjoyable. She should meet with the elders and discuss the ramifications. Pushing against his chest, she separated herself from him, feeling a sense of loss at the lack of touch. She would need to get that reaction under control. It did not bode well for a leader to be out of control of their physical reactions. Lucius was far too distracting.

Brushing away a tendril of hair which had fallen loose, she turned toward the door. "I will call a meeting. It is time for me to step into this role."

As she passed, he ran an arm across her back and reached the other behind her knees, lifting her into his arms. "Lucius!"

"The first thing a leader needs to know is when to rest. And you need to rest."

Grace blushed and didn't know quite what to say. He was telling her what to do again, but it was deliciously wonderful. Perhaps she would let him get away with it this time. "But what about you? Do you not need rest as well?"

"I do indeed. I will be resting right next to you. Do you think you can keep your hands off of me, Grace?"

Her mouth fell open and immediately shut at the teasing glint in his eyes. Playful, but no less intense. Her breath caught in her throat. "I do not know. Can *you?*"

"Dude, does anyone have a phone? I need to call Jason and let him know everything is ok, but I can't find a stinking phone anywhere." Hailey entered, stopping short when she saw Grace tucked against Lucius's chest. "Ok, so I'll just go see if anyone else can help me." She grinned, did an about-face and left the room.

A chuckle came from Lucius's chest and she looked up into his rich brown eyes, the steel replaced by a tenderness which took her breath away. He said, "I do not believe even the most talented *tiresian* could have seen the way things have turned out."

Grace thought back to the dreams she'd had of Lucius long before she met him. "Oh I do not know. I think a really talented *tiresian* may have known just a little."

Letter from the Author:

The Viator adventures have kept me on my toes, and I can't tell you how much fun it is to build with the twists and turns these characters keep throwing my way. I hope you have enjoyed Grace and Lucius's story and if you have yet to read Hailey and Derian's story you can find them in *Unexpected: Book One of the Viator Legacy Series*. As we move forward, I've been tormented by a certain Italian demanding that I tell his side of things. So, keep your eyes open for *Unrepentant: Book Three of the Viator Legacy Series* where we meet the wily librarian Lisa and learn quite a bit more about our favorite bad boy Carlo. To tide you over until book three is released late 2014, check out how they meet in the short story, "Shadows & Intrigue."
Cheers
Erin

About the Author:

Erin Lausten is a woman of many talents and seemingly varied hobbies. Her life is as busy and fast paced as her books. Working as an archeologist and research librarian in the recent past, Erin has a unique view of the world. She sees all possibilities and doesn't accept the limited scope accepted by society. Her favorite question is "Why not?" Join her, if only for a story or two, in her flights of fancy and 'what if' scenarios.

Books by Erin Lausten:

Viator series:
Unexpected
Unforeseen
Shadows and Intrigue

Steampunk:
Cibola's Promise
Cibola's Revenge

Other:
Love Uncommon

Discover Erin Lausten titles at
http://erinlausten.com

Find Erin on the Web:
https://www.facebook.com/erinlausten
http://erinlausten.wordpress.com/
https://twitter.com/erinlausten